The DELTA WAVE

RA Haskell

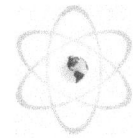

2024, TWB Press
www.twbpress.com

The Delta Wave
Copyright © 2024 by RA Haskell

Edited by Terry Wright

Cover Art by Terry Wright

ISBN: 978-1-959768-67-8

Dedication

For Ron M.

You always believed in this story, and that I could tell it.
The world is less without you.

Part I: Max Dyson

Chapter 1

Max Dyson had been dead seven times this year, and he'd never felt better. He walked, not with his normal leaning-forward shuffle, but with a high-kneed bounce, though he didn't know if it was because, after eighteen long months of winter, spring had finally come, or because he was walking toward Amanda. The cracked pavement flowed below him like burgeoning tributaries as he strode faster and faster toward her welcoming smile and pollen-stained fingers. She would complain about something and gesture wildly, as she cursed one too many times, but he didn't care. He was all too familiar with her stubbornness, and its manifested vulgarity, but it didn't matter, he simply enjoyed the sound; words were inconsequential in the face of her melody. It was the rhythm of her telling—the up, the down, and the crescendo of a sentence's end that did it. It was this that sent him dreaming, and in this day and age, there was no higher praise. Even though the thought of her brought a smile to his face, he wasn't sure he could do to her what he had wanted to do for nearly a month now.

Can I actually tell her I love her?

He passed the Department of Transportation Purification Plant, and a familiar siren blared, which caused a ringing in his ears. He soon faced an onslaught of haggard workers exiting the North entrance. Men who'd spent hours in waist-deep freezing water and reeked of lubricant slammed into him without care or apology. He slinked through, knowing that he too would carry that odor soon enough. The thought of the tedium nearly made Max slow his pace, but he recognized Amanda's street and, instead, hurried on. It was after he pushed past a second line of men, those waiting to receive their vaccinations, when he spotted her.

Amanda had busied herself with a ramshackle flower garden, and every now and then cast a sly, perhaps hopeful, southward glance down the street. When her gaze landed squarely on him, she turned away and paid attention to the coffee can at her feet. The tin contraption with ragged holes in the bottom was filled with street dirt, but like the others around her managed, somehow, to produce enormous purple tulips that rose up in a last hoorah.

Max bowed his head and smiled. He hadn't felt this happy since before the change.

As a man with a black trench coat crossed the street and walked toward him, he purposefully wiped the grin from his face. *Don't smile. Normal people don't smile. You'll look suspicious.*

The man, with rough wrinkled skin, passed, and Max nodded at him. He, typical of most everyone else, had a blank expression and empty eyes. It wasn't a look of sadness, for that would have been something. No, it was devoid of emotion, like he wasn't even alive. Max tried to think of the right word to describe him. *Automaton. Zombie.* Sometimes Amanda looked that way, too. He trembled at the remembrance.

She approached him now with feigned surprise, and Max thought she looked weary. He was going to remark upon it, but when she laid her dirty palm upon his cheek, crashing through the ruse of their usual greeting, Max cared only about kissing her.

She tried to wipe away the yellow smudge her slight caress had left on Max's cheek, but failed and only made it worse.

"Just leave it, will ya?" Max said, looking down at her.

Amanda licked the thumb of her other hand and moved it toward Max, intending to use it like an eraser on his face.

Max made eye contact and caught her hand in the same moment. "I said, leave it." He chuckled.

Amanda dropped the corners of her mouth and raised her eyebrows. She appeared, purposefully, to be considering his seriousness. He intensified his stare, and she decided that he was serious enough. He dropped her hand, and she relented, allowing it to fall to her side.

"You look good, Max." She cocked her head. "I swear every time I see you, you look better and better. What's your secret?"

"I look good, huh?"

Amanda snarled at him. "Let's go in. I've got stew on. There's only a little while longer for stew, you know. Pretty soon it'll be too hot. You can't eat stew when it's hot. I know people do, but it's just, you know, wrong."

Max grinned as she spun around, kicked a tulip can aside, and made for the door. After following her inside, he closed the door, and in the darkness of her apartment, rushed to her and grabbed her waist. That stopped her movement toward the stove enough that he could pivot around to face her.

She scowled with annoyance. "The stew needs stirring."

"Yeah," Max muttered.

"You're fucking bad at this stuff." She teasingly poked him in the side. "You know?"

Max cowered, shrinking away. "What stuff?"

She moved in on him, held him up, not letting him get away, though he was trying to melt into the floor. "You know what. You know."

"Yeah..." He somehow mustered the courage to blurt out, "You're my secret."

Tell her you love her.

I can't.

He froze, waiting for the outcome of his emotional outburst.

"Look at me," was her response.

He pointed his face in her direction, but his eyes darted about the room instead of staring into hers. He wanted to make eye contact, but he couldn't.

"Max, look at me."

Finally, he did and saw Amanda's lips were parted. Max's trepidation washed away. He placed his hand under the back of her neck and moved her hair slightly with the tips of his fingers.

She breathed out.

Max sucked in her breath to taste her. His mind was suddenly lost as she responded by kissing him with a wide open mouth and adventurous tongue.

As she stepped in and pressed herself against him, he knew, in that moment, that he'd have to wait to kill her.

Chapter 2

Amanda's head lay in the crook of Max's arm, as beams of setting sunlight shot through the window. Her black locks rejected the orange hues in some places but soaked them up in others. They had several hours before Max's shift started and, without speaking, mutually decided to go to The Raven. It was a routine familiar to them, as they frequented the establishment regularly. The club was only a few blocks away and, after dressing and eating a small bowl of stew, they headed out. The noise of the place could be heard for several blocks, and some claimed its vibration was felt for miles. Each night, this one being no different, The Raven was crowded, both inside and out. Masses of people packed themselves into the darkness, simply to have their chests hammered by volume, their sternums massaged by rhythm, and their ears mangled by the held notes of others expressing their anguish.

As Max and Amanda walked through the entrance, two people were taking the stage through thick smoke that signaled something had apparently gone wrong. The crowd, blinded by a swamp-smelling mass of steam, watched as the performers, unintentionally visible and *not* hidden by a mysterious cloud, argued with each other and yelled obscenities in the off-stage direction.

Whoever's making that fog must be on stagers, Amanda thought, as she took Max's hand and led him toward the bar.

The misdirected fog continued to take over The Raven, but the crowd bore it rather than move. Coughing and sneezing spread as the cloud moved throughout the club. Amanda spotted two patrons leaving their position, and she approached it with both a casual manner and a precise accuracy. Max leaned in first, and the barista ignored them until he met Amanda's eyes. She smiled, and the barista took their orders: two quads, grinds in.

Max took a tentative sip while his companion went to work. Amanda, keeping her mouth closed, smeared the bean fragments across her gums and sucked in. The grounds emitted their caffeine, and Amanda breathed in deeply through her nose so her lips would not part. She gave a second suck to tighten the seal and breathed out. Finally, her eyes opened, and she sipped again from the top of her small cup. She swished politely, swallowed, and then laughed. Though it rarely did, this time the swill had actually worked. She grabbed Max and kissed him, leaving a brown stain on his thin lips. She was going to wipe it away, but remembering Max's reaction to the pollen, decided to leave this one, as well. Max, this evening anyway, was her canvas.

Mark bumped into them in a stupor, smelling like bad bourbon.

"Mark," Max said, "you're a mess. Here, come here and lean with us."

"Wha? Oh, Max, an, and, Amanda. Wow. Okay, well,

hey. I've missed you guys." Mark said it with an inebriated sincerity.

"Missed us?" Max said. "You saw us yesterday. We–"

Amanda cut in. "It was two days ago."

"No, I'm pretty sure it was—"

"Trust me, it was two days ago," Amanda said with incredulity. "Forty-eight hours. The 13th of February. I pride myself on remembering what day it is, or was...whatever. Shit, you know what I mean, Max, right...that I know the date, that I know the damn day, that I haven't forgotten fucking everything?"

Mark swayed.

Max strained to keep him upright. "Yeah, *ugh,* I guess. Whatever." He grimaced and moved his feet to get better leverage. If Mark were to fall, Max was certain he wouldn't be able to get him off the floor.

Amanda was about to get angry when the perfect combination of a caffeine rush and a favorite song happened serendipitously. The smog had cleared, and the performers played their instruments. The spread was sparse: a tattered piano and a broken drum set, but they played them liked they loved them. And in reality, they did; those keys and skins had saved them more than once. They sang of exhaustion and the trickery of stagers, as Amanda, along with most of The Raven, grooved with their eyes closed. They all hoped to dance themselves into oblivion but knew that in just a few hours, the sun would rise and they'd do it all over again.

Max, deciding he'd had one-too-many quads, was headed to the bathroom when he ran into Nola.

She rushed to him. "Max, hey. Is Amanda here too? Where is she?"

Max leaned close to Nola's ear and practically screamed in it. "Yeah..." he motioned over his shoulder, "on the floor, where else?"

They switched positions in a common ritual, and Nola yelled back, "Okay. I'm gonna go find her."

They switched again. "Check up front. Hey, are the Sandmen back there? I gotta take a leak."

She nodded, shrugged, and went off.

Max waved to her and continued down the passageway of intensifying darkness. He rounded a corner and passed directly behind the stage, slowing to peer into the power room. A single bulb hanging from the ceiling by a frayed wire tether made this the only electrically lighted room in The Raven. Though the bulb was barely burning, the shine was enough to hurt Max's eyes, and instinctively, he raised his hand. Still, though, he could see the volunteers on stationary cycles, rowing machines, and other retro-fitted equipment doing their work to provide amplification to the noise on stage. As tradition demanded, he banged on the wall, yelling encouragements as he passed. Those giving up their precious energy for the sake of sound certainly deserved at least that. He turned again, readying himself for the Sandmen. He and two others entered the corridor together.

The Sandmen began their advertising well in advance. The lot of them, about a dozen, sang an atonal, though familiar, chorus.

"Stagers, man, these are the real deal...they get you

there, bro."

"I got remmers...four hours guaranteed."

"No thanks," Max said as powerfully as he could and pushed through.

"Oh, I see, a fighter...no problem, how 'bout some straight up crank? Cheap."

Max had passed, but the noise continued, and one of his corridor compadres was lured in. "Cyclers...the original, still just as good, sure thing."

Max pushed the door and entered the bathroom. There was the sound of running water, and in contemplation of its abundance, he sighed deeply. Another patron, standing in the usual one-arm-on-hip position, didn't notice when Max moved up alongside him. The line of men faced, and aimed their streams at a steel wall with a sheet of water pouring down into a trench. Every now and then, one would occasionally drop his head backwards, stare at the ceiling, and let out sounds of relief. The lip of the trench was too small to contain the deluge from above which crashed down like waves on a rocky coast, sending urine-laced spray onto everyone's shoes.

Max's right shoulder touched the wall of the only stall. The stall emitted a moan, and Max, surprised, accidentally bumped into the man next to him. "Sorry."

The man didn't look at him but retorted with a conciliatory grunt.

The noises from the stall stopped, and Max figured it was some totally inebriated kid trying to pass out from alcohol. Max had tried it himself a few times, years ago, and remembrances of the nauseating recoveries made him pity the poor bastard. Suddenly, above the running water, came first the sound of breaking glass, then the repetitive *tink tink* of a small hollow piece of plastic bouncing on the tile. The stall suddenly shook as moans turned to growls, interrupted only by incoherent and volumetrically increasing mumbling. Max leaned down a bit and saw what remained of a nasal inhaler. He stopped peeing without trying.

"Oh shit," someone said. *"Walker!"* Another guy zipped up quickly and ran out the door.

Max hurried, as well, and just as the stall door burst open, Max was exiting. He glimpsed the poor soul's eyes, filled with an otherworldly rage and, ironically, a familiar melancholy. A small drip of blood ran from the man's nose as he made, unsteadily, for the door. Max wished he could have helped the man, but at this point, not much could. The thought of existing in equal states of total insanity and perfect lucidity sent a shiver down his spine, even as he rushed back toward the body-heated Raven. He strode past the power room, banging the wall as he passed. "Walker," Max yelled.

A steel pocket-door slammed shut, followed closely by the definitive *thud* of a thrown bolt. Not all Walkers became violent, but one never knew.

Max slowed, knowing that the Sandmen would take care of the guy; Walkers were bad for business.

When he saw Somnus and his minions enter synchronously from every door in the club, he knew he didn't have much time to find Amanda.

✕✱✱

Word of Somnus's arrival traveled quickly, evidenced by the increased bustling at the doors of the Raven, patrons pushing, shoving, and generally clamoring to gain entry. Max couldn't see it, but the crowd was stymied, as men with serious eyes blocked the doors. The surgical masks covering their noses and mouths magnified the intensity of their stares. They looked as if their eyeballs had been cleanly removed, kept in perfect working order, and simply placed upon a thin white shelf.

One such man passed through the crowd like a droplet of oil in a glass of water, reaching Somnus untouched. He leaned in and whispered something that sent Somnus toward the stage. Max, not as slippery as Somnus's aid, bumped into people in every which way, as he simultaneously scanned the crowd and kept watch over Somnus's progress. Somnus, like all of his clan, wore the surgical mask, but he donned a blue shirt of The Doctor's, as well. *That's his* trademark, Max thought, *makes him instantly recognizable and respected.*

As more masked men took up flanking positions along the stage, Somnus mounted it without assistance and raised his left arm above his head. The throng responded vocally with shouts and cheers rising, now and then, above a steady gentle rhythm of clapping. The applause wasn't raucous nor simply polite, but somewhere in between. As Somnus approached the microphone to speak, Max found Amanda who, along with Nola, held their hands together in front of them. Amanda smiled over her shoulder, as Max slid his arm around her.

"We should get going," Max said, trying to strike a

delicate balance between casual fearlessness and a real desire to be as far away from the Raven as possible. "I've got a funny feeling. Let's put some distance between us and the Raven."

Somnus motioned to the crowd for silence, took the mic, and jammed it into his mask. "Citizens, we are the Eight Hour Knights, and we come to you in this..." he looked around and swept his hand in an arc, "darkness, that you may see the light. Right now, my fellow Knights are distributing these masks." He held one up. "And we encourage you to wear them at all times."

Most people took the masks offered them, but only a few actually put them on.

"We believe the doctors on the other side of the wall are filling the air with new poisons, that they are inventing new ways to control us, and that soon they will release an invisible pestilence for which there is no vaccination. And you..." he pointed at the crowd, "are letting them do it."

Some subtle boos could be heard, but it was impossible to discern exactly where they came from because they were soon drowned out by cheers of support.

Max tugged on Amanda. "Let's go."

The cloak of bravery he'd worn, however uncomfortably, fell with each word until he stood metaphorically naked in the middle of the Raven. Max thought he might as well have had "SISSY" scratched into his chest, and he looked down quickly just to make sure he didn't. Amanda didn't seem to notice, slapping him lightly saying *just a minute*, without actually speaking.

Somnus kept on. "Yes you. You, who come here to

forget, who come here to hope, it's you who are letting them do it through your own *inaction*. Do you think they will stop?"

The response from the crowd was becoming louder, more frequent, and more diverse as additional voices were joining the fray.

Somnus's voice bellowed and echoed. "Do you think they will just stop out of some kindness? Some *philanthropy?* Ha. The time when Doctors care for others is over."

The mass moved closer to the stage, and Max felt the wave behind him, pressuring him to lunge ahead. He eyed Amanda.

She acknowledged that now was the time to move. She tapped Nola who followed them as they weaved away, slowly and arduously through the enthralled mass moving toward them steadily.

Somnus had found a rhythm better than the music that had played before. "The Doctors care about who? You? Me?"

Like a preacher versed in call and response, voices answered, "Nobody" and "No" and "No."

"No, the Doctors care about the Doctors while all of us are paralyzed by fear. We're paralyzed by an idea...the unthinkable thought of our total annihilation, the unfathomable idea of extinction. But, my friends..." He stepped forward. "The Eight Hour Knights are not afraid. We have conquered the true enemy, our trepidation and our cowardice. If you join us, you too can be free from that which truly keeps you oppressed—"

"Liar!" Somnus was interrupted by a loud voice from the back of the club, followed by a gun blast into the air. The shot resonated with concussive effect throughout the club, and the panic it caused traveled faster.

Max and Amanda, with a small head start, ran along as Somnus's crew drew weapons from their coats, waistlines and boots. Max, Amanda and Nola kept their heads down as shots rang out in every direction. The noise was booming and disorienting, made worse by the echoes that ricocheted throughout every corner of the Raven. On the way to the exit, Max's thoughts accelerated like a toddler running downhill, unsteady and out of control.

Who's attacking?

The American Dreamers? The Rock-a-Bye-Babies?

Doesn't matter. Same outcome.

No knives.

No chains.

Those take real strength.

Guns.

Lots of guns.

Any one of us could take a bullet.

We gotta get the hell outta here.

The threesome had nearly reached an exit when one of the Knights who'd previously been guarding the door leveled a pistol at Amanda. Max kept running forward, even though he felt frozen. His left ear was suddenly in agony, and he was momentarily blinded. Someone, standing right next to him, had hip-fired a shotgun. Max stumbled and fell, nearly bringing Amanda down with him. She lurched forward. The Knight fired. A shotgun blast tore into the Knight's chest. Max, lying on his back, deaf, blinking wildly, and groping for Amanda's hand, saw what had happened. An armed man who'd been behind Amanda was stealing away now. Max noticed he wore the markings of a clan, though he didn't know which one. The Knight had sought to bring him down, but the man's compatriot had put a hole in him first. Had he not, Amanda would have been caught in a deadly crossfire. As Max rolled forward to raise himself, he saw the man who'd done it, the man who'd saved Amanda. In truth, as Max laid his eyes upon him, it was no man at all, but a boy. The innocent looking kid slung a shotgun with most of its single barrel sawed off.

Max made eye contact with him and mouthed, *Thanks.*

The boy nodded and turned around against the tide of humanity crashing upon him. Max's hearing was slowly returning, and he heard himself yell Amanda's name when he at last realized they'd become separated. He quickly raised himself and looked around frantically.

Amanda looked backward for Max and was amazed at how fast he moved. Max seemed strong, unfazed by the ugly tumble he'd taken.

People rushed past, bumping into him as he tried to maintain his footing. He spotted Amanda and Nola several steps away to his right. They'd been caught up in the momentum that pushed them toward the doors. Max wiggled his way toward them like a ship tacking into the wind. He finally caught her outstretched hand.

"You okay?"

"My ears are ringing," Max yelled.

She squeezed his hand tightly, and they exited the Raven. The three of them poured into the alleyway and kept moving until he felt they were safe.

Amanda spoke first. "Why do those assholes always end up shooting each other, for Christ's sake?"

Max started to respond but realized there wasn't much he could say in the face of Amanda's bluntness. Instead, the trio just laughed. They knew it was mostly a needed release—that Amanda's inquiry wasn't truly funny—but they guffawed just the same, and heartily. As the laughter trailed off with long sighs, Max offered to walk Amanda home.

"No, I'll be okay. You have to work, anyway."

Nola spoke up. "Don't worry, Max. We'll walk together."

Amanda stood on her toes to peck Max's cheek and tug on his ear. She whispered, "Come over after work, okay?"

"It'll be late." He returned the peck. They parted and walked in opposite directions.

Max smiled while plunging his hands into the pockets of his long tattered coat. He brushed a runaway lock from his eye, looked up and inhaled a chest-full of crisp air. Spring had arrived, but winter wasn't going away without a fight.

***

Max Dyson stopped at a crowded sidewalk diner that served food of all kinds throughout the day and night. He ate a sweet roll with white icing and washed it down with several cups of strong coffee. The patrons were subdued, talking in short spurts about the change in weather but mostly concentrating on the vast array of sweet confections. The place also served eggs, bacon, ham, and other hardy foods, but almost no one ordered them anymore; the quick sugar rush afforded by the pastries couldn't be passed up. A small child in a booth directly in front of Max, however, was just being served a large plate of scrambled eggs, and when Max smelled them going by, he salivated. "Excuse me," he said to the passing waitress.

"May I help you?"

"I think I'd like some eggs today." He jabbed his finger in the air with each of his next words. "Just like those."

"That's a lot to digest," she said. "Gonna make you dog-tired in about an hour. You sure?"

"And bring some bacon too."

When his order arrived, Max ate ferociously. It was, he realized, the most enjoyable meal of his life. He wasn't eating simply because it kept him alive; he ate because he could taste it like never before. He savored it, taking a bite of the eggs and augmenting them with a salty nibble of bacon. The flavors exploded in his mouth, and he was nearly brought to tears from the simple pleasure of it. He filled up quickly...his stomach not used to such gorging, but he sat there for an extra ten minutes until he'd finished every bite.

The waitress was absolutely right about the food's effect. Standing in the inoculation line before starting the night shift at the plant, his knees buckled under a sudden wave of fatigue, and Max caught the wall with one hand and held the other to his belly, grimacing. By the time it was his turn, and a technician was inserting a needle into the back of his neck, however, his body surged with warm blood, and his muscles easily bore his weight, and it seemed to Max, they could easily bare more. Yes, he strangely had strength in reserve. He held the cotton at the insertion point to stem the bleeding and held out his other arm. Another technician swiped Max's card through a small magnetic reader. The reader beeped pathetically, and the man handed the card to Max with a feigned smile. Max pocketed the card and walked onto the main plant floor where the smell and sound of running water became more and more apparent.

Max worked for the Department of Transportation Purification Plant and was enveloped by a familiar darkness. He continued across the expansive space, and squinted mightily as he passed through the bright beam of light coming from the raised control room in the middle of the floor. He'd been inside there once, and as its light blinded him now, he remembered the experience. His quest, to deliver a message from one of the foreman, had sent him climbing up the hundred stairs to their apex. Having never entered *Control* before, he'd been instructed to don an oversized pair of super-shaded goggles, similar to what he wore while working, but much darker. Despite whatever protection they afforded, the intense brightness of the room still hurt his eyes. He'd never been in a fully electrically wired space before, so his mouth dropped open at the blinking, multi-colored lights that covered every square inch of the walls. He was surprised, even jumped, when an alarm went off, and amplified instructions boomed out of speakers from the structure's roof. He delivered the message and hurried out of the din that assaulted him both visually and auditorily.

Max passed through the light and under the raised building that seemed to hover above hundreds of three-foot wide trenches that stretched from one end of the facility to the other. Men, spaced about twenty feet apart, stood in the trenches, wearing goggles with colored lenses and holding poles with a cylindrical device on its end. The cylinder measured about two feet in length and eight inches in diameter. At its midpoint, in three evenly spaced locations, small triangular fins stuck out about two inches. The men wore thick rubber suits extending from chest to feet and long gloves reaching past their elbows. Max, along with several others, pulled their suits and gloves on, grabbed their goggles and poles, and walked in tandem to station number seven.

"Hey, Max." A burly man walked up from behind him and slapped him on the back.

"Hank, what's up?"

"New guy starting today." Hank grabbed a young man with short red hair and freckled face by the arm and dragged him to his side. "Dale..." he pointed with his entire hand, "this is Max."

"Hello, Max." The winsome kid put out his hand.

Max shook it, observing the hand carefully, noting it was devoid of cracks or roughness. It was like the skin of a newborn. *Not for long*, Max thought.

"Max," Hank said, "is gonna show you the ropes."

"Happy to." Max dropped the smooth hand and smiled.

When they arrived at their station, Max leaned down and leapt into the water. "Dale, stay dry for now, and I'll show you how it all works."

An alarm like a baritone whistle sounded briefly, and all the men in the trenches leaned forward, seemingly to Dale, with anticipation of something. Suddenly, the end of the trenches facing them opened, and water rushed in. The white-blue colored wave knocked some of the men in adjacent trenches over, washing them backwards. In seconds, the men left standing were nearly chest deep.

Max looked into the water through his specialized, tinted lenses and swept the pole back and forth with a slow rhythm. "Nice steady motion like this. The fins on the cylinder create drag." The device spun around the pole counterclockwise, then clockwise as Max moved it to and fro.

"The rotation gets converted to energy, and that energy gets forced into a heating element that raises the temperature of the water. It's only a few degrees, but that's enough to startle any algae from stasis. The water doesn't often contain these microscopic little guys, but finding them is critical. I once worked on a transport tube infected with the stuff, and I gotta tell ya, their reproductive abilities were inspiring. In just a day, a droplet of them had grown thick enough to jam a tube and bring the entire hydraulic transportation system to a halt."

"Wow." Dale stood there with his hands on his hips,

watching Max.

"I hope you like the cold, Dale. The water's near-freezing temperature keeps the algae in a state of suspended animation, but these heating units are just enough to trigger the phosphorescence reaction when they awake."

"What's that smell?"

"That's Hank."

"Fuck you," Hank shouted from the other side of the trench.

"What? It's true. Well, sorta. After we stir it a few times, a lubricant gets added, that's what Hank is doing down there."

"It smells like rotten oranges."

"You get used to it. It sticks to your clothes and in your hair too. I've always thought it was like a lemon peel boiled in beer. Anyway, that's the last step."

Suddenly, all the water rushed out behind Max as a hatch had been opened, and the whole lot was then flushed out. The lubricant stench, unfortunately, didn't go along with it, instead, it clung to the air with intense pungency.

When the next wave rushed in, Dale noticed, the ambient temperature of the massive work floor actually dropped several degrees. "Did it just get colder in here?"

"By four degrees. The water arrives from the *glacial main*, a worldwide infrastructure of pipelines that originated at what remains of the polar icecap. A massive undertaking, it took nearly two decades to construct, and my own father was one of the thousands who'd eventually given his life for it."

"Wow, that's amazing," Dale said. "That's something

to be proud of."

"Yeah. Sure is." Max continued his work, methodically, and lost himself briefly to happy memories of his dad.

Dale watched him.

Max held the heat-stick primarily with his left hand, using his right to maneuver its butt-end to either side of his body and for leverage. He would position it against his left side when his torso canted right and then lean into the stick to force it through the water. With his torso now leaning left, his right hand would move the stick across him to the right. It was somewhat awkward, but Max had done it for years, which explained why he appeared weirdly graceful in its execution.

"You've really got it down," Dale said.

"Practice. My dad called this the *Trench Twist*, and despite that cutesy name, it does have the added benefit of keeping you warmer than just standing here like a statue. My father, in the crowded watering holes of the temporary camps where I grew up, would teach the local men, those who would eventually stir the water, about his dance. He'd stand on a chair or table and demonstrate with a broom handle while the men laughed and asked him to demonstrate again and again." As a batch of water drained behind him, Max could still hear them:

"I'm not sure I get it, Samuel. You mean like this?" a stout fellow exclaimed as he gyrated across the dirt floor to thunderous laughter.

"Sure, sure, joke all you want, but I'm telling you boys, you haven't felt cold like this."

The man halted his romp. *"You haven't met my wife."*
Max's dad cut through the laughter. *"Oh, but I have."*
The crowd hushed.

"And she assured me that if I give any classes on this technique..." Samuel writhed again, but this time pumping his hips, *"she'd sign you up for the lessons herself."*

Mouths opened as fingers and rising choruses of *ohhhhhs* were directed at the little man who'd been outwitted. He smiled, too, and nodded at Samuel with a slight wink.

Max was suddenly shaken from his reverie, as a new wave, for which he was totally unprepared, swept him off his feet. He dropped his heat-stick and fell backwards, arms flailing. The water rose up with deafening quickness, and Max tried, without success, to remain calm. He had one foot planted and raised up, when he stumbled slightly, and his head went under. Some water leaked into his suit, and Max's brain became as scrambled as the eggs he'd eaten. He panicked and soon forgot where he was. He struggled with his current predicament, as he recollected, with textured detail, the horror he'd experienced just several months before. Images flashed before him, and he wasn't sure if they were images he was living, or images he was remembering.

He climbed but was overcome. The current pushed him against something hard and unforgiving. He grabbed something that hurt his hand. He bled. The river opened up to swallow him.

He swam with no effect. Darkness. Cold. The taste of water. Sideswept. A piercing sound. He coughed and spat.

His arms flailed about as Hank dragged him sideways by the collar. Max's eyes were closed when he flopped himself over the side of the trench, leaning and breathing heavily. He regained his senses just as he started shivering. He noticed a high-pitched alarm, and all the trenches were prematurely emptying their lots from the side. Several seconds later, he heard someone ask if he was okay. It was Hank, the oldest member of their trench. Max let out a wet "Yeah."

Hank slapped him on the knee, handed him the fallen heat-stick, and climbed the steps. "Kinda freaked out there, eh, man?"

"Yeah." Max said, climbing. "Hey, thanks."

"Think we'd let you drown, pal? Heck, we need you if we're ever gonna catch sixteen." Hank moved away slowly.

"Hey, kid," Max said, looking at Dale, "*that* is an example of what *not* to do." He smiled, admitting his failure had made him feel both calmer and slightly ridiculous. He was caught off guard, that was all. Max jumped back into the trench. An alarm sounded.

"Is that...sixteen again?" he yelled over to Hank, motioning upwards while spinning his finger toward the alarm noise.

"Yep. Another critter for sixteen. Those bastards are either lucky as hell or have eyes like a hungry condor." Hank shrugged and scratched his shoulder.

Max understood why the trenches were draining when they'd only just refilled. Through their glasses, one of the men in trench sixteen must have seen the unmistakable sign and hit the alarm. Max's job was drudgery, but spotting one of the dormant organisms was invigorating; there was a brilliant green burst that glowed with the intensity of an emerging star. It was dazzling, fleeting, and wonderful. After seeing one, Max always imagined himself the God of a watery universe, waving a magic wand that called forth life and light at once.

"So," he looked back up at Dale, "the alarm opens the side gates." Just as he said it, the sideways current caused Max to lose his footing and skid sidelong. "The water will be emptied, flow under us to the *purification* level. There, it will be carefully electrified to eradicate any sign of life. And then, all trenches on this main level will need to undergo microscopic inspection...a meticulous process that takes hours."

Max climbed out of the trench and walked, signaling for Dale to follow him. They passed by the gear-laden inspection team and made their way to change into dry clothes and stand in queue at the supply depot.

"Yo, Dale," Hank yelled from behind them, also in line. "You come with me and I'll walk you through this part."

"Okay."

"See ya later, Dale."

"Later, Max, thanks."

Max was handed a manual crank-light, and then headed off for a series of metal-rung ladders that stretched down each sidewall of the establishment.

Each ladder led to an interlaced puzzle of catwalks that zigzagged and connected high above. A large board on the face of the control tower was suddenly in motion. Like an enormous old-fashioned digital clock with flipping halves of plastic numbers, the board shuffled the men's assignments. Max found his trench number and swallowed when he saw what slowly appeared next to it: *NW Main Tube, 9*. It wasn't an irregular occurrence that NW-M-9 rotated into the maintenance schedule, but it still made him nervous.

Max pushed ahead of many of the other men and climbed the correct ladder much faster than anyone else. He couldn't recall if he'd remembered the small spray bottle he'd vowed to carry with him and checked his pocket as he went. He sighed with relief, as the familiar shape pressed against his thigh.

Max caught up with the man ahead of him, but luckily he exited at a lower level, freeing Max to ascend as rapidly as he could move his hands and feet. Main Tube 9 in the Northwest grid was his team's responsibility, but all Max could think as he climbed himself breathless was that, in reality on any given day, it was *his*.

Max reached the entrance before anyone else. He slid the levers of the crude, though durable, locking system into the correct position and then spun the metallic wheel, releasing the airtight seal. A slow hiss escalated to a gust that moved Max's hair. The plant was soon filled with a symphony of repeating hisses and overlapping bursts of air. He eased the massive door ajar with the help of a smaller wheel, this one handled and connected to a creaky gearing mechanism. The door was almost open when another member of his crew, Mr. Stansbury, a balding middle aged guy, came striding down the grated catwalk.

"I'll take section eight, Mr. Stansbury," Max said hurriedly. Nobody knew Mr. Stansbury's first name, and he seemed quite content with the formal salutation. "I don't mind, and it makes sense, you know, start from the back."

"You are a section eight, buddy." The man hmphed. "Whatever you say."

The rest of the team arrived as Max disappeared into the slippery darkness. He cranked his light, and it beamed for a few seconds before slowly dying out. It was enough light for him to get his bearings and to see the breath shooting from his nostrils. Max walked for several minutes, guiding himself by running a hand along the wall. The immense tube was flawlessly smooth even though it appeared constructed of poured concrete. The tube was rigid, with barely any give at all underfoot. He walked briskly along and soon heard the hollow sound of water running through pipes. Max gave the light a few spirited cranks and ascertained that he was getting close to section eight. He stood at a junction point, and the flushed bolts rotated around him in a circle with geometric precision.

A metallic whistle echoed throughout the pipe. He popped open the back of the flashlight, and from a small compartment, a tarnished cork whistle dropped into his palm. Another whistle echoed, then another, another, and another, each louder than the last, as it traversed NW Main Tube Nine. When Max's turn came, he blew his whistle to signal his presence. He returned the whistle to its home and cranked the flashlight again. Walking a bit farther, he at last spotted the striations of red that marked his arrival at section eight. All around the interior of the tube, for several yards, were thick bands of bright crimson. The color looked painted, but Max knew of no dye that could withstand the conditions inside the glacial main.

Realizing where he was, Max ignored the red mystery and went straight away to his secret. He walked and cranked his dying light, counting quietly under his breath.

"One. Two. Three..." At twenty seven steps, Max's light shined upon it. To him, it looked as if the tube had been gouged with a ragged gardening tool, though in truth, it was barely noticeable. He rushed to it, looking worriedly behind him. The incision he'd made several months earlier was under the junction of another main tube, and the noise of water was overpowering. If someone were to approach his position, he could be taken totally unaware. The noise was necessary when he cut through the tube, but now it was a liability to the safety of his regular inspections. He cranked the light wildly to maximize its luminescence as he held it close to the damage. His chest heaved, and he breathed a sigh of relief, as the patch he'd constructed seemed to have remained soundly in place. His confidence eroded though, as he came closer. The area was about seven inches in diameter, and its corner had pulled away slightly, revealing something metal. Max pulled the spray bottle from his pocket and squirted, with hesitant delicateness, a gentle mist of adhesive onto the flap. Doing this always worried him; he was scared he might make it look worse. With the liquid applied, he blew visible breath to accelerate its adhesion. A rubber band held a small bit of grit-laden paper to the bottle, and he removed it. He glanced behind him, and then he smoothed out the adhesive continually testing it with his fingertips until he was satisfied.

A double whistle blow, indicating that their inspections were to commence, sounded far away down the tube, and Max replaced the paper with the rubber band, and stowed the bottle in his pocket. He then began a careful search of section eight. He did this job with utter sincerity; if a leak, crack, or infestation were found in NW Main Tube Nine, he'd be found out, for sure.

Chapter 3

Amanda smiled as she approached the door of her childhood home. Actually, it was her mother's childhood home, as well.

We've been lucky to have retained a tangible piece of our own history. Most everyone else's had been flooded from existence a generation ago.

The house was small, but Amanda loved it. She'd learned to plant flowers in its tiny backyard, once broke her wrist trying to climb out the second-story window, and, it seemed to her now, almost every stone, every corner, and every blade of grass in the yard held a vivid memory for her. She opened the door, which was always unlocked, and walked in to find herself standing on her mom's favorite welcome mat. It was the funny one, the one that said *Apparently, We Still Have Miles To Go.* What Amanda's mother was passionate about was obvious the moment she walked in. Books were everywhere. They were piled all over the place, teetering towers of books actually obscured the furniture. In the case of the coffee table in the living room to Amanda's right, the books had overtaken it all together.

"Mom, hey, it's me."

She wasn't greeted by the usual smell of homemade candy or laughter for no reason. Today, only silence.

Amanda walked through the house and was immediately concerned when she saw the kitchen. It was disheveled, ransacked, and Amanda feared Walkers or other miscreants were to blame. She kept going because she heard the shower running and felt relief. She increased her speed and burst into the bathroom with every expectation that she'd look her mom in the eyes and tell her about what happened at the Raven. She was right about one thing.

Her mother looked directly at her and stuck out her tongue. Amanda was pushed backward by hands that weren't there, but crushed her chest just the same. Her mother had several layers of cheap kitchen twine wrapped around her neck. It was looped over the shower head and held her body just an inch off the floor. The skin around the string was raw, broken and bleeding in places. It bulged out from between the taunt strands. Her eyes were open, gawking at Amanda. Her swollen tongue, now too big to go back in, dripped with the running water that ran down from her matted hair. The small ledge leading into the shower was smeared with blood, and more could be seen on the lower walls of the stall. Amanda looked down at her mother's bare foot and knew what had happened. Her mom had ripped her toenail off, likely in a struggle to gain footing, and it bled all over, as she searched wildly for footing she had been careful to make sure wasn't there.

Amanda, in shock, picked up a note from the toilet seat. She slid down the bathroom wall, succumbing to the agony of grief as she read it:

Perchance to dream... Love, Mom

***

Max closed his door and locked it in a single motion. The sun was almost fully risen, and he didn't need to head over to Amanda's until later; the time of day was perfect. He breathed deeply at the thought of it, at the impending coldness, but walked with determination toward the basement hatch. After what had happened to him at the plant, the irony wasn't lost on him, but he strode with purpose anyway. He was talking to himself like a sports figure from the lost decades.

"C'mon, Max. You can do this. Not like that stupid wave, you're in control here. You're in control."

You do this, *you* do it.

He repeated the self-encouragements as he descended the rickety stairs into the damp underbelly of his home. The faintest swath of light entered from a tiny window on the right. He felt along the wall until he reached another door. He took a chain from around his neck, used its key to open the padlock, pushed on the door, and entered a large chamber. More natural light streamed into this room, but it was mostly contained to one side of the space. Very high ceilings curved upwards in a dome-like shape. Max had once looked up the blueprints in the library's archive and learned that the room had once been part of the city's internal infrastructure, but had been abandoned for a decade. Its location, he'd thought at the time, was perfect, and so he'd made the decision to transfer his living quarters so he could reside more proximately.

He threw his coat on a hook and unbuttoned his shirt as he walked toward one corner of the room. His shirt was mostly off, as he checked on the position of a large piece of broken mirror connected to a manual timing device. Max carefully wound the device, as he bent down, squinting one eye to line up another mirror across the room. In fact, there were several mirror pieces scattered throughout the room, each about three feet square, though none with clean edges. Max looked up to the grating where the morning light shown through and estimated he had about five hours before the sun would be correct. He set the timers accordingly, removed his shirt fully, kicked his shoes off, unbuckled his pants, and walked toward the contraption that would kill him. He ensured that the steel table was in place as his pants dropped to the ground. The table was six feet long with two vertical pieces of metal soldered directly onto the top, creating a V shape. The table-turned-trough had, at one end, a hole cut into it about eight inches in diameter. The edges of the hole were covered thickly with gray tape. The end of the table closest to Max's machine was raised, making it purposefully unleveled. Max leaned down and stuck his hand in a yellow bucket. A viscous liquid dripped from his fingers, and he slathered it on the table. He wiped his hand with a dirty rag next to the bucket.

Max, wearing only a tight pair of white underwear strode toward a second timing device, this one attached directly to the machine. He wound it, set it, and closed his eyes. Max clenched his fists, gritted his teeth, and breathed out quickly through his nose. He was tall and slender with pale skin and little body hair. A small tract of it ran down his sternum ending just south of the ridges of his prominent, though not big, pectorals. He breathed again and popped his eyes open. He was ready.

Max ascended a small step ladder, and from its perch, climbed into a half-tube shaped container suspended by chains perpendicularly over the steel table. The container had a clear plastic door, and one could imagine that if closed, a cylinder would form. Max reached down and shackled his feet in place, making absolutely sure the trip-wire was connected properly. Having his feet bound was the part he hated most, but his movements showed no sign of hesitation, at all, though he wasn't graceful either, often fumbling what he was doing, forcing him to repeat the motion.

He stood upright in the half-tube, and from right to left, wrapped a three-inch thick fabric strap around his thighs and attached its end to a large Velcro patch. From a grommet at the strap's end hung a lead weight. With his other hand, Max held the weight and then inserted it into an open metallic shelf just above the Velcro. He repeated this process with a strap about his chest. Without fanfare, Max reached out, grabbed the door, and pulled it closed, which caused the cylinder to swing slightly in the air, creaking each time it pivoted downward. Max inspected the seal by running his hand down the crease and then, looking dead ahead without a hint of emotion, threw the internal lever that sent the water rushing in.

He could never get over the arctic-like cold. The lever he'd yanked had popped open the valve he'd installed in NW Main Tube Nine. It sent water, hovering just above freezing, rushing down an intake, filling the tube. When it hit his feet, there was a flash of pain followed by numbness, followed by pain on his shins, followed by numbness, followed by more pain, and more numbness. He sometimes passed out as it rose up around his genitals, but this was not one of those times. As the frigidness hit his belly, a familiar panic made him start to hyperventilate. Max knew it wouldn't last long.

***

The evening was at twilight's end, as Max walked along the familiar route leading to Amanda's. The sky's first stars blinked at him, and the air smelled clean. As he walked, he tore off a strip of paper from the sandwich he carried. The street vendor had wrapped it so that he could peel it down, bit by bit, and eat as he went. He took a bite and marveled again at his taste buds enlivened effectiveness. He hummed a quiet guttural note of satisfaction and licked his lip. An inoculation station with a line that snaked haphazardly out the door, forced him to cross the street. The faces of those waiting ranged from blasé indifference to squint-eyed, head-holding anguish. Max knew the blinding pain they felt, for he too had occasionally waited too long between sticks. His job with the purification plant had all but ended that excruciating inconvenience; the Department provided all employees with easy access to shots. Max crossed back and tossed his food wrapper in a corner trash can, wiped his hands on his pants, and turned onto Amanda's block.

Nola was out front, lighting a cigarette with the butt of her last. She paced in front of Amanda's door. Max called to her, and Nola bounded at him, flicking the new cigarette into the street without looking.

"Max, where have you been? I've been looking everywhere for you. I went to your place but you didn't answer and—"

"You went to my place? Just now?"

"Yeah, but whatever, you weren't there, I guess, anyway, listen." Nola's eyes were intense and full of angst.

Max saw that something wasn't right. Nola was talking, but he peered over her, looking at Amanda's door.

"Amanda's mom is dead."

He suddenly paid attention. "What? How? Wh—" he stammered.

"Last night. Amanda found her today. She came home to get some things and told me to find you, then went back to her mom's."

Max shook. "Okay, well I've got to get over there." He started to turn when Nola grabbed him.

"Max, she hung herself. She hung herself from the shower."

"Christ," he uttered.

"It was a shocker." Nola sighed, lowering her head.

"I need to get to her, Nola," Max said with anxious determination. "I'm going."

"I'm coming with you."

They walked quickly and silently for several blocks until reaching the transport station, and then they descended the stairs without holding the handrail. The station was dark, damp, and to both Max and Nola, smelled sour. The air seemed saturated with the odor of pickled cabbage.

Nola vocalized her dislike. "Yuck."

The pair made their way through a complicated set of unlit passageways, causing them twice to have to double-back and re-navigate. There were no attendants, or fees to pay, or turnstiles to pass through, so they simply kept going. Nola and Max approached a fork partially lit from above. High up, at the end of a vertical tunnel, the purple sky of dusk poured in through an opening several feet wide. This also allowed for fresh air to enter, so the vinegary cabbage odor dissipated somewhat. Nola sniffed in mightily, savoring the cleanliness of the breeze. Max, without stopping, simply bore left, continuing farther down into darkness and passing a lone traveler. They excused themselves as they went by, and the elderly man nodded. *Finally,* Max thought as they reached the platform. Similarly constructed, a series of rooftop holes in the cathedral ceiling allowed oblong patches of light into the stone and steel expanse. The platform had several other people waiting, but no one was speaking. One man hummed to himself, and a woman leaning against the wall drank from a cup. Max looked around the spartan room— flat with metallic siding and a smooth stone floor—but didn't find a place to sit. Droplets of condensation occasionally joined forces and, with new-found gravity, rolled down the walls and onto the shoulders of people leaning there. Max looked at the center of the room and saw two trap doors, about three times the size of a service elevator. The doors were side by side and inset into the floor. He leaned on a waist-high fence of plexiglass around the perimeter in order to get a better look. One set of doors had a clearly marked queue by additional plexiglass and painted arrows. The other set of doors had the same, in mirror image.

Max, nervous about what he was going to say to Amanda, swayed back and forth and picked at the palm of his hand every few seconds. He felt like they'd waited for hours even though only a few minutes had passed. Max's eyes darted around the station then back to his hand. More people were filing in through the entrance he and Nola had used, and he was hopeful this indicated a transport's imminent arrival. As the room became more crowded, people started lining up inside the plexi labyrinths.

Max tapped his foot and smiled meekly at Nola. The sucking sound of wet friction started faintly and increased, as the transport pod was hydraulically pushed into the station. The doors in the floor split open to reveal the inside of the transport pod, the tops of other riders' heads, and a staircase leading to the deck. Max and Nola filed down the stairs along with everyone else and found a handle to share. The doors closed, and the sucking sound began again. Max sighed deeply.

Nola spoke to him. "I lost my uncle that way, you know," she whispered, leaning into him. "And a couple friends, too."

"My cousin, and my friend's wife." Max rested against the side of the pod and blinked slowly. "Mark's wife, actually, you know Mark, don't you?"

Nola looked surprised. "Yes I do. Wow, I had no idea."

"It was a long time ago."

They remained silent until arriving at East station.

Exiting, Nola led him to the home of Amanda's mother. The door was open, and several others were already inside. People stood, mostly couples talking to each other, but a small crowd encircled Amanda. Max caught her eye and raised his hand slightly as he bent his fingers in a small wave.

Amanda raised her hand, too. Her eyes were swollen and her face colorless.

Max and Nola chatted about nothing for several minutes until the people talking to Amanda hugged her politely and walked away. Amanda wiped her eyes with the back of her hand as Max and Nola approached her. Max hugged her tightly but Amanda's arms remained flaccidly at her side. He kissed her cheek and whispered, "I'm sorry."

"Thanks. I didn't see this coming." She sighed heavily. "I mean, at *all*."

Nola held her next, and this time, Amanda returned the embrace. "Oh fuck, Nola." Nola hung on to her longer than Amanda expected.

She crinkled her face and then wept violently into Nola's shoulder. The outpouring didn't last long.

Max knew these incidents were responsible for the way Amanda's eyes looked.

She pulled back from Nola, and the skin around her sockets looked even more irritated and inflamed.

Max set his hand over his heart, suddenly panged at the sight of her anguish. He tried to touch her again, but this time Amanda shrugged away and mumbled something about having to speak to someone across the room.

Max and Nola waited for several hours until they were alone with Amanda in her dead mother's house.

"Have you eaten anything?" Nola asked.

"No, but there's nothing in this..." Amanda looked around, "pigsty anyway."

"If I get you something, will you eat a bit?"

"I don't know, maybe."

Nola gathered her coat and slipped it on as she went out the door. "I'll be right back," she said, looking at Max.

Amanda walked by Max, avoiding his outstretched hand as she went. She slumped into a chair and cupped her face in her hands. Her shoulders heaved with sobs, and Max felt utterly helpless.

"Amanda, I just, well..." his voice was getting weaker, "I just don't know what to say except to tell you how sorry I am."

"There's nothing you can say." Her voice was muffled in defeat, and her shoulders started jerking again.

Max walked to her and knelt down. "It's going to be okay."

Amanda stopped crying and looked directly at him. "And, how, exactly is that going to work? In what fucked-up universe will this ever be *okay*?"

"I don't know, I-I was just saying," he stuttered, "uh, something."

"If a bunch of goddamn platitudes and niceties are all you can come up with, then just shut the hell up."

"Okay." Max stood and moved to the side.

"Oh, great, now you're wounded and pissed." She stood and pivoted to face Max. "That's just what I need after finding my mom hanging in the fucking shower." A tear formed, rolled down, and puddled in the wrinkled puffiness that buttressed her eye.

"Hey, I was just trying to make you feel better."

"You're too afraid for that, Max."

"What the hell does that mean?"

Amanda raised her voice and clenched her jaw. "Don't you understand that I'm dying? My mother may be dead, but living with it is *mine*. *All mine.* It doesn't have anything to fucking do with you."

"Okay, I get it, but why am I afraid?"

"You can't make a dying person feel better, Max. You just have to be there. You have to sacrifice a little bit of yourself. Some of you needs to die, too. This isn't something that will ever go away. Nothing will ever be the same. Get out while you can, Max. Run away from me."

"I can be there for you, Amanda. I *want* to."

"Bullshit. Ever since I met you, you've been afraid."

Max knew she wasn't all wrong, that he'd talked with her about ambitions, but lived up to almost none of them. He managed to say, "Hey, that's not fair."

"Fair? You want fair? Fucking perfect."

"What can I do?"

"Nothing, Max. There's nothing you can do. Just go."

"Really? You want me to leave?"

"Yes."

Max almost said, "I'm not leaving, and I'll never leave." Instead he fumbled with his coat and mumbled, "Can I come see you later, at your place?"

"Whatever," Amanda said, sitting again.

"Okay, then I'll see you later, all right?"

"Yeah, later."

"Amanda, I love you."

"Okay, thanks." She nodded and smiled with one side of her mouth.

Max gently closed the door. He heard Amanda sobbing, as he walked away down the street. *Maybe I should kill her now*, Max thought as the door fell into place. *No. She's not ready.*

Chapter 4

Brock Patterson made the same pilgrimage every year on the exact same day. He moved slowly through the streets, reliving the worst day of his life, ten years ago. But, he remembered, the whole story forced him to go back even further than that. Three full years after *the change,* he was ready for it all to end. He didn't feel alive and, with every sunrise and sunset, he became more convinced there wasn't any point to continuing on. He knew his parents would be devastated, but they'd gotten over his brother's suicide, so he was confident they would get over his. They might even understand it, given that what he was considering would have made it a family tradition. In reality, he didn't care. He just wanted it all to be over. The thought of passing out of life and into whatever lay beyond was actually a comfort. Even if nothing at all was waiting for him, oblivion must be better than the colossal weight of his fatigue.

Then, he'd just stepped over the railing at the apex of the Franklin bridge on a breezy spring day when she'd spoken to him. He was so focused he'd not seen that a young woman was already over the railing and facing the water. She was only six feet away but partially obscured by a green riveted bracing that jutted out. He could see her face clearly.

Now, Brock stepped off the curb to cross the street, as he allowed the memories to play out in his head like a staged performance. He attended this play every year on this day, and the emotions were always the same. Intense happiness, soiled by the knowledge that he knew how it ended. Still though, he could hear her voice as if she were strolling alongside him at that very moment:

"I suspect," she said, standing on the ledge with her arms outstretched behind her, *"we're thinking the same thing."* She smiled nervously, her lip quavering.

Brock force-smiled back. *"Oh, yeah,* and *what's that?"*

There was a long pause, and Brock half-expected her to say nothing. He thought that rather than speaking she might simply slip away from the edge and silently tumble the two hundred feet beneath them to the water's unforgiving surface. He imagined the sound of that impact, not the carefree, refreshing sound of a summertime dive into cool depths, but a brutal *smack*, like a baseball bat making the perfect connection with a raw turkey carcass thrown at fastball speed. He expected her to fall. But she didn't. Her glassy eyes, peering at him from just around the green iron bracing, were full of sadness, though not devoid of hope.

"I thought it would be easier to let go," she said.

She could have said any of a million things in that moment, and any of them would have been appropriate. *What I wouldn't give for a good night's sleep. Oh to be a child again. I just want it to stop. This is going to kill my parents.* Any of those would have, in a way, been true. But what she'd actually said was the truest of all. Brock really did think the whole thing was going to be fluid: step over and jump, in one continuous motion. It hadn't turned out to be that easy. A strong breeze that smelled of riverside mud and wildflowers whipped across their faces and blew the young woman's bright red hair all over her face in dancing strands.

"How old are you?" she asked.

"Twenty two. You?"

"Twenty six."

"You made it a lot longer than I did. Does it get easier, like they say?"

"Not really." She looked down at the rippling water. *"You could get more used to it, I guess."*

Brock also stared down, thinking only of a baseball bat smacking a hurled turkey. The *thunking* against flesh with the coterminous crunching of bone. His bones. He looked to his right only to find that the redhaired woman was already looking at him. In the matter of minutes, he knew, his life had changed.

"I'm Brock," he said, surprising even himself.

"I'm Shirley."

Neither of them could remember exactly how or even when they'd stepped back over the railing. Their memories were, however, synchronized on the moments that followed. They took each other's hands and walked aimlessly through the city, talking. They shared an enormous piece of chocolate cake at a small bakery near the river they both had just come close to dying in.

Brock rounded the penultimate corner and knew he would reach his destination in just one more turn. He slowed his pace so that the performance playing out in his mind could make it through the final two acts.

Their love had been immediate, passionate and deep. Brock had never connected with another person as closely as he had with Shirley. It was mutual, and the strength of their emotion sustained them for four blissful years. As Brock strode along the cracked sidewalk, he closed his eyes and inhaled. He could smell her. Closing his eyes and tilting his head back, he raised his face toward the sky. He smiled and imagined her smiling back at him. In his mind's eye he saw himself running his hand through her fiery locks, as she grinned back at him with her one crooked tooth. He opened his eyes again as he made the final turn. Act three, the final act, despite his desire to avoid it, would now play out.

Everything changed when Shirley's grandmother had passed. Her mother died during childbirth, and she'd never known her father, so it was her grandmother who'd raised her. The death sent her into a downward spiral. The tiredness their love had distracted them from had come back with a vengeance. Her depression, with no way to escape it even for just a few hours, soon became a raging contagion in their relationship. They stuck together, but the fatigue soon began to affect them both just like before they had met. They tried everything to overcome it. Back-alley grain alcohol. Knockout rooms where supposed experts inflicted just the right amount of head trauma to make you lose consciousness and fall on the padded floor, but not enough to inflict serious injury. Street drug concoctions. None of those had worked. They were both nearing the point of exhaustion that had been responsible for their meeting in the first place. In an act of desperation, they made the decision to save their money and try a coma parlor. Brock rode a stationary cycle for four hours a day, charging batteries for a merchant who sold them at ten times what he paid Brock. Shirley put in extra shifts at the diner where she waitressed. After three long weeks, they'd saved enough for the procedure.

Brock finally arrived at the place where he'd last seen Shirley. He waited across the street from the parlor and kept an eye out for any possible patrons. If any came along, Brock would quickly intercept them and tell them about what happened to him here a decade ago to the day. In the past ten years that he'd told his story, probably a couple dozen times, the majority of those he told went inside anyway. But not all of them. The coma parlors told a good story: that drug-induced comas were used purposefully and successfully in the past as a healing and restorative medical technique; that they were safe and effective. Brock found out the hard way that those were lies.

He and Shirley only had enough money for each of them to get four hours under, but that sounded like heaven back then. When he'd awoken, foggy and dazed, two people were standing over Shirley's bed, and she was shirtless. Her small freckled breasts were exposed as they pumped on her chest and squeezed a device over her nose and mouth at regular intervals. Her mouth was wide open, her eyes closed, and her lips, usually thin and pink were puffy and blue. Brock couldn't hear well, as if he were fully immersed underwater, but he could make out a distinctive sound that haunted him still.

Beeeeeeeeeeep.

Shirley never woke up.

Just then, a young man climbed the stairs out of a transportation stop cattycorner to Brock's position. He carried himself just as Brock and Shirley had all those years ago, shuffling and slouching, as if the weight of the entire world rested upon his shoulders. Brock crossed over, introduced himself, and told his story.

Chapter 5

At Mark's abode: "Come on in, shithead," Mark said with as much seriousness as he could muster. "Thanks, crap face."

"Crap face?" Mark slammed the door. "Is that the best you can do? Jesus H. Christ, you can't swear for shit."

"Fuck you, man. I can too."

"You've got no creativity, no head for it. It's an art form, you know."

"Yeah, well, blow it out your ass."

Mark walked toward Max. "You fucking seriously suck, dude. I tell you what, though...Amanda's got a knack for it. That girl'd give a sailor a fair run."

"Yeah." Max sank into a kitchen chair. "I've noticed."

"Christ, what's wrong? You look as if somebody just knocked the piss out of you." Mark sat in the chair directly across from him.

Max explained what had happened. "I'm sorry to have come here with all this." He looked at the kitchen table then raised his eyes to Mark. "Especially, here. I'm really sorry, man."

"It's okay, Max. I'm all right. And this is the perfect place for you to come. You know why?"

"Because you're my friend, you have experience with this in a very personal way, and because of that, maybe you can help me."

Mark raised an eyebrow. "No, you fucking pansy, because I have whiskey."

They laughed.

Mark shot up from his chair, opened a cabinet behind him, and extracted a bottle and two glasses. He set them on the table then reached over to Max's shoulder. "And..." he lowered his voice, "because of that other shit, too."

"Thanks, but I'm not sure I should drink any liquor right now."

Mark cocked his head, furrowed his brow, and started unscrewing the bottle.

"Seriously, Mark."

"Uh-huh." Mark lined up the glasses and poured the drams.

Max folded his arms. "Hey, are you not hearing me over there?"

"I hear you."

"Then why are you pushing that glass of whiskey on me?"

Mark took a long pull from his glass and *ahhhed* with satisfaction. "That is because I'm not listening to you."

"But do you hear me?"

"Hear? Yes. Listen? Not so much." Mark smiled.

"There's a difference?"

"Yes. One ends in whiskey, and the other doesn't." Mark took another sip.

Max sighed. "It won't do any—"

"Hey, listen. Are you depressed?"

"Yes, sort of."

"Got any friends around?" Mark held his free hand in the air and pointed at himself gregariously.

Max chuckled. "Yes."

Mark shrugged and held up his glass of whiskey as if to say *ta-da*.

Max scowled, grabbed his glass, tapped it on Mark's glass, and took a big swig.

Some of Mark's whiskey sloshed onto the table. "You're such a klutz, man." He ambled to the sink, took a dirty towel off a nail in the wall, and walked back. There came, suddenly, a rapid and hard knocking on his front door. His conviviality vanished in both perceptibility and reality. He set down the glass and dropped the towel next to it then hustled through the kitchen, diagonally across the living room, and straight through the small foyer to his front door.

Mark was a large man, both in height and girth, and as he walked, Max noticed that a layer of flesh resting above his considerable rump teeter-tottered in rhythm with his gait. He pulled the door open, spoke briefly, and moved aside.

Two people, on either side of a third, entered.

"Put him on the couch over there."

The two men dragged the third into the living room. He tried to walk but was terribly uncoordinated and appeared, with his legs bouncing about randomly, to be a hindrance to his own movement.

Mark looked at Max. "Do you mind?" He followed the trio while pointing at the couch.

Max jumped up, and the utter mess that was the

decorum of Mark's apartment struck him all at once. He moved to the couch and swept away a pile of paper, clothes, food wrapping, magazines, two cans, and a dirty plate with a fork stuck to it.

The two men deposited their friend on the clear space Max had provided. They stepped back with worried faces, and Max noticed that the man on the couch kept bobbing his head as if his neck were skin with a rubber-ball core. The man's eyes were in a similar state and refused to focus on anything for longer than a second or two. They rolled about in his head as if unattached.

Mark inquired of his friend's, "How old is he? Twenty? Twenty-one?"

"Nineteen."

"Yeah, that's what I figured. Those first few years are the toughest. Christ, I remember them myself."

Everyone in the room nodded unanimous agreement.

One of the other men spoke. "He said today made three years. He wasn't sure of it exactly, but that's what he said."

"That's about when everyone cracks." Mark leaned down toward the quietly writhing mass on his couch. "Ah, you're a mess, kid." He tilted the boy's head back and looked up his nose. "No blood, that's good." He grabbed the young man's face and held it still. "Hey. Hey."

The boy focused on Mark.

"What's your name?"

"J-Jack," was the slurred reply.

"That's right," one of the men said.

"So tired, so, so..." Jack was blubbering.

Mark again took control. "Jack. Do you know what year it is? What's the year, Jack?"

"Uh, yeah, it's..." His head rolled about in every direction. "Twenty-one, uh, sixty four, wait...three, no it's twenty-one sixty—"

"Close enough, Jack. What's the nation's capital? Jack, hey."

"W-Washington."

"Not bad, Jack...you're right. It's mostly underwater, but Washington it is. Jack, hey, Jack."

Jack was now blithering with total incoherency, and his body quivered.

"Shit," Mark said, "thought I could bring him back with cognitive stimulation. Apparently Jack isn't game." Mark straightened and looked at the others. "What'd he take? Do you have the inhaler?"

One of the men reached into his jacket pocket and handed Mark a plastic inhaler.

Mark took it, smelled it from a distance, and shook his head. "Empty but...hmm." He frowned. "Max, under the sink in the kitchen, bring me the bag. It's in the back."

Max moved away.

Mark pondered the nebulizer he held. "The human being is a truly remarkable creature, his ability to survive seems equaled only by his ability to invent new ways to fuck himself up."

Max soon returned with a worn brown leather bag. It was as big as a shoe box with a large zipper down its middle and no handles. A simple strap was sewn into one end, but holding it that way would cause the bag to go vertical and all its contents to shift dramatically. Instead, Max carried it with both hands and delivered it gingerly to Mark.

Mark kneeled and dug around in the bag, as if he were stirring stew: things clinking and clanking together. His hand withdrew a dropper with a clear liquid. He unscrewed its cap and placed a droplet of the liquid into the chamber of the device. It immediately turned aqua blue.

"Cycler." Mark put down the items and stood again. "That's good, actually, much better than stagers. Those are nasty concoctions. Not much you can do about a stager."

"What's the difference?" Max asked.

"I'm no chemist, but then again, neither are the raving assholes who cook up this junk." Mark was looking around in his bag as he spoke. This time he came out with a packaged syringe and ripped it open with his teeth. "Anyway, a Cycler is pretty old fashioned. It's a cocktail of harmless drugs...don't ask me which...aimed at inducing a state of massive fatigue. It's supposed to take the brain out of cycle..." he made quotation marks in the air with his fingers, "and keep it, well, *on hold*, I guess, until the drugs wear off, and then the brain can return to its previous state."

Mark sat on the couch. "That's it, really. It sort of works as you can see." He motioned to the listless man next to him as evidence. "The benefits are negligible, though some think losing your ability to think straight, or stand up straight, for that matter, helps." Mark slid next to Jack, who was staring at his hands lying face up in his lap, and started taking off Jack's coat. The young man offered no resistance.

"Stagers are entirely different...and dangerous. They literally assault the brainstem with a brew of chemicals in an attempt to shift the brain from one stage of consciousness to another...stage one to two, two to three, and so on." Mark rolled up Jack's sleeve. "It never works, but it sure can fry you. Lots of people end up similar to our friend here, but all too often those chemicals literally re-wire the brain and you have—"

"*Walkers*," Jack's two friends said in perfect synchronicity.

"Yep. Basically, they're the walking dead. Sort of like a drug-induced cerebral e-e-edema." Mark stuttered over the last word. "I think I'm pronouncing that correctly." He took the syringe out of the plastic and slid closer to Jack, who was singing softly to himself.

Max asked, "What's that?"

"Your brain drowns in your body's own water. Not good. High altitude mountain climbers...can you believe people used to climb mountains on purpose? Anyway, climbers used to get it, and they'd just sit down on the mountain and die. They'd understand totally that they were freezing to death but wouldn't do anything to save themselves. When that happens, you're pretty much a goner." There was silence as each man thought about what a frozen mountain climber must have looked like.

"Will you guys be able to stay with him for few hours after I do this?" Mark asked.

They answered positively. "What is that?" one inquired.

"Adrenaline. Works like magic...you'll see. Gonna make him nauseous at first, though. Max, hand me that bucket."

Max picked up the dull yellow plastic pail next to his feet. He looked inside, and saw that the bucket had a thin layer of something white dried to the bottom. As Mark reached out for it, Max signaled that something disgusting was already there by tilting his head. "Nice."

Mark folded his fingers down, leaving the middle one fully extended, and then he smirked. Jabbing the needle into Jack's arm had almost no effect. His head moved slightly toward Mark and carried with it a stupid-looking grin under bloodshot eyes. Seconds later, the eyes widened, and his muscles contracted; even the ones in his face flexed with vigor. Jack took an enormous breath and blew it out hard. Mark backed away, leaving the bucket in his patient's lap. Everyone stared as he sprung up, sending the bucket tumbling down. It was as if the couch had suddenly become hot under him. Jack looked at each of them. "What happened?"

His friend was about to answer him when the pallor of Jack's face in an instant went from dull to bleached. He stepped forward, kneeled, grabbed the bucket, and vomited from deep within his gut. He continued vomiting, and they continued staring, mouths agape, until Mark said, at last, "He'll be at that a while, guys. Gonna feel like shit, but he'll recover."

"Hey, thanks. I'm John, by the way. This is Wil."

"Nice to meet you, John. Wil." Mark shook John's hand.

"How much do we owe you?" John asked.

"What have you got?"

"A few world dollars and a half-pint of bourbon."

Mark, looking over his shoulder at Max, smiled widely.

Chapter 6

Brock Patterson had succeeded in getting the younger man's attention. "She died?"

"Don't believe what they tell you. It isn't at all safe, and it doesn't even work. I made it out, but I wasn't any better after it. The drugs they use have side effects that counteract any benefit you might have from being unconscious."

"But, but..." The young man struggled to talk. "I have to do something. I can't go on like this."

"Yes you can."

"How? How do you do it?"

"Because I know the secret of survival."

"Oh yeah, and what's that?"

"Purpose. You must find a purpose. Find that and you can survive anything."

The younger man hadn't noticed they had stopped walking, but Brock was conscious of it. He was hoping the man in front of him would make the decision to forego his plans, so Brock was employing every countermeasure he could. He was telling his story, but he had also physically placed himself between the man and the coma parlor; a physical barrier in addition to the emotional one he was conjuring.

And it worked.

The man agreed to sit with Brock and hear him out. Brock may have saved the man's physical life, but now it was time to offer him a way to spiritual salvation, as well. It wouldn't bring Shirley back, but he knew she'd have been proud of him.

Moments later, the two found themselves at a sugar bar that served overly sweet drinks all containing a simple syrup, the recipe for which its owner guarded like some secret weapon. Brock's drink was clear with a yellowish tint while the young man's was fire engine red. They sipped them through wide straws.

"I'm Brock Patterson," he said before taking a long pull from his drink. "I love this place. Best sugar rush in the whole city...in my opinion." The wide straw dropped from his mouth, which was adorned with a finely trimmed goatee, mostly brown with flecks of gray like small spatters of paint.

"Never been here before," the young man said, "I'm Kyle. Kyle Green."

"It's nice to formally meet you, Kyle." Brock held out his hand.

Kyle shook it. "So..." he paused to suck down nearly half his drink, "oh, that is good. What's *your* purpose?"

"I'm an Eight Hour Knight." Brock answered him has plainly as he could, but a sense of pride came through anyway. Kyle Green sat up straight-backed and his eyes widened. "Really?"

"Yes."

"Where's your mask?"

Brock chuckled. "That's certainly part of the brand,

but we don't generally like to advertise ourselves in that way. So we wear them inside our cell's headquarters or for public appearances."

"Oh, like at the Raven the other night?"

"I wasn't there, but yes. Like that."

"Is it true?" Kyle finished his drink with a long pull ending with a loud slurping sound. The other patrons made similar noises, as they polished off their sugary potions, and Kyle suddenly understood how the place got its name. *SLURP.* "Is it true what they say about Somnus?"

Brock was drinking, so he couldn't respond immediately. His eyes connected with Kyle's and signaled for him to continue his interrogative.

"Has he really seen the doctors on the other side? Has he been over the wall?"

"I don't know, but I believe that the key to changing our fate lies on the other side, and that is the very premise of Somnus's perspective, as well. I don't know if he has all the answers, but I think his ship is the one pointed in the right direction. The other factions are too busy quibbling over territory on this side of the wall."

"Is it also true that Somnus has medical records dating back years that might provide clues as to our...our condition?"

"I don't know that either." Brock paused, considering just how honest to be. He decided his best chance to recruit Kyle Green was to go all in. "Actually, I've never met him."

"Wait. What? Your purpose is to follow this man on his mission...and you've never met him? You mean to tell me that, if you fell over him, you wouldn't even recognize him? You wouldn't know him if you saw him?"

Brock leaned back in his chair. "Oh, I'd know him."

"How?"

Brock raised his palm toward Kyle. With his thumb he rubbed a metal ring on his ring finger. "Because I have this."

Kyle stared wide-eyed, amazed. "Is that an authenticator ring?"

Brock nodded. He partially unzipped his jacket, and from an inside pocket produced a small pad of paper with an attached pen. He jotted on the pad, ripped it cleanly off, and handed it to Kyle. "Come to that address tomorrow at noon. Buy something to eat from the street vendor. You will be met by two of my men who will escort you to our cell. Let me show you around. Introduce you. Maybe our purpose can become yours."

Kyle Green took the paper. "I'll be there."

Chapter 7

Max stumbled out the door into the morning light and nearly fell. Miraculously, he clambered forward and found the cold metal railing leading up the staircase to the street. He clutched it desperately, steadied himself, and turned around, still hunched.

Mark had both hands locked on the door jam, held himself up precariously and swung his hefty hips in and out of the door. "Whoa there, brother...careful." Mark teased him.

"I'm fine, you asshole."

"Where you headed, my friend?"

"Home," Max said.

"Why's that?"

"Where the heck else would I go, ya jerk?"

"Amanda's."

"Wha? Amanda? You must be joking? I don't think she wants to see me. She made that very clear."

"Really? I don't think so."

"Trust me, Mark. You should—"

"Hey! I think you should go. All I'm sayin'."

"Well..."

"Seriously, man...just go."

"Okay." Max righted himself, turned, and in the same

RA Haskell

moment, made a significant decision. He didn't know if the drink had given him the courage, but he didn't care. He had decided to tell Amanda everything, to reveal himself, to love her without reticence. The decision unlocked something in him that scrambled his brain like the eggs he'd eaten days ago. His head was suddenly on fire with a concoction of emotions. He made it up the stairs with a purposeful mind that he couldn't control, a mind he'd unleashed by simply accepting the fact that he needed this woman, a mind full of love and regret. A mind full of sympathy and fear and hope. A mind full of hatred and compassion and lust. A mind full of dominance and inadequacy and omniscience. A mind full—literally full—of Amanda's earthy scent. He ran to her place.

The corner of her apartment door caught a bit of the morning sunshine, and Max felt guilty before remembering that it wouldn't matter at all; he loved this woman and was now going to tell her with drama. He was going to espouse and make a fool of himself.

Jesus, I'll sing to her if that's what it takes.

He planned on doing something difficult. He planned on showing himself to her and telling her about his greatest secret. His intentions would reveal his vulnerability, and he'd become more vulnerable in its doing. She'd be able to kill him with a wink, wound him with a whisper, and bleed him with a thought. As he grew weaker from the revelations, he hoped, *they'd* grow stronger, and that's what he wanted. He pushed her door and it opened without a sound. Max went in. Her scent smacked him squarely, and he smiled with pride. He tried to contain his anticipation but cried out anyway, "Amanda, I'm sorry I didn't come sooner. You should have seen Mark last night, he was..."

Max shut the door and immediately noticed the silence. "Amanda?"

Her apartment matched, absolutely, the memory in his mind. The flower pots were positioned perfectly to capture optimal sunshine; those loving the morning sun were beginning to open, bend back, and bask as Max walked casually by. Amanda was not meditating in her chair; neither was she cooking. Max looked about and called again. "Amanda? Amanda, where are you?"

Max stopped dead when he heard the shower running. He breathed in quickly but not because he needed oxygen. In fact, he needed less, far less; his heart was racing. Max ran to the bathroom with every expectation to find Amanda there, strung up and wet. He regretted the whisky, willfully trying to ignore its effects. He burst through the bathroom door and was accosted by thick steam. Max waved his arms and blinked over and over.

"Amanda?"

He yanked the shower curtain back, but the stall was empty. He heard a whimper from below.

There she was, sitting on the floor with her back against the sink's cabinet. Her hands rested by her sides, palms up. Her right hand held an empty inhaler and another was on the floor. Amanda's head was leaning to the right, and her eyes, like slot machine cherries, rolled up and down.

"Oh, no. Oh, fuck, no," Max shouted. "Amanda, oh God, oh my fucking God."

Amanda didn't move.

Max fell down to her and grabbed her face with both hands. "Honey! Babe! Amanda, talk to me. Amanda. What'd you take?"

Amanda tried to speak but simply let out noise and drool.

This isn't happening.

Max slapped Amanda's face with both hands, as if applying aftershave, and her eyes stopped rolling for a split second. Max increased the intensity of his slapping and Amanda spoke at last. "I need to, need to..." Amanda's speech was slurred. "I need to..." Her eyes were unfocused. "Sleep," she muttered at last. "Must sleep." Amanda's eyes teared as if the very thought of rest made her ache with longing. And, in reality, that was exactly true.

Max battled panic and alcohol. "I know, I know, but..." Tears rolled down his face, and mucous filled his sinuses, lacing his words with an unwanted lisp.

Amanda receded back into her previous state, and Max hit her again. "What's the capital? Amanda, what's the capital city?"

She didn't respond.

Shit. Fuck. Damn, was all that Max could think. Desperate, Max hit Amanda much harder.

She righted her head. "I need sleeeep," she whimpered.

"What did you take?" Max screamed at her. "Was it stagers?"

Amanda's head nodded up and down three times.

"Oh, Christ."

Max looked around to the left, then looked around right, then stared at Amanda. He wiped tears from his eyes and sniffed vigorously. Max made his second important decision of the day and grabbed Amanda. As he pulled her up, he saw a small droplet of blood trickle from her nose.

"Oh, no. C'mon Amanda, we've got no time. You need to walk, honey."

Amanda didn't cooperate, and Max had to drag her outside. He knew he couldn't carry her the whole way.

What the hell am I going to do?

The sun hit him in the face.

He spotted Amanda's wheelbarrow, lifted her into it, and grabbed the handles. "Hold on," he said, though Amanda had already begun to show signs of transformation and, therefore, didn't hear him.

He rolled the wheelbarrow into the street and ran for home.

The fastest route took him past the plant, and having lost track of time in the chaos, all he could do was pray there wasn't a shift change. To be seen pushing a wheelbarrow at full speed that had a woman's arms and legs flopping out from the sides would have surely meant Amanda's end, and maybe his own. He could see, blurrily, through the sweat that dripped into his eyes, his front door in the distance.

Amanda's eyes, on the other hand, snapped open and focused angrily on him. He tried speaking her name, but she appeared either not to hear or not to understand and instead, grabbed the sides of the wheelbarrow and squeezed it until her knuckles turned white. The wooden sides, weathered by seasons of rain, snow, and sun, crunched under her grasp, and splinters pierced her skin, puncturing it raggedly. She squeezed harder in an attempt to stand, and tiny blood trails ran down the sides of the silvery-gray wagon.

Max reached the door and stopped short.

Amanda fell back to a seated position and breathed heavily. She tasted a droplet of blood that had run down a dried track leading from her nose to the top of her lip and smiled in a way that chilled Max to the bone.

He didn't think about what was happening to her, he only cared about getting her downstairs as fast as possible. He picked her up, and she scratched his face, as he tossed her over his shoulder. He staggered into his home as Amanda clawed his back and kicked a half glass of water off a side table. It smashed. Max rushed her downstairs, fumbled with the padlock, and at last entered the stone room. He crossed quickly, climbed on the stepstool and shoved Amanda into the cylinder that hung in the shadows. He held her against the back of the device with a firmly planted hand on her chest, strapped her in, placed the weights, tied her feet down and slammed the door.

She gritted her teeth and growled at him like a wild beast.

Max was glad to have her secured. The cylinder swung in a nerve-wracking arc, creaking, as Amanda pounded it from inside. Max found the external part of the lever and managed to throw it.

Amanda stopped entirely when the water hit her feet.

Max climbed the stepstool so that he could look into

her eyes. She glared back at him and barred her teeth. When the rising water, ice cold, reached the delicate skin of her stomach, she screamed, a high-pitched scream full of vitriol and fear.

"I love you." Max stroked the clear cover just under her face. It was cold already and the water continued to rise.

Amanda looked down, then back at Max. She, all of a sudden, appeared more normal and whimpered at him. "Max?"

"Amanda?" Max yelled, putting both hands on the cover. "Amanda!"

She tilted her head up to keep breathing air for a second longer but was soon overcome. Her shape was distorted through the imperfections in the door, but Max could see she was still squirming. He backed away as the water spilled out over the top and ran down the sides.

The water collected in a collar that wrapped around the cylinder at approximately Amanda's waistline. As it filled, it slid down the cylinder. Several feet above the top of the device's opening was a water-tight lid, slightly concave, with a metallic sphere attached. It resembled a chess-set bishop haphazardly carved from scrap metal. The lid was attached by heavy-gauge cabling to the collar, now filled to capacity. As it slid, it pulled the top down with a squishy thud. The top locked-in, automatically, and clamps clicked into place. The round weight on the lid's top pitched the cylinder forward and it rotated toward Max. The valve in the glacial main was still open and, no longer funneling into its receptacle, water rushed out in a forceful stream and spattered against the stone floor, making an echo that could not be distinguished from the original sound.

The cylinder came to a creaking and abrupt stop in a parallel position, about two feet above the steel table. It would have kept going had its bottom not struck a backstop, which had the simultaneous effect, due to a gearing system, of throwing a lever that forced the valve to shut, cutting off the deluge from above.

The room was suddenly quiet.

Max scrunched under and wiped off the frost so that he could confirm what he already knew. Amanda's eyes were open and her mouth agape. A small trail of bubbles exited at the right joining point of her top and bottom lip. Max sighed and placed his face in his hands. At last, he'd killed Amanda.

Chapter 8

Kyle Green stood on the sidewalk with his left hand jammed into his pocket. His other hand held a recently acquired peanut butter and jelly sandwich on crustless white bread. The sandwich, a triple decker bestseller, would have more accurately been called a jelly and *hint* of peanut butter sandwich. He was taking his third bite when, quite suddenly, two young men who looked about his age appeared out of nowhere. They ended up on each side of him nearly touching shoulders.

The man on his left spoke. "This way."

Walking quickly down the sidewalk, they moved, three abreast, for ten solid minutes, zigging and zagging down streets, through alleyways, and across what used to be a park, now nothing but open space with scattered benches looking out to half-dead trees and brown grass. Spring may have come, but this neglected park showed no sign of it. They rounded another corner and walked down the street halfway. There, they stopped, and the two escorts swung their heads from side to side as if ensuring they hadn't been followed.

They took a staircase down from the street level and entered a stone building with several broken windows. A red door was held open for them by a man with a surgical mask. They strode over a metal-grated gangway and into a large industrial kitchen, every inch covered in dust. Brock Patterson, masked, stood in the center of it with an outstretched hand. Kyle was delivered to him, and they shook hands. The two escorts took three steps back and remained still.

"Welcome," Brock said. "This is Carlos..." he motioned to the man on Kyle's left, "and this is Joseph. Guys, this is Kyle. I'm going to show him around."

"Hey, Kyle."

"Hi, Kyle."

"Hi."

Carlos and Joseph left the room.

"This..." Brock swung his arms out, "is the bunker. There's only one point of direct entry or exit and no windows." He indicated for Kyle to follow him out the doorway in the back of the kitchen. They passed under an archway and took a right. As they turned, he pointed down the hallway they would have taken had they continued straight ahead. "Back there is an old wine cellar. It's the most secure location in the entire building but not very exciting beyond that. Let's go up a level where there's much more to see." They took several more steps until, on their left side, they stood in front of an elevator door. The door had a large metal latch attached to its right side, and a weighty padlock secured the door to the wall. Brock fished around in his pocket and produced a key. With the lock unhinged, he reached for a crowbar that hung on the wall, suspended by a metal chain. He wedged the bar into the elevator door and forced it open. The car had long been dismantled so all that remained was the shaft. Brock wore khaki colored pants of a stiff, tough fabric. There were multiple pockets on each leg, and Brock unsnapped one and reached in. Out came a walkie-talkie. He flipped the device over and unfolded a recessed crank. He rotated the crank several times, folded it back into its recessed seating and then switched it on.

"This is Brock. We're coming up to one. Acknowledge."

He released the walkie button and held the device to his ear. Moments later, the response: "Acknowledged. Coming up."

Brock jumped on the ladder attached to the far wall and ascended. Kyle followed.

They arrived at the first floor, and Brock pounded on the metal door once. Seconds later, it was forced open, and the two men climbed out.

They stood in a similar looking hallway, though this time there was natural light pouring in. They stood for a moment outside the elevator shaft and scanned their surroundings. Brock, intimately familiar with the layout, was deciding which way to go while Kyle surveyed the space simply to ascertain where he was. The walls were a light brown marble with a hint of rose. On each side of the elevator opening, fluting rose up to a cantilevered ceiling. Kyle rubbed his hand against the wall, confirming that it felt as smooth as it looked. He looked up to see art-deco detailing of interlocking geometric shapes carrying along the upper part of the wall. He looked down, his hand still caressing the wall and saw that the tile floor had a black border that ran against the walls, stretching out along the hallway both to the left and right. Inside the border was a simple ecru tile, every other one adorned with an inset triangle matching the rose hue of the walls. In front of them was an expansive foyer, the far end of which, through a large archway, opened up to an enormous outdoor courtyard. There was much commotion out there, people moving about, but Brock instead led them to the left down the hall. They walked through an entryway and ended up in a large cafeteria. The air was filled with scents of food preparation. The yeasty baking of bread. The saccharine of maple syrup. The earthiness of grilled onions. There were long tables in the middle of the room, and several people were seated in groups, scattered throughout. A line of men and women against the right wall waited to enter an opening against the far wall, and another single file line strode out the left side with trays in hand.

"We serve two formal meals a day," Brock said, "but the crew always sets out snacks. It's pretty good grub. You hungry?"

"No, I'm good."

Brock nodded, about-faced, and strode out, turning right and continuing to the end of the hallway. He pushed a door and went through it. Kyle found himself in a large room that smelled, not of cooking, but of sweat. The salty air penetrated his nostrils at the same time he realized that it was easily ten degrees warmer. The explanation for this was immediately obvious, as the room was full of men and women on stationary bikes, treadmills, and other jury-rigged exercise equipment all wired to a central panel, which in turn had a bird's nest of wiring that led out to a series of batteries that occupied half the floor. A crew of three others monitored the batteries, pacing amongst them, and decoupling the fully charged ones and replacing them with, what Kyle presumed, were dead ones. The room was noisy with squeaking bikes, heavy footfalls, and heaving breath. Over it all was a monotone humming, an electrical one-note melodic line that told the tale of physical exertion transforming into stored power.

"Everyone," Brock said loudly enough to be heard over the din, "puts in three shifts a week."

Kyle nodded.

Brock headed over to the wall on his right where a large bulletin board was hanging. He removed a push-pin and took down a wad of stapled papers. He flipped through them until he found what he was looking for.

"Including me," he said pointing at the paper to show Kyle. "I'm up tomorrow from three to five."

"Keep it up, Knights," Brock shouted as they exited the doorway.

He backtracked down the hallway and turned left into the foyer. On each side were grand staircases leading to a common landing on the second story.

"This apartment building was originally built in the late 1800s," Brock said as they walked. "Back then, some of the city's most influential people lived here. Right up until it became abandoned, it continued to house the elite. I learned, from some old files I found, that the basement was, at one point, rented out to a popular restaurant. It had been completely uninhabited for about a decade before we settled our cell here. The living quarters are all above us."

He pointed up the stairs. "One hundred twenty-five apartments in total with only about ten uninhabited at the moment." Brock stepped out into the courtyard and looked up at the blue sky. "Room to grow."

He sighed and stopped.

"Out here," he motioned, as if drawing a loop around the entire space, "is where we train."

Kyle saw young men and women sparring in various locations throughout the courtyard. Some did so without any weaponry while others had a variety of violent tools. Knives. Bo staffs. Wooden swords. Some sparred alone, while others clearly had coaches or trainers alongside them. "Looks tiring."

Brock moved again, toward the back of the courtyard. "That's why we only train in hand-to-hand once a week on a rotating schedule."

They reached the back of the courtyard, and Brock swung open a metal gate that opened into an alleyway. He motioned for Kyle to step through.

Brock followed. "But this..." Brock pointed into the alley. "We practice every day. This alley is the beginning of a shooting course that winds all the way around the block." Brock reached behind himself and pulled a handgun from his waist. "You have much experience with firearms?"

Kyle shook his head. "Only a little. My dad showed me, and we shot targets together, but he passed away when I was fifteen."

"I'm sorry to hear that." Brock handed the weapon to Kyle. "Give it a try while I'll observe and give you some pointers."

Kyle took the gun, turned around, and flicked the safety off. He peered into the alley, and looking more carefully, saw that a series of targets were scattered around the area in various locations and in varied amounts of cover. The targets, he could tell from the sunlight bouncing off them, were metal and well worn. They approximated armed assailants but in nearly all the cases, the paint was so faded, and there were so many dents from repeated bullet strikes, that it wasn't always clear what the images were supposed to be. On the right, behind a green dumpster, a target crouched, preparing to throw a hand grenade. In a window on the second story on the left was the entire torso of a man with a shotgun. Kyle took a position, spreading his feet apart, raised the pistol to the shotgun man and squeezed the trigger. He missed.

"Widen your stance," Brock said.

Kyle repositioned himself, pulled the trigger, and was rewarded with a high-pitched *ting* as the bullet struck the target.

"Good. Now move to get a better angle on the target behind the dumpster. You're going to have to fire while moving to get him. If you miss, fire again."

They continued on through the course, walking through a labyrinth of alleys. Brock pointed out targets and commented on Kyle's form as they proceeded. Brock noticed a wide grin forming on Kyle's face and a glimmer in his eyes, which intensified with each and every *ting*.

This shooting course, Brock thought for the hundredth time, *is my best recruitment tool.*

Suddenly they were interrupted by Carlos, who ran up to them, breathless. "Brock. Sir," he shouted as he ran. In his hand he carried a piece of paper. "This message just came in. You won't believe it, sir."

Brock took the paper and read it quickly. His eyes widened. "Is this legitimate? Did it come properly coded?"

"Yes, sir." Carlos regained his breath. "Properly coded and double-authenticated. It's real, sir."

"What's going on?" Kyle asked.

"Somnus is retaliating against the Rock-a-Byes. He wants our cell to do it."

"Do what?"

"Take out their leader." Brock lowered the paper and breathed deeply. "He wants us to kill Sedgwick."

Chapter 9

For the next several hours, Max paced, sat, slathered the table with lubricant, checked the table's position, adjusted the mirrors, checked the sun's location, paced some more, wiped off frost to look at Amanda, wound and set the timers, paced while mumbling, sat while humming, and finally sat without moving. He stared at the cylinder for what seemed an empty eternity; he'd never felt so totally alone.

He stared at it through dry eyes, only occasionally, as mostly, the tears ran plentifully. He tried to console himself by thinking that there was no other choice he could have made, but his doubt was intrusive, interrupting his train of thought with difficult inquiries for which no satisfyingly definitive answers could be given. Max sat on a rickety folding chair normally used for his own recovery. Its resting place was in the shadows, near the tank, but he'd repositioned it directly in line with the alien-looking table and cylinder that floated above it carrying his Amanda.

The first timer went off, and Max turned his head at the sound.

Only a few more minutes.

Max watched the timer trip a small latch that opened to release the piece of mirror it held. The mirror fell backwards and pivoted left, until stopping when another snap-latch grabbed it. The mirror lit up like a diamond, as it captured the intense beam of sunlight carried by the network of other scattered mirror pieces. The beam shot across the darkness and illuminated the steel table in front of Max. The shimmer made him squint, and he could instantly feel its heat.

Max sat perfectly still, hunched forward with anticipation. His elbows rested on his knees, and his chin was held up by his folded hands. Max was no longer crying and barely blinked. He stared intensely and breathed only through his nose.

He waited.

At last, the final timer made an unceremonious *click,* and Max's eyes opened wide as he leaned back and sat straight-up in the chair.

This is it.

The clicking had pulled a trip-wire, freeing Amanda's feet and opening a valve in the aft portion of the device that held her. The water dumped out onto the floor and embarked on a slow twisting journey toward the side of the room where it would slowly seep away. Seconds later, the frosted door of the cylinder dropped open. Amanda's arms hung down limply for a few seconds until the weights skidded out of their cubbies and ripped the Velcro straps away from her.

Amanda fell out in a gangly shape of pale skin, wet hair, and ecru fabric into the wide groove of the steel table below her. Her body slid down the table with a sloshy squeak until stopping prostrate, with her face peeking through the taped-up hole in the table. The last of the water dripped onto the floor, and the door of the cylinder creaked to a halt.

Max held his breath. He held his breath so that he could remain perfectly still and look for any sign of movement in Amanda. He cast his eyes up and down the backside of her body repeatedly. Max hadn't had the time to remove the dress she'd been wearing so it clung tightly to her now. The dress was cotton with simple lace detailing around the calf-length hem. The bright reflected sunlight revealed curves Max knew well; the tomboy back of her knees, the hard crease at the top of her thighs, the proportioned roundness of her buttocks, the deep trough at the small of her back, the too-sharp peaks of her shoulder blades, and the always hair-covered nape of her neck. She didn't move.

Max waited.

When he thought he saw Amanda flinch, he breathed in as lightly as he could. He stopped in mid-breath and waited. He wanted to reach out to her, but his superstition was too strong to allow it.

Max's eyes, despite several internally issued commands, welled up. A tear rolled down over the flushed apple of his cheek, and he was seconds away from crumpling, both emotionally and physically, when Amanda choked violently. Water gushed from her mouth and splattered on the chamber floor. She breathed in with a gasp and Max did the same. She coughed, spat and muttered, "Fuck," before she coughed and spat again.

Max smiled at the sound of her voice, and at how perfectly she used the word. She'd only said one syllable, in fact, but there was enough of Amanda behind it to know exactly how she was feeling, and, more importantly, he recognized her, the real Amanda, not the would-be Walker that had growled at him just hours before. He rubbed Amanda's back to warm it, and she shivered, coughed again, and rolled over. His trepidation for touching her, that he might jinx the recovery, was still there, but he ignored it. When he was coming back to life, he'd so often wanted a human touch, and he was happy, now, to provide it to Amanda.

"Cold," she said, through chattering teeth.

"I know...come here." Max reached out to her, and her thin forearms wrapped around him as he leaned into her. She was slippery, so he held her tightly, pulling her forward until she fell off the end of the table into his arms. She was shivering uncontrollably.

"You're hypothermic," Max said. "I need to warm you up."

"What happened? What was *that*?" she managed to ask, cricking her neck slightly aft.

"Later. I'll tell you everything later."

She shivered. "Sooo...cold."

He helped her walk over to another area of the room that he'd prepared with blankets. "It's those wet clothes. I'm normally in my skivvies."

"You've done this...to yourself?"

"Several times."

"Jesus, why?"

"I told you, I'll tell you everything later, right now though, you've got to get warm." Max took his shirt off.

"I don't really feel in the, the..." she stuttered, "moo-moo, mood, right now." She managed to crack a smile.

Max looked at her with a smirk, gently reached around her, unzipped her dress, and pushed it off her shoulders. The soggy fabric clung to her, and he had to wrench it down bit by bit as if it were too tight. She wore no bra, and he soon exposed her small white breasts. They were textured with gooseflesh and fine blond hairs standing on end; the nipples were more erect than he'd ever seen them. He was amazed that, now, even though she could slip into shock at any minute, he could still become aroused by the sight of her. He thought he should have felt ashamed at the inappropriateness of his lust, but he didn't.

She shivered from head to toe and coughed.

He pulled her in, pressing his warm torso against her, and wrapped a large blue blanket around them both. The moment that her icy body hit his bare chest, all amorousness left him in an instant. He removed her dress the rest of the way, and they sat on the pile of blankets he had prepared. With his legs around her waist, and her chest tight against his, he rubbed her back vigorously. They remained intertwined for several minutes, basking in the warm sunlight that shined down on them.

She raised her face to it, but kept her eyes shut.

Max continued rubbing her back, arms, thighs, and fingers until her shivering subsided and a petal-pinkness bloomed in her face. "Do you feel better?"

"Yeah, a little...actually..." She was having trouble reconciling what she knew had happened, and how she felt. "I feel pretty good, considering." She smiled.

"You feel rested."

"Huh?"

"*Rested.* You've been resting for a little more than five hours."

"You mean, I..." *died?* Amanda couldn't speak the word, as she choked up at the very thought of it. "You mean, I-I slept, right?"

"No. You were dead."

"Christ, Max, what the hell are you talking about?"

"Let me get you upstairs, and I'll tell you the whole story. You need some dry clothes, and you're probably hungry."

Amanda realized how right he was. "I'm fucking starving, now that you mention it."

"Wait till you taste my pancakes."

Chapter 10

B rock Patterson needed time he didn't have. Somnus's instructions were very clear...he wanted to retaliate *immediately* against the Rock-a-Bye Babies. In matters of war, Brock knew, *immediately* was up for interpretation. Even still, he couldn't wait much longer. He'd known for a long time the location of the enemy's stronghold.

Three interconnected row homes on Cresthill Street acted as a castle wall for their encampment. Behind those homes was a vast vacant lot littered with storage containers, sheds, and other small buildings.

The man who presided over this fiefdom was known only as Sedgwick. His first name, at least, outside the faction itself was unknown. He was rarely spotted out in the city, rumored to be a bit of a shut-in due to an exaggerated sense of paranoia. Somnus had the one photograph of the man that existed delivered under heavy guard to Brock's hands.

He stared at the picture, wondering how he was going to get this done. He knew the answer, but hated it. They were going to have to breach the compound. It was going to be bloody. He set the photograph on the table in front of him. It landed just to the left of a series of black and white pictures of the row homes from a variety of angles. He placed his hands on his hips and sighed. One of the pictures was badly blurred. "What happened here?"

Another man, with a camera strapped around his neck, stood across the table from Brock. "Sorry. Somebody came out the door as I was shooting that one, and I had to take off in a hurry."

"For Christ sakes. Isn't there better technology than this?"

"Used to be everything was digital. But that was before the grid went down. Now I'm left with my trusty Pentax thirty-five mil, and the darkroom I built. Film is getting harder and harder to come by."

Brock dropped the fuzzy black and white on the table and stepped backwards. "We're not ready." He sighed. "We're just not ready." He walked away from the table and rubbed his hands, then intertwined his fingers over his head.

Silence.

"Just too many questions unanswered. How many are in there? What kind of weaponry? Do they have reinforcements? If so, how far away are they?"

The photographer stepped forward. "When I was shooting..." he rummaged around the table, clearly looking for something, "I noticed this." He'd found a map and centered it. The location of the three row homes had been circled in red marker. The man grabbed a pencil from the table and etched a mark on the map. "An old office building two blocks away. Excellent sight lines but far enough away, I think. What if we could perch somebody up there for a full day...even two...with a scope to record and document everything they see. Points of entry. Egress. Number that come out, number that go in. Does Sedgwick ever come out? If we put them up high enough, we might be able to see into the back, too. It's not a complete set of intel, but it's better than what we've got now. We could encode a message to Somnus that the strike is at least *planned* to satiate him and buy us the time."

Brock returned to the table. "I agree, that would be very helpful." He tapped the map. "But it's a dangerous mission. If they have lookouts or snipers, and our man gets spotted, they could surround that building pretty quickly. On top of that, there's not a great escape route, you'd have to weave through a decent part of the city on foot. Tricky."

Kyle Green stood from his chair. "I'll do it."

Chapter 11

Amanda ate three stacks of pancakes drowned in blueberry syrup without speaking. Her nearly climactic grunts after each bite were enough to keep Max quietly entertained, and cooking. At last, she slumped back in the chair and let out a satisfying, drawn-out sigh. "Wow. I've never tasted pancakes like that."

"You've never tasted anything like that, and trust me, it gets better."

"Okay, Mr. Mysterious, I'm not in the mood. Just tell me what shit you've dragged me into."

"It all happened by accident, really. It was the end of summer, last year. Do you remember that time?"

"I didn't know you then."

"That's true, but what else do you remember?"

She picked at her tangled hair. "Was that the seven-month summer?"

"Right."

"All the water systems were shut down because of an infestation. Even the fields weren't irrigated. We lost a lot of crops."

Max sat down across from her. "The infestation. That's right." He continued telling the story he'd carried with him for months, but never had the courage to tell. "It was November and still hot and humid as hell. I was with the rest of my squad, we'd been deployed in the upper quadrants of the city's water transport system...the above ground network stretching down from the aqueducts. It'd taken us several hours of intra-tube navigating just to reach our assigned location. The infestation, the worst algae outbreak in decades, had been so bad that all shifts had been ordered into non-stop rotation. The combination of steady humidity, warm temperatures, and inferior detection processes had brought the city to a grinding halt. Transportation, hydro-electric generation, plumbing systems, and irrigation were all completely shut down. Man were we tired."

"I bet."

"I'd never been that run down. The whole team was fatigued by the time we'd made the several mile trek through the pitch-black tubes. I was lagging behind, numb from exhaustion, and not just because of the work. I felt that I'd simply reached the end of my stamina. All I wanted to do was sit down and not move. I wasn't just tired. I was also depressed, and not because I was tired, I was always tired, but because I felt helpless to remedy it. The guys, you know how they get, with the banter. The teasing and the cajoling to cover up the misery and make it through the shift. Eventually, that wasn't working. Then Hank came up to me. He shoved me in the shoulder. *Max, look up there*, he said. I looked ahead and was preparing to crank my light and shine it in the direction Hank indicated, but Hank put his hand on my light and pushed it down. I looked up and saw a neon green glow coming from around the bend. *There it is*, someone said ahead of us."

Max paused and rubbed his eyes.

"Go on," Amanda said, "I'm listening."

"I turned the corner and stood in front of a glowing garden of algae. It coated every surface of the tube and pulsated like it was breathing. It made a distinct squishing noise when we walked on it. The algae's procreation created heat, and this section of the tube was warmer than the expanse of it we'd already traveled. Mr. Stansbury told me to take the last subsection and was very specific that I not leave the tube. *Understand*, he'd said, *if they flush another one, you need to be on this side of the hatch...see?*"

Max took a deep breath and let it out slowly.

Amanda sensed the story was becoming more difficult for him to tell.

"So, as Mr. Stansbury pushed me gently ahead, some of the other guys sprayed the algae with wands connected to backpack tanks, while others hand-pumped their cisterns before strapping them on. The algae offered no resistance to the toxins; its phosphorescence was simply extinguished without fanfare. I felt almost sad for the creatures as I squished my way through the glow. I continued for a few minutes, until reaching the end of the tube. My shoes, coated with the stuff, glowed for a while until I rounded the last corner. Natural sunlight poured in through the wide-open hatch, as did fresh air, which I took in, I don't know, *reverently*. That air seemed to come from heaven, if there is such a thing. I slung my pack off onto the floor and pumped my tank. I wondered if the moss felt any pain when the chemicals ate it alive. I was in mid-stroke with my hand pump when a strong breeze whipped into the tube, pressing my shirt against my back and sending my hair flying into my face. It felt so good. Like a higher power had reached out and touched me. I smiled, and realized it had been the first time in a while that I'd done so. I turned my head around to let the wind hit me again."

Amanda's eyes sparkled as she stared at him.

"I can't believe I'm telling you all this."

"What happened next?"

"I've wanted to tell you for so long."

"So get on with it."

Max grinned. "I enjoyed that breeze until it died down. Then I went back to work, pumping. As soon as I'd restarted, another gust entered, as if tapping me on the shoulder. I let the tank go and turned myself fully around. I hesitated, only for a second, before deciding to leave the tube. Perhaps the sunlight in my eyes would wake me, or fool me into wakefulness, I'd thought. I took several steps and was soon standing at the threshold of the exit. The massive round hatch, some ten feet above me, was swung out, and it cast an oblong shadow out into the dry aqueduct. I left the shade and entered the bright light. The aqueduct sprawled out on both sides of me, and its overwhelming height took my breath away. Have you ever seen it?"

"Never been up there."

"Trust me. It's gargantuan. Titan. The walls were stone-grey, steep, and pock-marked with hatches, doors, and pipe ends, all placed with a, I don't know, *randomness*. To my left, the trough dropped sharply downward over the crest of a hill. The walls remained high, but the floor of the duct dropped *literally* out of view to reveal the cityscape in the valley below. I walked toward it, underestimating the distance, because of how big everything was. I walked diagonally across so that I both approached the drop off and revealed more of the city with every step. Standing still in the middle of the aqueduct, I peered down. The cityscape was perfectly in view from that vantage. I was able to see the flooded parts and those parts at higher ground. The great wall was completely visible. The whole thing from the city's north, at the river's mouth, through the center, and all the way to the west, ending at the bay. Have you ever seen the other side of the wall?"

"I don't know anybody that has."

"Actually, you do." Max smiled. "From that bird's-eye view, it appeared a little different. Both sides had massive bucolic tracts with expansive fields of grains, though only the western one looked tended to. Both seemed to have buildings in varying states of disrepair. Both had the same basic topology of landscape."

"There must have been some differences."

"There were. While distinct signs of life could be seen in the part of the city we live, the eastern part seemed still. Upon further inspection, the smaller east city had, centrally, an enormous building with two bulbous rooftops. I think it was an Atmospheric Stabilizer. It was the only thing I could think of that would be that big."

Max leaned in. By now, his voice was nearly a whisper, as if what he was going to say next was some kind of secret.

"Suddenly, I heard a faint whistling sound. I moved my head from side to side in an attempt to figure out where it was coming from. I tilted my head, heard it again, and then understood that my team was calling for me. I also realized that I'd left all my gear back in the tube, including the flashlight with the embedded whistle. *Damn*, I thought, without my whistle, I can't answer. I started to run back. I nearly stopped dead when the faint whistling turned into a series of overhead screeches. I knew what those sounds meant so I started booking it. I was pretty far away from the hatch when it started to close. It moved, not smoothly, but with a bumpy ratcheting motion. I was terrified and my heart pounded. I knew I wasn't going to make it in time. I yelled, but there was nobody there to hear me."

Max sat back in his chair and lowered his head.

Amanda reached across the table and took his hand.

"This is the worst part." He sighed.

"I'm here."

"The sound of rushing water drowned out the alarms and, even though I was running as fast as I could go, I felt as if I were standing still. The floor of the duct started shaking. I looked frantically around for an escape. The only option was to climb the steep embankments of the duct and hope to get high enough in time. I reached the bottom seconds after the hatch's air lock sounded. Too late. I scrambled up the side. I dug my fingers into whatever crevasses I could feel. Every second or two, I looked left. Seconds later I saw it. A surging river. I felt like it was hunting me. I completely panicked and started clawing at the sides. It didn't help. My grip faltered and I slid down, I don't know, five or six feet. The foaming head of the monstrous river rounded the corner...headed straight for me. It looked alive. I froze and my body tightened, ready for the impact. I closed my eyes."

Amanda squeezed his hand.

"When the raging water slammed into me, I was no longer a person. I became a small twig, engulfed in the natural journey of a violent tide. The wave sucked me down at first, twisting me this way and that. I kicked like crazy, but it didn't do any good. By some miracle, I emerged and sucked in a mouthful of air. The water cascaded over the drop-off, and I fell along with it, my head going under repeatedly. I struggled to stay afloat. At one point I was traveling backwards, and it was just as I turned around to see where I was going that I felt a sharp sting. The water was freezing cold, and I was shivering even as I swam vigorously to keep my head up. Ahead, I saw that the canal was closed off. Maybe I can make it, I thought to myself. Then, the flow crashed against a wall and began pooling. I was no longer bobbing along in the rapids of a white-capped river, but now I was rising steadily upwards. I swam for the side, hoping I could pull myself out. My teeth chattered. I was so cold. Without warning, I felt as if a sack of sand had been shackled to my ankles. I fought it with all my might. I managed to reach out for the tip of a metal pipe that peeked just above the water's level. I grasped it hard at a connection joint and a piece of jagged flange cut my hand."

Max turned his hand over, and at its first sign of rotation, Amanda let it go. He used his other hand to extend a finger and run it down a scar on this palm. Amanda also traced it with her index finger.

"I bled like a stuck pig, but I hung on to that pipe anyway. I grabbed it with both hands and looked behind me. A vortex in the pool had appeared due, I knew, to a hatch having been opened. The thing was like a black hole. That tube, some forty feet down, was drinking in the water as fast as it could. I'll never forget that sound. That roar. Anyway, the whirlpool grew in size, and power, until I couldn't hold on any longer. I was pulled under."

Amanda stared at him.

"I remember being underwater. I remember the power of it...the pull. I swam and swam, but it was no use. I kept sinking down. Man, it was strong. I was scared, right up until the end. I didn't get that euphoric peace everyone talks about. I was just scared. I don't remember taking a breath, but I did drown that day, that's for sure. I do remember a terrible pressure in my head...I mean, forty feet down, that's a lot.

Amanda stroked his face and frowned. "What's this?" She touched his fresh scratch.

"It's nothing, don't worry about it. It happened when I was helping you."

"Did I do that?"

"No."

"Oh, good. Then what happened to you, after you drowned?"

"All I remember was waking up, freezing and lying on a metal grate some feet below an exit valve. The sun was shining down on me, not directly because the day was ending, but the grate was warm. I couldn't stop coughing or shaking."

"What do you think happened?"

"I got sucked into that tube, I'm positive of that. When a tube has been disinfected they generally send a few million gallons through it and then funnel it back to the very top of the filtration system. I think I must have traveled that whole way and been dumped out at one of the exchange points."

"That's very interesting," Amanda said as sugary sweet as possible. "But how did you survive if you're so sure you actually drowned?"

"I don't understand it exactly, but I must have been suspended or something."

"Like those little buggers you look for all day with that big stupid stick?"

"Well, it's not stupid, but yes, exactly."

"And that's how you got the idea."

"Yes." Max sighed with relief, as the secret was finally revealed, and best of all, revealed to the one person he really wanted to tell. His journey had finally come to an end.

Amanda smiled and stood up. She walked over to the window, and then, in the light of the mid-day sun, turned around to face him. "We need to tell everyone."

Chapter 12

Kyle Green couldn't see his own hand in front of his face. On this moonless night, the city was shrouded in utter darkness. Carlos, Brock, and several other Knights had walked most of the way with him using hand-cranked flashlights. But this last part he needed to do on his own, no flashlights, no company, totally alone in the blackness.

He crouched and blinked hard, trying to force his eyes to make out *anything* ahead of him. Pressing his palms against his eyes first, he did it again. He couldn't see it, but his pupils were as dilated as they'd ever been. His eyes, normally blue, he knew were now totally black. As he remained close to the ground and stared ahead into the void, eventually he could make out outlines. He managed to cross the street, step up onto the sidewalk, and place both hands on the cold stone building, the footprint of which took up the entire block. He'd memorized the route and now knew that he was two blocks from his destination. Using his hands to guide himself to the end of the block, he crossed another street and repeated the entire procedure until his hands were against the smooth glass of his architectural quarry. He'd arrived.

He found a door and pulled at it. Locked. He spent thirty minutes circumnavigating the building and trying every door he came upon. Finally, on the opposite side of where he'd initially arrived, he found one that opened.

Kyle knew that on the ground level, owing to the surrounding buildings, nobody at the Rock-a-Bye encampment would be able to see him. As he ascended, that would become less and less true. For the moment, though, he unslung his backpack and reached inside, removed a hand-powered light, and cranked it vigorously several times to illuminate it. He cast the beam across the building's lobby. Papers were scattered about the floor. A large square reception area was in the middle of the room. He cranked the light again and the beam intensified. He ran the light along the walls until he found the doorway to the staircase.

He climbed up twelve flights, arriving heavily winded. The building directly in front of this one was eight stories, so the Knights had decided an extra four should be enough to provide clear lines of sight. Before exiting to the floor itself, Kyle stashed the flashlight. He wasn't going to risk it; darkness made his mission more difficult, but also provided safety. He opened the door, and it creaked loudly, echoing throughout the empty space. He stepped into a hallway. A useless bank of elevators stood to his right, and beyond that a set of double doors. His mark, however, was in the opposite direction, to his left. He hand-guided himself down the corridor and around the corner to the right. Glass double doors opened to a large office space with cubicles in the middle, and several conference rooms edged around the perimeter.

Using the walls to guide him, he headed to a

conference room directly across from his current position. He pushed the door open and entered. A foul smell assaulted his nostrils. A black plastic trash can right inside the doorway held the source of the odor, unrecognizable under a blanket of fuzzy mold. When Kyle moved the bin, and consequently the rot inside, it cast the scent more widely, causing Kyle to gag. He moved the can outside the room, and with his foot, pushed it away. He gagged again and looked around.

A large wooden table with armed swivel chairs took up nearly the entire room. Directly ahead was a large window looking out over the city to the east. That was exactly the vantage point he'd wanted. He rearranged the furniture, pushing it back against the office-side wall so that he created enough room on the floor for him to set up.

From his backpack he removed a pad of paper, pencil, a high powered scope, and a tripod. As he sat down on the floor, he removed his pistol from this waistband and laid that next to him. Soon he was lying flat on the floor with the scope to his eye. He positioned it, adjusted it, and soon three row homes came into focus. The middle one had an outdoor light aglow but unevenly, going from dim to bright with a rhythmic regularity. Similar rhythmic light emitted from a few of the windows. Kyle looked at his watch and then wrote on the paper.

1:27 a.m. 1 outdoor light. Several lit windows. No activity.

When he finished writing, he gazed into the scope again. No changes. He then looked through the window and cast his gaze over the city. This building, he knew from studying maps, was squarely in what used to be the city's business district, so it was totally blacked out. The row homes he observed were at the very edge of one of the closest residential areas, but he couldn't see any deeper in. He sighed. He looked into the scope. No changes. He sighed and realized something he hadn't considered before. He was tired. Of course he was. Everyone was always tired. But he hadn't noticed it for a while. The Kyle Green that had nearly walked into a coma parlor was a different Kyle Green than the one who laid on the floor now.

This Kyle Green has a purpose.

***

Max, with a furrowed brow, started to mumble just before being interrupted.

"How many times have you done this?" Amanda asked as she rushed back from the window with a sprightly gait, plopped down, and looked as if she weren't really interested in Max's response.

"Well, a few, I guess it's been about *eight*," Max said with a false stutter, as he knew the exact number.

Amanda wasn't listening. "How long did it take you to build that, that..." Amanda stood again, still not looking at Max. "Contraption?"

Max was still stuck on her last statement. "Hey. What did you mean that we should, you know, tell *everyone*?"

Amanda turned around and looked at Max. He saw her eyes aimed at him, but felt as if she weren't seeing him, at all. She was, he realized, looking *into* him. Max's greatest fears, the ones he kept locked in an inner crypt, were suddenly at risk of exposure, because in that moment, Amanda's eyes transcended seeing, in that moment, Amanda appeared to have the only key to his dark treasure. She seemed even more powerful than that; she hadn't found the key, but forged it from the intensity of her own convictions. Max shivered.

Amanda, rather than playing Pandora with his secrets, shrank and sat back down. "I only mean that I wish more people could feel *this*." Her hands, palms up, moved in an arc from her top to bottom as if she were on display. "I wish more people could feel this hope you've discovered."

"I haven't discovered hope, Amanda, I've cheated, and that's all." Max sighed.

"That isn't the way I feel."

"Plus, I don't think this is exactly...safe."

"I haven't felt this rejuvenated for years." Amanda realized the rightness of the word and said it again. "*Rejuvenated*. That's it. Not since before my change have I felt this alive. I guess we fool ourselves that it was just the fact that we were kids...you know how we were, right, Max? All that energy...that go-go-go? But it wasn't free, was it? It was the *sleep* that gave us our youth."

"Yes. I'm learning that you're right."

"What do you mean?"

"Well, the other day, I saw a young boy eating an enormous breakfast...you know, bacon, eggs, the whole deal."

"Yeah?"

"Well, I craved it."

"Really?"

"Yes, badly. I used to think that those kinds of passions were the gifts of youth. That, once we changed, once we became men and women, that the gradual fading of those desires was totally natural. But recently, after, well, what I've been doing, they've been coming back."

"Max, do you realize what you're saying?" Amanda leaned in. "You're saying that those cravings *aren't* cravings...they're *living*."

"But at what cost, Amanda? At what cost? Are you saying we need to die to live?"

"Fuck, yeah. Why not?" Amanda sounded serious.

Max thought about his crypt, and her key. "You are actually proposing that we, what? We teach people to tie their feet down and drown in freezing water?" Max laughed at the sound of his own statement.

Amanda stood. "Perhaps you didn't hear me, but *fucking-a* yeah." She put one foot ahead of the other. "Jesus Christ, Max. Don't you get it? You've got the fucking solution to the world's misery in your goddamn basement."

Max stood to face her. "Amanda, that's insane...I mean, it's fine for you and me every now and then, but do you think I'd advocate this for anyone else?"

"Why the hell not?" She scowled.

"Because it's killing people," Max yelled back

"So fucking what?" Amanda's face turned red. "As if what we've got is living anyway. What's down there might have saved my mom, Max. Did you ever think of that?"

Max hung his head. "No. I didn't."

"It might have."

"Okay."

"Will you listen to me now?"

"Yeah."

"Someday, if I ask you to, can you build more of those?"

Max chuckled. "Not easily."

"Why not?"

"It took months. Designing it was easy...I have a knack, but finding the parts was a total bitch."

"The parts shouldn't be a problem." Amanda smiled.

"Trust me, will ya...the materials for the cylinder were difficult to come by. They look simple, but those components haven't been manufactured for decades."

Amanda spun around. "Don't worry, I've got a *knack*."

Max wagged his finger at her cleverness. "I spent months scrounging around all over this city for what it took to make that one, so you can do better?"

"I know someone who can help."

"Really? Who's that?"

Amanda didn't pause. "Somnus."

"That kook?"

"He can get this stuff, and you know it."

"Maybe, but he's friggin' nuts. He's dangerous...remember the, uh, shooting?"

Suddenly, from upstairs, there was thunderous knocking on Max's door.

"You should get that." Amanda looked upward. "Quickly."

Max turned and moved. "Amanda," Max was on his way but stopped short. "I know you're feeling better because of, well, everything, but I'm worried that you...well." Max felt as if he couldn't say more and cast his eyes down.

"What, Max? What is it?" She looked at him, as she sat.

"Well, we haven't talked about your mom. Shouldn't you be mourning her?"

Amanda smiled widely as voluminous tears ran quietly into the corners of her mouth. "I am. In my way, I am."

Chapter 13

Mark dropped his leather bag at his feet and stood in awe, as his friends described the way the machine had killed them. He was only partly surprised that they'd committed suicide; after all, he'd witnessed the aftermath of countless attempts. The grotesque consequences of people who'd tried to end their sleepless suffering used to haunt him, but now they simply existed in his mind as casually as thoughts of rain. Both Max and Amanda saw his look.

"Do you think we've gone off the deep end?" Max asked.

Mark smiled. "I've always thought that."

"Well, you look surprised," Amanda said. "Listen, I know it's kinda stupid—"

"No," Mark cut her off. "I'm not surprised that you'd do it."

"You're surprised we survived."

"No. I'm surprised this hunk of shit actually works like you described. I mean, *look* at this thing." Mark walked around the device, poking at it irreverently.

"Hey, I built this *hunk of shit*, you know."

"Yeah, I can see that." Mark chuckled.

"Screw you, man." Max looked at the cylinder from top to bottom. To him, especially in the skipped patterns of yellow light, it looked beautiful, a work of art. He sighed, remembering how he found each component. He'd twisted them, pounded them, soldered them, and glued them. He'd built the thing out of frustration, exerting more power than he'd thought he had, hoping secretly it would break him before it killed him. But it didn't. It had kept him alive then, and it was keeping him alive still. He recalled lugging those damn lead weights halfway across the city, not stopping though his arms ached and burned. Blinking, he remembered his fright when, after breaking into an abandoned pet store, a flashlight shot through the darkness and landed on his startled face. He stood there for a second holding a massive pane of acrylic glass until he dropped it on his foot and ran away crookedly, not knowing he'd broken two toes.

"Seriously, Max, this thing is about to fall apart." Mark picked at the cylinder between two of the rounded front panes. "This silicone is literally crumbling at the seams." Mark wiggled his finger, and big crumbs of dirty white rubber fell easily to the floor and bounce-rolled around his brown shoes. He raised an eyebrow. "See what I mean?"

Max cracked a weak smile and stared at his supposed friend who was now criticizing his most precious possession in the whole world.

"And these rivets holding the bottom on, Jesus, how'd you install these, with a cannon?" Mark walked around to the back. "And this gearing system looks like..." Mark struggled with something out of view until a crunching metallic sound made Max jump.

"Hey. Cut it out," Max yelled at high pitch while running toward Mark's position.

Mark came back around, slightly surprised at Max's sensitivity.

Max was also surprised at the new way he saw his device. It was always so perfect to him, so pristine. He may have dreaded the experience, but there was no denying the power of its affect. It was for that reason, he realized awfully in that moment, that he never saw its flaws: the cracks, the leaks, and the corrosion. When he descended the stairs into the darkness of his rebirth ritual, it was sacred in every way and, he knew right then, that's why he never saw the cylinder with impious eyes, he only saw salvation. "So, maybe it needs some touch-ups, or something."

"Touch-ups? I'd say—"

"Mark," Amanda cut in quickly. "The condition of this thing is not the issue. We can deal with that later. The issue is, or rather, the question is, is it safe? Can we keep doing this?"

"Oh, that. Safe? Hell no. I'm surprised both of you aren't dead. No, this isn't safe at all. It's suicide, plain and simple."

"Well, then, how is it we're not dead?" Amanda asked, her voice stern with annoyance.

Mark pondered the inquiry for a second, rolling his eyes up for a second or two, then: "The water comes in fast?"

"Yes." Both Max and Amanda answered with an undeniable believability.

"I would guess, and this would just be a guess, that

it's a combination of the *diving response* and the fall."

"The fall?" Max glanced at Amanda and shrugged.

"This crazy thing pitches forward about two feet or so above this table and then you drop out onto it, right?"

"Right."

"The fall."

"Oh."

Max and Amanda stared blankly at Mark.

"Okay, it's like this. There are several documented cases of cold water drownings where the victims were successfully saved without exhibiting any brain damage after their recovery. Well, not much brain damage anyway." He grinned at Max.

Max gave Mark's drippy sense of sarcasm the finger.

Mark chuckled. "It's because of the diving response, which, when cold water hits the body, makes the blood immediately recede away from the skin so that it can be used exclusively for vital organs like the brain."

Max and Amanda nodded. "Huh?"

"But here's the thing, these cases, mostly in cold climates like Michigan or Alaska or Maine...these people didn't just suddenly wake up. They were resuscitated. Mostly by machine, but at least through manual methods at a minimum. So, I'm theorizing, your fall onto the heated table acted like that. It shocked your heart, your protected heart because of your body's response to the cold water, into rhythm again."

"Cool," Amanda said.

"No, it's not cool." Mark scowled. "It's dangerous as hell. And it's only partly right. This theory could explain why you didn't die the first time and maybe the second, but how many times have you done this, Max? Eight? You should be dead."

"But, I'm not. In fact, it makes me feel better."

Mark rubbed his chin in thought. After a few seconds, he chuckled.

"What?" Amanda asked.

"It could be," he paused, "that..."

"What?"

"Before the doctors left and before the white wall was constructed, some research was done to study the sleeplessness epidemic. Not much work was done on it, go figure, but what I've read was pretty interesting. Chronic inability to sleep does all kinds of things to people, and one thing it does is increase the amount of stress hormones in our bodies. One of the stress hormones is Norepinephrine. That probably doesn't mean anything to you."

Both Max and Amanda shrugged.

"But epinephrine is a resuscitative drug. It was used to resuscitate people when their hearts stopped. I use doses of it to counteract some of the street drugs people take."

"So, you are saying that we all may have elevated levels of this stuff that helps to resuscitate us?"

"It's possible, yes, but—"

"But what?" Amanda asked.

"If that's true, then it is also possible that by doing this, you are lowering those levels, meaning that each time you do it, there is a greater chance that you can't be resuscitated."

"But if *you* were around to resuscitate us, it could be

safer, right?"

"Well..."

"Well what?" she pressed.

"Safer, yes. But not safe. Definitely not safe."

"Could anything make it safe?"

"Are you not hearing me? It isn't safe, not at all. If you keep doing this, you'll die, sooner or later. It's suicide delayed but not denied. I don't mean that as a metaphor either. It really is suicide. It's killing yourself on purpose."

Amanda's eyes watered, and she dropped her head, somewhat defeated. "I understand completely."

"Maybe..." Mark spoke under his breath. "If you had a defibrillator..."

"What's that?"

"It's a device that shocks the heart, literally sends a shock right through the muscle in order to bring it back into normal rhythm. I'm not saying it would make this stunt safe, but it might give someone a better chance if shit goes south."

Amanda looked at Max with genuine excitement; she stood up on her toes grinning. "Let's get one of those fibulator things."

"You are truly crazy, Amanda."

"You, of all people, have very little—"

"Okay. We'll try." Max sighed.

"Try what?" Mark asked.

Amanda stepped back, pointing at Mark. "Just stay here, okay?"

"Only if you tell me where you are going and what's going on."

"I have no idea what's going on," Max said, then followed Amanda, who was already out the door. "But we're going to see Somnus."

"Now *that's* suicide." Mark grumbled.

***

Kyle Green sipped water from a bottle and munched on chocolate-covered raisins. He threw them into his mouth one at a time, catching them first then sucking off the chocolate and finally chewing the dried fruit. He'd arrived twelve hours ago, and he filled up his first pad of paper with notes. His mission had, so far, been extremely fruitful. He had meticulously documented the comings and goings of the Rock-a-Byes. Lunchtime had been particularly productive. A group of six men and one woman had exited from the complex and returned about thirty minutes later with bags of what, Kyle assumed, were lunch containers. Using the high powered scope, Kyle zeroed in on the containers and counted them. This intel combined with his notes about each and every entrance and exit would surely provide the necessary variables against which some military mathematics could be applied to estimate the size of the force they'd be assailing. He had also documented the security procedures used if someone outside the faction came calling. He'd witnessed someone knock on the door and then seen a series of steps before the person gained access. He had also, importantly, noted that this enemy definitely had some kind of regular patrolling routine, in groups of two, always and only in twos, members would follow regular routes around the streets which surrounded them. The patrols occurred predictably, and they followed the same routes, depending on their starting direction. He had drawn the routes on several sheets of paper and hoped that, once he reunited himself with a map, he would be able to add the proper street names. These bits of intel would surely be invaluable.

Kyle's only regret was that his location did not allow him to see behind the row homes and into the mysterious jumble of buildings that he knew were there.

As the sun had come up and visibility improved, Kyle did notice that approximately five more stories up in the building from which he conducted his reconnaissance, there was some kind of observation deck that jutted out and away from the building. He could only see the bottom of it, of course, but he guessed that out and upon it, one would have a perfect view into the back of the compound. Gazing into his scope and seeing nothing to report, he made the decision to check out that high deck. He gathered all his belongings into his backpack, slung it, and walked toward the stairwell.

Moments later, he slid back a door that granted him access to the observation deck. It was an open-air balcony with tall glass panels on three sides. The roofless top allowed fresh air to flow in, and Kyle welcomed the breeze on his face. White clouds rode on the breeze at a steady pace across the sky. As he approached the front glass panels, he smiled as his hunch suddenly came true. The back of the Rock-a-Bye complex was visible. He immediately set to work. As he peered through the scope, he didn't notice any movement. He noted that the high wooden fence that ran the perimeter of the space had extra braces, huge wooden beams that angled out at regular intervals and were inset to the ground. But, he noted further, the bracing was only along the back.

A minute later, he saw two men head for one of the storage containers. They swung open the two metal doors and left them agape. One of the men walked inside, and Kyle gasped at what he saw next. The man who went inside emerged atop a four-wheeler. The machine rolled out, and both men appeared to check on a few things, and then the man drove the vehicle in reverse back into the container.

How they managed to find fuel for it, Kyle couldn't imagine.

The men then walked over to another building, this time a shed, and opened its doors. Both men carried out a huge machinegun. It was the kind that used belts of bullets and rested on a metal tripod. One of the men inspected it while the other pulled a cigarette out of his pocket. Kyle was attempting to focus the scope so that he could see past the shed doors and into the shed. Just then, and at the exact time the second man was staring out over the city to light his smoke, the sun came out from behind a cloud and glinted off the lens of the scope. It temporarily blinded Kyle, who quickly looked away. After rubbing his eye and blinking profusely, he stared back into the scope. The smoking man was pointing directly at him and talking to the other man. Then they ran inside.

Kyle Green didn't wait to see if a group of Rock-a-Byes would next come running out of the row homes. He knew they would. And they did.

Chapter 14

In early evening, Amanda and Max exited the transport station. Tall buildings of the once bustling industrial center reached skyward, but very few people were about. Those that Max spotted must have been lookouts, as they were ensconced in shaded corners and made obvious and often clumsy maneuvers to stay out of view. The buildings were empty, and every footstep echoed off the walls for far too long, making both Amanda and Max uncomfortable. They walked the three blocks toward the hospital without speaking.

Rumors of Somnus's ridiculously paranoid security precautions seemed to transform into reality by the second. The Eight Hour Knights were well known in name, but not in detail. Members of Somnus's gang, for reasons equally unknown, never attrited; they stayed for life or died for the cause.

As they came closer to the hospital entrance, both Max and Amanda knew they were under intense surveillance, though it wasn't conspicuous.

They continued on unencumbered, and a confident, perhaps simply determined, Amanda led the way. About twenty yards from the main entrance, a single gunshot rang out. It echoed with similar trajectory to their footsteps, bouncing off the same building walls, the same hollow concrete parking garages, but it did so with considerably more decibels and with increased speed. They found it impossible to determine from which direction it came, and Max and Amanda jumped and then ducked defensively. Immediately following the shot, and even before the echo had escaped the labyrinth of building walls, a voice was heard, again seemingly out of nowhere. "Stop!"

They waited behind a tree, but no further warning came, only silence.

"We want to—" Amanda started to say, but was cut off immediately by the same voice.

"Shut up." The voice was loud, but not angry, controlled, and authoritative, without rancor. Comfortable that it was in total control.

Amanda looked at Max and he shrugged slightly.

Suddenly, from an open window about two stories up, Max noticed a blur of blue color. At nearly the same moment, something was hurled from the window and was falling right toward them.

"Look out," Max barked and moved Amanda aside. He squinted and cringed, expecting to be blown to bits. Instead, a soft package wrapped in plastic harmlessly fell in front of them. It looked like the sweater Amanda had given Max for his birthday or a blanket for a newborn boy.

"Take your clothes off. Put those on."

Amanda gasped. "What? Here in the street?"

"Put those on or leave," the voice said matter-of-factly.

Max shrugged at her again and ripped open the package. It wasn't sweaters at all, but some kind of paper-thin robe. He put the package back down and started to undress. The couple soon stood in the street, shivering in the wind that twisted its way through the corridor of buildings and pushed the blue paper against them like a flimsy second skin.

"My ass is hanging out," Amanda said out of the corner of her mouth.

It was, and Max had already noticed. He gave it a gentle pat. "Nice."

"Hey!" Amanda scolded him in a gruff whisper.

"What?" Max feigned innocence.

She crooked her neck back and caught a glimpse of Max's derrière. "Not bad, yourself."

His butt cheeks clenched.

"Walk forward," the voice boomed again, still without anger. "Go through the glass doors. Stop in the square." The window from which their new attire had descended slammed shut, perhaps unrelated to the instructional voice.

They strode forward, Amanda looking to the right and Max to the left. They saw no sign of anyone and finally arrived at a set of glass double doors. They pried them open with much effort and finally slipped in. Another set of doors, steel, faced them and on the floor a square was roughly painted with sloppy brush-strokes of green paint. They stepped into it and stopped.

Nothing happened.

"Now what?" Amanda asked.

"Maybe they just want to stare at your ass." Max harrumphed nervously.

"Or yours, maybe."

Another steel door slid noisily across the floor behind them, quickly covering the glass doors through which they'd just passed. It blocked out the light and amplified the sound of their breathing.

They stood in place, and Max shifted his weight to his left foot. He breathed out through his nose with a gurgling sound that Amanda noticed but didn't acknowledge. He reached up to wipe his nose just as a small slit in the ceiling opened, shooting bright light down on Max's head. Another slit opened in front of them, and they both saw an eyeball glaring at them, shifting rapidly back and forth. Max snapped his head to the left when another three slits opened in succession.

Amanda's breathing was rapid, approaching hyperventilation, when another dozen slits opened all around them. The steel against steel grinding sound of the openings was enough to unnerve anyone, but it was the singular darting eyeballs that truly made them shiver. The irises of green, blue, hazel, brown and black scanned them, and violated them with an intimate anonymity. They bounced around every inch of them, and Amanda reached behind herself to close the opening of her thin garment. She remained perfectly still as her eyes swelled and reddened with pent-up rage. "What are you guys, a bunch of perverts?"

Max bit his lip. *She's going to get us killed.*

The voice came again: "Are you Yawners? Rock-a-Byes? Dreamers?"

"N-no," Max stuttered.

All the slits closed with a series of clinks, clunks,

scrapes and scratches. The foyer got darker than before.

The steel doors in front of them opened, and a long hallway stretched out before them. A burly man with a white surgical mask approached and stopped. Max's knees were shaking.

"Who sent you?" The burly man spoke in a voice matching his girth.

Max responded, "We're not with any organization—"

"That you've ever heard of," Amanda jumped in. "We're, uh, new."

"A new gang, huh?" The burly man *hmphed*.

Max was puzzled but followed Amanda's lead. "Yeah, new. We're the...the...Dead Tired Crew." Max had blurted out the first thing that came to him.

Amanda smiled in approval. "We're here to make Somnus a proposal."

The man scoffed. "Tell me all about it, and I'll make sure Somnus gets the message."

Amanda held her hands up, assuring the onlookers of her non-violent intent and approached the man. "We'll speak with Somnus directly."

"Nobody sees Somnus."

Max was amazed at her serenity and the steadiness of her motion. He was simply trying not to urinate all over himself, and he wasn't sure he could move, even if instructed.

"Look..." she pressed, "after seeing what happened at The Raven a couple nights ago, we've decided to declare our allegiance to Somnus." She paused purposefully to eye the brute as if fear wasn't in her DNA. "I'm sure he'd like to discuss this matter with us personally."

The man shrank from her a little, as if thinking and standing tall were too much to handle at once. He raised an eyebrow as if the synapses inside his thick cranium tried to decide between the veracity of this petite girl's persona and Somnus's temper, and what might happen to him if he let them enter.

Max poked the bear. "How long do you think she's going to wait for you to make up your melon? She's got a legendary short fuse."

The man spoke to two masked men standing by. "Guard them."

They shuffled into flanking positions beside Max and Amanda just as their burly keeper turned to walk down the hallway. "Follow me."

Max and Amanda followed silently, without looking at each other, though they were both thinking exactly the same thing:

Great. We're going to see Somnus. Then what?

The floor was cold under their bare feet, as they walked quickly forward through the dark hall. Amanda, on the right, saw darkened rooms through open doorways, every ten steps, or so. The windows had metal plating roughly bolted over them, and every now and then a brilliant shaft of orange dusk cut into a room where its window had a different covering: two plates and a handle so it could be slid open.

Max, on the left, noticed the same layout. The dark rooms appeared not have been entered for years. They were filled with overturned tables, broken chairs, and the floors were covered with bits of paper, plastic, and other packaging materials, as if boxes had been hurriedly opened, one after another, their contents removed, and what protected them was jettisoned without care. Often the walls were covered with empty shelves reaching all the way to the ceiling. He imagined they once held the boxes whose guts now decorated the floor.

Max, Amanda, and their masked escorts continued down the hallway. Thin swaths of setting sunlight from the windows made crisscross patterns ahead of them, like the girders of a heavenly bridge.

Amanda imagined Max confidently walking along the beam of the ethereal conduit, as his footfalls landed perfectly on each intersection of crossing beams on the floor. She smiled at him.

He took notice. "What?"

Amanda was going to say "nothing," but a sharp antiseptic smell made both of them crinkle their faces and wave at the air in front of their noses. "Ewwh," she whispered.

"Keep going," the man beside her said.

They reached the end of the hallway and stood in front of a bank of elevators. Max spotted a doorway to his left with a sign: *STAIRS*. He pointed to it.

"Just wait," his escort said.

The burly man looked up into the right hand corner of the hallway and removed his surgical mask.

Suddenly, the far right elevator light illuminated, and then, after a pause, beeped weakly.

Amanda gasped.

Max's eyes widened. "Wow."

The burly man extracted a flat piece of metal from his waistband, approximately six inches in length with a hooked end. He forced the device between the doors and turned it until the hook was caught firmly. Keeping a solid grip on the metal flange, he pried the doors apart until they were about halfway open. "This way."

As they squeezed through the opening, their dreams of an actual ride in an elevator was squashed. The roof had been completely removed, and a set of stairs was bolted to the floor. The stairs led up to a metal-rung ladder inside the towering shaft.

"You first." The burly man pointed at Amanda. "I want to keep an eye on you guys."

"How far?" Amanda asked.

"All the way."

Amanda looked up the shaft's full twelve stories and gulped. "It's dark...I can't even see all the way."

"You wanna see Somnus?"

"Of course."

"Climb, then."

"You realize I'm not wearing anything under this." Amanda tugged lightly at the thin blue outfit that hung like a square tablecloth off her slim shoulders.

The burly man smirked. "Like I said, you first."

Amanda, for the second time in only a few minutes, again felt violated. Her desire to meet with Somnus and her vision of a different future ushered in by Max's machine was, for a moment, more powerful than her modesty. She mounted the first step with her right foot, but stopped short before her left foot rose to meet it. *He thinks he's going to get a show...I'll give him one.* Stepping down, she turned around to face the burly man who now wore a satisfying grimace.

"What's your problem, lady?"

Amanda stared at the man, smiled sweetly at him, untied her garment, and slipped it off completely, then placed her hands on her hips.

Max was stunned, but he simply waited to see what would happen next.

She scowled and spoke plainly. "You might miss something with all that climbing we've got to do, and we can't have that, now can we?" She spun around, facing Max and the other two men. She backed up against the far edge of the elevator, beside the stairs, so that they could all see her clearly. And there she stood, fully exposed with her hands on her hips and a sly smile pasted on her lips. "Let me know when you've seen enough."

The burly man coughed uncomfortably. "Get dressed."

"Seen everything so soon?"

"Get d-dressed," he said with a nervous quiver in his deep voice.

"Are you sure?" She sounded saccharin, but not fake enough that one would doubt the sincerity of her sweetness. "I don't want you to get distracted up there. It's a long way up. You might as well lay your gaze upon me now, while both feet are on the ground."

"Ma'am," the burly man muttered, lowering his head, "please get dressed."

Amanda's smile vanished, and she looked at the man with a disdain that Max had never seen before, a scorn so powerful it appeared that Amanda had accessed it from a locked-away reserve deep inside her, one of those emotional vaults that she knew was there but resisted opening for fear that once liberated, it might be impossible to wrestle it back from whence it came. Whatever it was, it was out now, and it filled the elevator while she robotically slipped the flimsy garment back on, tied it closed, and mounted the stairs.

The burly man looked at Max, but without making eye contact. "You go ahead. Wait for us at the top."

Max climbed behind Amanda, and they made their way up the twelve stories while their three escorts climbed some distance behind, never looking up, but instead, staring straight ahead at the greasy gray wall.

***

Amanda and Max's feet were raw from the textured metal rungs of the elevator shaft's ladder. They both sat, slumped down to the floor, exhausted and in pain.

The burly man and his compatriots arrived seconds later and immediately parted ways, the pair shooting off down to the right, and the burly man headed toward Max and Amanda's position. He strode by them without looking. "This way," he barked. He turned his head, coughed without covering his mouth, and continued on.

Amanda and Max quickly raised themselves and followed. The corridor was similar to the one they'd traveled down before, but this one was completely lit by pinkish-purple light from the crest of sun left on the horizon. It poured in freely without obstruction of any kind. The floor wasn't as cold, the light having warmed it. Their battered feet, slapping noisily with each step, were soothed by the warmth.

Each side of the hallway had standard rooms spaced evenly apart. There were beds with metal railings, carts on wheels, and a curtain that divided the room in two. Each room was identical and each was dusty, a fine layer that covered everything evenly, like a summer-weight blanket freshly unfolded from its package.

Sound echoed easily down the hall, bouncing around the rooms, in and out, zigzagging, and whenever the burly man coughed, its tenor rattled through, sounding to Amanda like the rumbling of voices. She shivered in the wake of the man's increasing attempts to loosen whatever was holding on inside his chest. Max noticed she was looking behind them nervously and he touched her shoulder, gently. It helped.

The burly man reached the end of the corridor and gave the two wooden doors in front of him a quick nudge, and they swung inward, away. Max and Amanda hurried through before they swung back. This corridor was absent natural light, but amazingly, had three electric bulbs equidistant throughout the length, dangling from the ceiling. They flickered like candles, intensely bright, then dim, then somewhere in between. The effect was unsettling, as the different light levels made the corridor grow, then shrink, grow, and then shrink again. Max thought it appeared the hallway itself was breathing.

The hallway, drawing breath or not, was lined with thick wooden doors, all shut tight. Some of the doors had tarnished golden rectangular frames positioned at eye level. Max noticed that the rectangle was incomplete, that the left side was missing and that it was consistently missing on each door; it was as if something had once been slipped in there. Max became sure of his deduction when he passed under the middle light bulb during a burst of illuminating brilliance and noticed that the wood inside the frame was noticeably darker than the rest of the door.

A door opened and slammed at the far end of the hall, but Max couldn't tell which it had been. The two men who'd escorted them to the elevator soon approached them from the front. They walked past quickly, pausing only to whisper something into the burly man's ear. He nodded an acknowledgment and then coughed with a violent shudder that made him stumble. The burly man stepped awkwardly aside and thrust his left arm out, searching for balance. His rough cough continued until it took his breath completely, sending him careening sideways until his hand at last reached a shut-tight door, and he could steady himself. He coughed on, and it sounded to Max as if the poor man's chest were full of melted rubber bands and marbles. When the burly man's knees buckled, Max rushed to him and caught him up. The burly man coughed again, and this time, productively. His cheeks puffed with air, as his lips pressed closed to prevent expectorating on the floor. He seemed very concerned with the possibility and moved his hand under himself to, supposedly, catch whatever may fall from him despite his effort. His eyes bulged, and Max decided to raise him. Max's hamstrings and the triceps muscle in his right arm pulsated under the weight of the crumpled burly man. Amanda saw them quiver and wondered if she should help too, but too quickly, Max had erected them both. The burly man's eyes cleared, and with a visible struggle, he swallowed. He nodded repeatedly, breathed in deeply, and moved slightly away from Max.

The door that the burly man had leaned on suddenly swung open, and another masked man stood defiantly in its frame. He made eye contact with both Max and Amanda. They stared back at him blankly, managing to catch a glimpse of the background scene. The room was filled with functioning electrical equipment: white lights, green lights, screens with blips, screens that *bleeped*, screens with pictures of Max holding the burly man, and screens with Amanda looking at screens of Amanda.

Amanda's mouth opened slightly, and her finger pointed at herself. "That's me."

"Yes, Amanda," the masked man responded without looking, "that's you."

Amanda, with some difficulty, stopped looking at herself and stared at the masked man. "And who are you?"

The man removed his mask. "People call me Somnus."

Chapter 15

Kyle Green ran for his life. He threw his belongings in his backpack with shaking hands, making sure his notes were the first to go in. He was trying to calculate how much time he had, knowing it wasn't much. The Rock-a-Byes needed only to cover the distance from their row homes to the base of the building while, Kyle needed to descend twelve, no, now seventeen stories and *then* outrun them. There was a very good chance that he might run right into them. He considered hiding somewhere in the building, but what good would that do? His enemy would only stake out the building and wait for him to emerge, or conduct a room-by-room search, or maybe, set the damn thing on fire to drive him out. Escape was the only way out. He needed, somehow, to get away.

He crashed through the stairwell door at full speed and took the steps two at a time, and then leaped to the landing, rounded the corner, then attacked the next flight with the same haste. He did this all the way for seventeen floors. By the time he reached the ground floor, his forehead dripped with sweat and his shirt was soaked through. At the lobby door, he cracked it open and peeked through.

Shit.

Two Rock-a-Byes were coming through the door. *I'm*

fucked.

His mind raced, but was clear. The situation had his life hanging in the balance, but in that moment it was simply a puzzle to be solved. A murderous, real-life brain teaser. Kyle was extremely thankful that, before deploying on this mission, he'd spent so much time in front of the building's schematic. He was equally thankful that, given its precarious location, the team had developed an escape plan. He just hoped he could make it.

Kyle turned around and quietly negotiated the staircase down to the basement. He cracked the door, and seeing no one, slipped through. He took a right down a long hallway without any doors. If someone rounded the corner ahead of him, he'd be trapped. He thought about pulling his weapon but decided not to waste a single second. *Escape. Get away,* were the only thoughts in his head. They had discussed it back at headquarters and Brock Patterson's words played on repeat in his head.

"Look, Green. We need that intel, so no matter what, you gotta get back to us. If it comes down to it you're a hundred percent flight and zero percent fight. One hundred percent flight."

Kyle moved quickly down the long hallway then turned left. The loading docks would be down this last hall and off to the right. He rounded the corner at full speed, and bright sunlight blinded him for a second. He kept running through the large doorways, onto a short ramp, and jumped off. The pavement made his knees buckle, but he gritted his teeth, willing himself forward.

He exited the loading bay and turned left. Just before

turning, he saw two men come around the corner of the building to his right. He had, perhaps fifty feet of straightaway down an alley until he could turn right down the street. Those fifty feet seemed long, especially when the gunshots rang out. His two pursuers fired at their mark as they ran. If they'd stopped, positioned themselves steadily, and taken proper aim, they probably would have killed Kyle Green. But they ran and shot, making the marksmanship calculus nearly impossible to solve.

The sonic sound of a bullet whizzing by his ear suddenly gave him the incentive and adrenaline to increase his speed. He was only two turns away from the escape plan hatched by Brock but, if there wasn't enough distance between himself and those who hunted him, it would all fall apart.

Faster, Kyle. Faster.

A bullet struck the corner of the building as he dashed around it, sending dust and bits of grit into his face, which stuck to the sweat that beaded on his brow. He spat and wiped away what he could without slowing down. His legs ached from the lactic acid that surged through them. Kyle Green kept sprinting. *It can hurt tomorrow.*

He ran down the street until reaching an alleyway. Had he been just a second quicker, the two men chasing him wouldn't have seen him make the turn. Another bullet struck the stone, creating yet another cloud of dust and grit. This time, though, Kyle was ahead of it. Halfway down the alley another intersected, and Kyle entered it.

Based on internal calculations Kyle had been doing, he estimated that the disappearing act he was about to attempt wasn't going to work. He needed another ten or twenty feet of headway. The men behind him were just too close. He thought about his family, and his heart dreaded the notion of never seeing them again. He thought about his new family, the Eight Hour Knights, and how many of them were going to die because of his failure to get away with the intel. Just ten or twenty feet. Why hadn't he been able to run faster? He thought of his younger brother and how they would never again laugh at their mom who cranked up the old vinyl record player and belted out songs in their kitchen. They'd never again throw a baseball in the unkept diamond across the street from the home they grew up in.

Baseball.

Kyle Green had an idea. He leaned forward and ran with everything he could muster. *It can hurt tomorrow. It's going to.* The end of the alley was just ahead.

The night before, in the cover of darkness, just before Kyle set off on his own to enter the building, he, along with Brock and Carlos, had removed the manhole cover that sat in the middle of a T-junction at the end of this alleyway. Two other alleys, leading to two different streets respectively, led off from here. Both alleys were short, and both interconnecting streets were quite long in each respective direction. And that's why they selected the location. It was proximate to the building, but not too close, and the juncture created two equally likely paths.

The open manhole was now about ten feet away, and Kyle, bracing for the pain, entered a sliding position just like the old ballplayers his granddad had told him about.

His granddad had a set of these cards he had inherited, in turn, from his dad. One of them featured a player "sliding into home," as he'd called it. Kyle and his brother memorized that card and practiced the slide on the decrepit field across the street from their house. Of course, the sliding back then had been done in smooth brown sand, not rough black pavement. The pain was immediate and intense. The concrete tore the cloth of his pants and his shirt. He knew he was damaging his body, but his escape math had reached the only solution that would square his predicament.

He slid, almost entirely flat now on one side of his body, only his head lifted slightly, across the hard surface as it tore raggedly at him, tearing off skin layer by layer by layer. He imagined that his ankle and hip, the two areas which hurt the most powerfully were scraped all the way down to bone. In the case of the former, he was right.

Finally, and just when he didn't think he'd be able to refrain from screaming any longer, he plunged into the hole. His momentum slammed him against the ladder affixed to the far wall. When he felt the impact he grasped wildly with both hands and managed to find two holds. He climbed up two rungs and steadied himself. He used both of his hands, over his head, to quickly and quietly close the cover. He held his breath and waited, frozen in place. Blood dripped from his shoulder, knee and ankle. The backpack weighed a ton.

He heard footfalls and voices. More footfalls and more talking. Then footfalls. Then nothing.

***

Somnus's face was young, tight, and even a bit shiny, Amanda thought. He seemed shorter than she remembered, but perhaps that was only because he was leaning down to slip the burly man's arm over his shoulder. They looked awkward, as Somnus labored visibly to aid the much bigger man who depended on him heavily and dragged his feet. Somnus dropped him into a chair beside a desk and leaned in. Max and Amanda remained just outside the door, watching as the burly-turned-pathetic man breathed inconsistently and noisily. Somnus spoke to him. "When was the last time?"

"About...two or three..." he wheezed, "days ago."

"Which was it, two, or three?"

"Two."

"Okay, two. And the pain this time, dull or sharp?"

"Sharp."

"Sharp like needles or sharp like a knife?"

"Sharp like..." the wheezing burly man paused, "fire."

Somnus smiled. "Okay, Leon, okay. Sharp like *fire*."

Max and Amanda looked at each other, smirking, as they mouthed in unison, *Leon?*

Somnus crossed the room and, from a tall pile of askew papers, crinkled notebooks, and bent manila folders, took a small hardbound black book with a red ribbon from the pile's top. He tugged at the ribbon, which opened the book to his mark, and with a pen he grabbed from a cluttered desk, scribbled as he whispered, "Two days...two days...two." He made an emphatic motion as he underlined something. "Hmm, it should have been three days and dull pain. Why two? Why sharp?" He scribbled wildly again, and started moving around the office quickly, searching for something. He moved folders, knocked over stacks of papers, and, all the while, muttered, "Two, two days and sharp pain, why two? Why sharp?"

At last he managed to extract a leather-bound ledger. He opened it carefully, nearly reverently, and bent toward it gently. He ran his hand down the left side of the book and then stopped. He moved his hand toward the right and stopped again, his index finger balancing delicately on the page. He leaned in farther, and with his right hand, finally scrawled the numeral, "2" and the letter "S."

He closed the ledger and directed his attention to Max and Amanda. "Amanda, you I know...seen you around the Raven before, but..." he motioned to Max, "you, I don't know."

"I'm Max Dyson," he paused then threw in, "sir."

Somnus chuckled. "Please, Somnus is fine." He waved to a row of three chairs. "Take a load off."

Amanda claimed a chair closest to the desk. "Is that your real name?"

"No, it is not," he answered with a steadfast confidence, a confidence that said, *that is not my real name, but it* is *who I am*. He took a seat. "I'm sorry for the stringent security measures, but you know how things are around here, so many factions, so much violence. Anyway, my people tell me that you've got something important to say. Amanda, apparently you've joined up with some group called the..." Somnus looked over at Leon who had recovered somewhat from his wheezing fit. "What was it, again?"

"Dead Tired Crew," Leon said.

"I've never heard of them, which is the only reason you're sitting there."

Amanda smiled for a second, then: "Can I have my clothes now?"

Somnus nearly leapt from his seat. "Of course. I'm sorry." He looked again at Leon who acknowledged, stood up laboriously, and left the room.

Amanda adjusted in her seat, gazed around the room and then looked at Somnus. "This equipment is impressive. Where do you get the power for it all?"

Somnus smirked. "You know, I'm sort of used to asking the questions around here."

Max grunted and rolled his eyes.

"We have an extensive battery system, and everybody works hard to make sure they are always charged."

"Everyone? Including you?"

"No. Not me," Somnus answered with the same confidence he'd wielded before. And again it spoke in his stead, *Believe me, I've worked harder than anyone else in this building.* Somnus looked directly at Amanda, brows cocked as if raising the stakes and calling her bet.

She didn't blink.

"Amanda..." he said slowly, "what is it you want?"

"It's not what I want, it's what I have to offer you."

"Fine. What do you have?"

"You want to defeat the other factions?"

"Yes, but the reason for it is far more important than the fact itself."

Max jumped in. "You need to defeat the other factions

so that you can gain control and keep your people safe."

"No," Somnus said.

Amanda tilted her head left. "You need their help."

"Correct," Somnus replied.

Max asked, "Why not just ask for it?"

Both Somnus and Amanda smiled.

"Because they want to defeat me so that they can gain control and keep their people safe."

"Touché."

"Look..." He stood and walked to a small window behind him. "It isn't about us at all. We've been fighting each other and killing each other for decades. It's not about us." Somnus breathed deeply and exhaled loudly. "It's about the doctors beyond the wall." He'd said this with a newfound calmness. "*That's* who we need to defeat."

Max frowned. "But they've never harmed us...we've never even *seen* them. Besides, all the leaders of all the factions talk about the *evil* doctors behind the great wall. They all perpetuate the rumors of the doctors who sleep peacefully in their beds each night. They all promise to begin a revolution and lead us to a world where our dreams of *dreaming* will be fulfilled. No pun intended, but it's tiresome. We don't even know, really, if there's anybody behind that stupid wall."

Somnus turned around slowly and faced Max. "I understand your skepticism, but hear me now. I *know* that there are people behind that wall, *and* I *will* begin that revolution...or die in its pursuit."

There was a solemnity in Somnus's gaze that made Max swallow uncomfortably.

Amanda had a different take. "I think you may have to die sooner than you planned."

Somnus spun around, grinning. "Oh, so now I see. You've come to kill me." He chuckled.

Amanda grinned equally. "Actually, that's right."

***

Kyle Green hobbled through the darkness. Every other step was agony. Putting weight on the hip, leg, and ankle that had been skinned by pebbled pavement caused nauseating waves of pains to shoot up his entire body. The first of those steps, an hour earlier, had caused him to vomit all over himself. Not only did the blood fill his nostrils with a coppery odor, but it was accompanied by the acridity of his own stomach contents. All he wanted to do was sit down. Even though he felt, as every step drew him closer to the rendezvous point, safer, he willed himself to keep going because, in reality, the Rock-a-Byes could easily, and at any moment, figure out his trick. If they did, and descended below the street and into this tunnel, he would be no match for them. He was barely able to stand, and stumbling forward took just as much heart as it did brawn.

Kyle came to a complete stop when, from the black, he heard a noise. A voice. *Was that from behind? Or ahead?*

Silence. And then: "Kyle?"

Beams of light shot from around the corner, and a second later, Brock Patterson's illuminated face was in front of him.

Kyle collapsed.

Chapter 16

Amanda had slipped behind a pile of boxes to change into her newly delivered clothes while Max finished explaining how his machine worked.

"Let me make sure I completely understand all this," Somnus said. "You've built a device. A tank."

"A cylinder." Max held up a piece of paper with a sketch of the device.

"A cylinder. Into which you've both, *on purpose*, drowned yourselves."

"Well, technically..." Max lowered his doodle. "I drowned her."

"And afterwards..." Somnus stood and walked around the corner of his desk. "By some miracle that you survived, this experience has somehow made you *feel* better."

Max nodded. "Well, yeah. Physically and mentally."

Somnus, backtracked, sank into his chair, and threw his head back as he exhaled. It was as if the force of the breath exiting him had made his head bobble. He put his hands on the top of his scalp and made intermittent eye contact with both his guests. "My God. You're both crazy."

Amanda returned fully dressed and looked at him seriously. "It might be crazy. But it *works*."

Somnus rolled his eyes. "Where is this thing?"

Max answered quickly. "Safe. Only Amanda and I

know where."

Amanda reclaimed the seat next to Max, surprised and impressed by his retort. *Good thinking, Max.*

"That's too bad," Somnus said.

"And why is that?" Amanda asked.

"Because I believe you...and you've left me with a decision I don't want to make." Somnus got up quickly and crossed the room.

Amanda and Max swiveled in their seats to follow his motion.

He reached the door and opened it. "Boys." The burly man, Leon, and the escorts from earlier entered quickly. Somnus moved to the middle of the room and faced Amanda and Max. He inhaled noisily through his nostrils and then ordered emotionlessly to his men, "Take her and keep her. If I don't return..." he paused to do some kind of mental arithmetic, "within twelve hours, kill her any way you want."

Leon looked at his wristwatch, making a note of the time.

Amanda looked at a clock on the wall. *7:00pm*

Two men pounced on Amanda and grabbed her violently. She struggled. Max stood but Leon shoved him back into his chair. Amanda put up a fight, trying to push the men away, but was finally subdued by the men who towered over her.

She stared hatefully with glaring eyes at Somnus.

"It has to be this way...too many people want me dead. It's just a precaution. If this *thing* exists like you say, everything will be fine. You have every right to be angry, and I only hope that the future brings a day that affords me the opportunity to earn your forgiveness."

"Fuck you," Amanda barked.

Somnus grinned. "Yes, maybe, or maybe the other way around. Max...let's go."

Max looked at Amanda. *This can't be part of her plan.*

"By tomorrow, Max, 7:00am sharp," Amanda said. "You'd better be here."

"I know. I will."

Somnus motioned, and one of the escorts, equal to Leon's girth, lifted Max from the chair and shoved him forward. The final man held Max's clothes and threw them to him. Leon, Amanda in hand, crossed in front of Somnus and stood in the doorway.

Max quickly dressed, and then he and Somnus, followed by the two escorts left the room. Leon stepped fully outside the door, closed it, and padlocked it.

I should have told her I loved her, Max thought as he was led away.

They did not follow the same route by which Max had arrived. Instead, they went through a series of doors until they reached a guarded staircase that was dimly lit and smelled like wet paint. The two guards silently went ahead of burly Leon and rushed down the stairs. Max heard footfall after footfall, as they clambered down flight after flight, the sound of their descent reverberating in his ears. Finally, they reached the end of the stairwell and Max, winded from the hurried journey, noticed two more people had joined their group. There were now Leon, the two stairwell guards, the rear escorts, and the two new men who were dressed identically to Somnus, wearing surgical masks, as well. The real Somnus approached the imposters, and after a few whispered instructions, the group broke into three: Leon and a Somnus-decoy went straight ahead, Max and Somnus went through a locked door to their right, and the remaining five-man entourage ran up one flight of stairs, drawing weapons as they ascended.

"C'mon..." Somnus said, "hurry up." He was walking swiftly down the dark hallway, cracking his knuckles on both hands, simply by clenching his fists.

Crack-crack-crack.

They passed by a room with a partially uncovered window, and Max noticed that they were on a basement floor, the window was at ground level, and the sun was now fully set. Max also saw piles of boxes—but these were unlike those he'd noticed when entering Somnus's lair—these seemed undisturbed. "What's in the boxes?"

"Stuff they left behind, mostly useless junk. We've already salvaged anything of value."

Max, remembering Mark's words asked, "I don't suppose you've got anything called a de-fib-ril-a-tor in there?" He sounded out each syllable of the word.

"Probably, why?"

"We need one."

"We don't have much time to get out of this part of the city."

"It's pretty important...it's for the machine."

"They took every bit of medicine, antiseptic, blood, instruments, anything they could carry, but left a lot of the equipment. We'll look in this room coming up on the left, if there's one there, you can have it. Otherwise we're getting out of here."

Moments later, with a moderately heavy box in tow, Max followed Somnus out of the room. They walked quickly until the floor sloped upwards, and then climbed the gradual grade, and Max breathed a bit more heavily under the strain of his awkward load. In front of them, at the end of the hallway, stood two doors, barricaded by a bird's nest of steel chain and padlocks.

Suddenly, from the other side of the building came the sound of shotgun blasts and pistol shots.

Somnus looked at Max. "Put that down and help me. Quickly."

As Somnus freed each padlock with a ring of keys extracted from his pocket, Max tugged at the chain, thrusting it aside into a great pile. The gunfire continued, and yelling voices joined the disturbing choir. At last, the doors were opened. Max grabbed the package, and they both ran out.

"Shouldn't we lock the door?" Max asked.

"My people will take care of it. We need to hurry." Somnus walked speedily, but carefully, moving his eyes up and down, and his head from side to side. He crossed streets, ran down alleyways, and turned corners until the sound of gunplay faded away and they reached a transport station. With a final glance around, they both scrambled down the dark staircase.

It was, in reality, only seconds, but for the inconspicuous boy who'd spotted his faction's nemesis simply walk without care, and seemingly without guarded escort, down the stairs of the transport station, it was long enough. As soon as Max and Somnus's heads had descended into blackness, the boy bailed from his perch in the doorway across the street, and ran, swinging his arms wildly as he went. He wished only that he'd make it in time, so that Somnus and his unknown but certainly harmless companion, couldn't board a transport and disappear. He dug his feet in and leaned forward, hoping he'd be fast enough.

He pictured the huge ice cream sundae all the kids in his faction had been promised if they could discover the whereabouts of Somnus.

***

Kyle Green winced, as the alcohol-soaked gauze pad touched his exposed buttock. He tried extra hard not to squeal in front of the young woman with silken hair and glistening blue eyes who tended to him. Yeah, real tough with half his ass hanging out, staring her in the face. She didn't seem the least bit fazed by the view and simply continued intently working on him.

Kyle lay on his good side in an infirmary, a room he'd not ever been in before, in the building where Brock Patterson had first introduced him to this cell of Eight Hour Knights. His injuries, the woman-cum-nursemaid had told him, from sliding at top speed across the concrete alleyway would not be life-threatening if the wounds could be properly cleaned. Left the way they were, teaming with dirt, grit and whatever else was on the ground in that tucked away city backstreet, they would probably kill him. Slowly. Infection, she warned, would beget infection and slowly, agonizingly, it would turn gangrenous. Even if they hacked off his arm—she'd made a striking motion while speaking—and amputated his leg in an attempt to save him, the contagion would eventually win. The woman, she'd told Kyle, knew these risks, which was why, despite how uncomfortable it was going to be, she worked at him meticulously, under the bright light of a battery powered lamp on wheels, with tweezers and gauze. She'd injected him in several locations with the only pain killer she had access to, Novocain, a local anesthetic, she told him, was once used mostly by dentists during tooth extractions. It was all she had, so she'd picked a few select locations and injected it.

"It's still going to hurt like a son-of-a-bitch," she'd said before commencing.

She was right. While the injections had numbed some of Kyle's body, it didn't work on all of it. Being picked at with the tweezers felt like hot needles being jabbed in him, while the alcohol gauze pads, of which the young lady had already used an entire box, felt like a blowtorch turned on him. Kyle tried to think about other things, but the only real distraction was how his arrival had sent the entire cell into a frenzy, like a bees' nest that had just been whacked with a big stick.

Brock Patterson stood before him, talking to Carlos. He then pulled over a chair and sat in front of Kyle. He looked him directly in the eyes. "Nice job." He smiled.

"Thanks." Kyle winced again.

"Sharon's going to fix you up. She's our head medic, so you're in good hands."

Sharon continued working, not looking up.

"I know you're not feeling great right now, but I think we should go over everything you learned. I'm concerned that, because they spotted you, they could vacate, fortify, or call in reinforcements. The time to strike is now." Brock turned toward Carlos. "Go find Joseph. Spread the word that we're moving out in two hours. We're hitting that compound at..." He looked at a wind-up watch on his left wrist, the glass face of which had a crack from end to end. "Sixteen hundred. Get everyone ready."

He turned back to Kyle and retook his seat. "Kyle, tell me everything. Every detail."

"Hand me my notes...in the backpack over there."

For the next ninety minutes, Kyle went line by line over every note he'd taken. Brock listened, transforming the information into strategies and tactical options. Actually, his brain was checking off boxes as he listened to Kyle.

Okay, we know the sentries schedules. We can avoid them. Check.

We'll need to cut off access to the vehicles and heavier weaponry. Check.

We know how to get them to open the front door. Check.

"Kyle, the one thing that worries me," Brock said while pacing, "is that we don't even know if the mark is in there. You never saw Sedgwick?"

"Nope, not once," *ouch*, "but, isn't he supposed to be

a recluse?"

Let's hope it's not just a rumor. We can't wait any longer. The longer we wait, the riskier it's gonna be. Somnus wants retribution and he picked us to deliver it. It's on.

Two and a half hours later, Brock's plan was put into violent motion. When the two sentries exited the row home and began their patrol, the Eight Hour Knights laid in wait. When the two men, casually chatting with shouldered rifles hanging uselessly on their backs, rounded the corner at the farthest part of their route, two Knights emerged from shadow. One of the men's throats was slit while the other man found that he had the point of a knife pressing against his neck and a hand over his mouth.

Brock stepped forward and looked the man in the eye. The sentry looked barely twenty years of age, and his bright blue eyes darted from side to side. Brock put a single finger, perpendicularly, against his lips. "Shhhh," he whispered. "What is your group called? How do the other groups refer to you?"

Brock looked at the man who's knife was at the sentry's throat. He nodded, and the man removed his hand from the sentry's mouth but kept the knife in place, making sure the blue eyed man could feel its sharp tip against his alabaster skin.

The sentry swallowed. "Blue regiment," he muttered.

"Is there a red regiment?" Brock asked.

The blue-eyed sentry shook his head ever so slightly, wary of the knife's tip.

"Green regiment?"

"Across town near the water."

"Thank you." Brock looked at the Knight with the knife and nodded again. The knife's edge brushed against the man's sparse whiskers and rotated from a vertical to horizontal position so it could slash the man's throat open. The blue-eyed sentry crumpled to the ground, grasping uselessly at the gushing hole in his neck.

The group moved in a choreography designed, mostly by Brock himself, that had them breaking apart into two separate, yet equally important groups. Half the cell went around back and crouched behind the large reinforced fence that reached up twelve feet. The wooden barrier, they knew, was buttressed with thick beams dug into the ground at approximately forty five degree angles. That detail, however, wasn't visible from behind the fence itself, so the soldiers that ducked there in that moment, all secretly thanked Kyle Green for his service. Beyond the fence, behind them, they now saw not just on a planning map, but for real, was a street running parallel, and across that street, a block of dilapidated homes, all of them with collapsed roofs. Previously they'd been squares on a page. Now, for those that gazed upon them, they were abandoned homes that begged questions about who might have lived there.

Brock's first of two brigades also looked up a perpendicular street that intersected the one running along the fence line, bifurcating the shanty houses into two blocks. Back at their building, when they looked at that street on the map and combined it with Kyle's intel about the bracing, a working theory had developed. That street was directly across from the middle of the fence, and

Brock, after hearing Kyle's description of the braces, figured that it was there in case somebody tried to drive a vehicle at high speed down that street and directly into the fence. Based on Kyle's description, combined with what they now saw in reality while crouching behind it, it probably would have held. When the theory was first introduced, someone countered that the chances that anybody would be able to find a working vehicle or, and even more remotely, the fuel to put in it, was next to impossible. As the men, with the large fence now directly in front of them, thought about how much work it must have been to both plan for and execute against such an unlikely scenario, all they could do was chalk it up to further evidence of Sedgwick's purported paranoia.

The fence was certainly an obstacle to overcome, but it also provided the Knights who knelt and crouched at its base, perfect cover while they waited for the signal. There's was the second riskiest of the jobs they all had today. They all knew that getting over the fence was imperative to the mission's success, but their enemy wasn't going to make it easy. Once sure that they had successfully taken their positions unnoticed, each Knight quietly donned a brand new blue surgical mask. The act of putting it on, when the second white elastic cord rounded the second ear, stimulated the heartbeats of the men and women behind the fence into a wild, uncontrollable detonation of percussion. Fifty two heart-drums of varying tenor created an organic, atonal concerto that inspired every one of them. They breathed heavily and waited.

Brock understood strategically, as he had studied the

RA Haskell

planning schematics, why the enemy faction had chosen this location, but now, upon seeing it, had an even greater appreciation for whomever had selected it for the Rock-a-Bye Babies. The three row homes, and its essentially vacant lot behind, was a little island that stood alone, surrounded by an ocean of cracked pavement. From the front there was no inconspicuous way to approach it. A wide street ran parallel to the homes, and beyond that street lay two lanes of track from an old, long abandoned public transit system, and after the track, another wide street which would have conveyed traffic in the opposite direction to that of the street nearest the homes. A crumbling building, half caved in according to Kyle's report but looked even worse in person, was cattycorner to the left of the homes, but its structure seemed so unsound that Brock had ignored it as part of his planning. Upon seeing its condition for himself, he was glad he'd made that call. The only way to stage an assault with any chance of success, in Brock's planning mind, at least, was to cause a diversion that allowed his forces to swarm from the side. As he stared at the quarry in front of him, he confirmed that suspicion. It wasn't impenetrable, but it was easy to defend and difficult to assail.

To the west of the complex, directly across a single lane one-way street, were the remnants of a strip mall. What had once been an independent grocer, a bakery, a Chinese restaurant, and a dry cleaner were now empty shells with broken windows, doorless entries, and in the case of the dry cleaner on the end, a collapsed exterior wall. The second group of Knights, led by Brock himself, like ants escaping the rain, scurried into every opening offered by the structure. Once inside and hidden, the one Knight who'd volunteered for the next part regretted his former bluster. *What the fuck was I thinking?* As his comrades masked-up and their collective hearts joined the symphony of percussion, he handed his shotgun to Brock and took the brown package from his hand. He exited the doorway, attempting to calm his nerves and feign casualness, while he mentally reviewed the steps and advice Kyle Green had relayed. Kyle had seen two visitors granted entry into the compound. He replayed everything he'd been told in his mind's eye. They both knocked on the door of the row home in the middle. Not the one to the left nor the one to the right. It appeared that they knocked one single time with an open hand. They'd slapped the door in the upper left corner and then stepped back, faced it, stood tall, and remained still. Each visitor had then moved their mouths, speaking. And no, Kyle had not been able to tell what they had said, only that they spoke multiple words. Was one of them a password or code or some other verbal authentication? Kyle didn't know and that lack of knowledge weighed heavily on the young man who now approached the middle door.

Both of the visitors Kyle witnessed had raised their hands over their heads and slowly spun around. The first visitor Kyle monitored waited, frozen in place, for a few more seconds after the pirouette, until the door opened and a man with a pistol used the gun to wave the man inside. He entered, and the door closed behind him. The man exited unceremoniously through the same door about forty five minutes later.

The second person Kyle had seen delivered a package wrapped in brown paper. He'd also been made to spin around, but the door had not opened. Instead, he placed the package on the top stair and backed away. When the man was fully out of sight, the door opened and someone retrieved the package and carried it inside. The knees of the young man who now mounted the first stair nearly buckled. He tensed all his muscles at once in an attempt to stave the quaking his body was doing against his will. He shook and thought he might fall down, but found the resolve to slap his open hand in the upper left corner of the door and step back. He held the package in front of himself.

"What's your business?" came a voice from inside the row home.

The young Knight hoped his voice wouldn't shake like his body was.

"Delivery for blue regiment," he said, a bit too loudly, but unquiveringly. *Whew. I said it.*

"From whom?"

"Green regiment."

"You know what to do."

The young Knight raised his hands over his head, the package cradled in them, and spun around slowly. He then placed the package on the top stair, turned, and walked away. Only when he had rounded the corner did the door open and the package make its journey inside.

Brock watched the door open through the lens of the same scope Kyle had used to learn about this procedure in the first place. He saw a man retrieve the package, bring it inside, and close the door.

"Get ready," Brock said. The whole mission was dangerous as hell, but this part made sweat run down his back. They were fifty yards away from the row homes, and there was no cover between them and the compound. As they traversed the distance they'd be out in the open, sitting ducks for their enemy to pick off. The distraction was going to buy them some time, but probably not enough. They'd all agreed back at HQ to take the risk.

Just then, as someone inside opened the package, Brock heard the explosion, and through the scope, saw the front door of the middle row home blow right off the hinges and fly twenty feet in the air. A large cloud of black smoke rushed out. *Now, hopefully,* Brock thought, *chaos.*

"Now!" Brock yelled, and he, along with the rest of his Knights emerged from the nooks and crannies of the falling-down strip mall and ran, guns raised, toward the row homes. In the back, along the fence, those Knights, also having heard the explosion, were now throwing their collapsible ladders to the top of the fence and climbing as quickly as they could. The first to reach the top, hooked ropes to the opposite side and used them to scale down into the lot. Not even half of them had made it over when the bullets started coming. Somnus's retaliation was underway.

Chapter 17

The journey with Somnus was especially long for Max, who thought only of Amanda and how absolutely infuriated she must be.

Sure, hold the woman hostage. Figures, he could imagine her saying. Max half-wished the tables were turned, that he'd been the one facing imminent execution and counting on Amanda to return and save him. He wasn't sure if he'd make it back in time, but he knew without question that she could have done it. Max, leaning the defibrillator box against himself, looked often at Somnus who stared back.

"How can you be so sure that the doctors are still behind that wall?" Max asked.

"Trust me. I know," Somnus responded, again with an eerie seriousness. Something about the way he said, *know,* curt and sharp, made Max believe him.

"Do you trust *me,* that I've invented this thing and that it works like we say?"

"No. That's why I need to see it. And, *that's* also why you should believe me."

Max thought for a second. "Okay, so what have you *seen?*"

Somnus looked around and noticed more than one glance focused in his direction. He held his finger to his lips. "Shhhhh," he whispered, "later."

Max and Somnus were silent for the rest of the journey. The prying eyes gave Max a sense of paranoia, and his heart was pounding vigorously. He then fully wished that the tables *were* turned so that all he had to do was await Amanda's return.

The transport arrived at Max's station with a hollow *squish,* and they exited. Somnus commented on the surprising number of people who disembarked, as well. "Popular stop."

"Not usually."

"Keep your head down," Somnus said, looking around.

They went up the stairs, and Max led him through a maze of alleyways and backstreets. It wasn't the most direct route, nor the fastest, but Max knew it was confusing enough to, hopefully, avoid being followed.

Somnus, quite skilled at urban navigation, must have found himself completely twisted around, because his head spun from left to right a few times and he mumbled to himself. *Right. Then left. No wait. Was it left?*

After several more twists and turns, including an awkward squeeze through a jammed doorway, they arrived at Max's front door at 8:00pm. *One hour down, eleven to go.*

A few moments after knocking, Mark cautiously opened the door, looking bedraggled but relieved.

Max lifted the package up slightly and moved inside toward his friend. He unloaded the bundle into Mark's outstretched arms and smiled. "Here's the de-fib-ra-thing, you wanted."

"Wow," Mark exclaimed. "I was half-kidding, but cool."

Max turned to Somnus. "Mark, this is Somnus. Somnus, this is my dear friend Mark."

Mark's mouth was suddenly agape. He placed the box on a wobbly table next to the door and tentatively reached out his hand. "Hello, Somnus."

Somnus took his hand and shook it. "Hello."

"Where's Amanda?" Mark asked.

"I'll explain later. Somnus is here to inspect my, uh, invention."

"A...a...and you came alone?"

Somnus replied simply, as if his coming alone were the most logical thing in the world. And, to him, it was exactly that. "Yes."

"And where's your mask?" Mark asked.

"You don't honestly think I wear it all the time, do you?"

"This way," Max said, pointing. He was already headed toward the back stairs, fully cognizant of the passage of every minute and what it could mean for Amanda.

The moon was beginning to cast rays of soft pale light into the chamber as they entered it. Max rested his hand on the cold cylinder. "Here it is. My savior."

"Deathtrap is more like it," Mark muttered.

Somnus turned to Mark. "You don't approve?"

"No. No, I don't. It's suicide."

"But, does it work?" Somnus placed his hand on the

plexiglass.

"In theory, very well. Death is the ultimate kind of rest. The brain doesn't even need to..."

Mark kept talking, but Somnus had already heard all that he needed to. *Something like this could fundamentally shift the balance of power. It could unite the factions. Or conquer them if it comes to that.*

When Mark ended a sentence with an interrogatory, Somnus's attention refocused.

"You understand?"

"Um. Uh. Yes, I understand. Go on."

Somnus walked around the cylinder, touching its various parts as one might stroke a coiled snake: carefully, curiously, gingerly.

How might this help us to rebel against the doctors behind the wall? It can make us stronger. I've always known that I would die in my quest to discover the truth. I never imagined it would be like this. I always thought it would be an epic moment of valor during a great battle. Not in an underground chamber in secret.

He returned his attention to Mark's voice.

"I think the risks far outweigh the benefits."

"There's only one way to know for sure," Somnus whispered. He folded his arms and looked at Max. "The Dead-Tired Crew. Good one."

Mark was going to ask what that meant, but Max waved his hand, signaling him to be quiet.

"Well..." Somnus proclaimed loudly, "let's do it."

Mark started to recite his cautionary mantra, but Max interrupted. "I'll show you. Nothing can happen to you, or

Amanda will die, remember?"

"Amanda will die?" Mark asked with a quiver. "What the hell are you talking about?"

Somnus stepped forward. "Max, I need to do it, otherwise I can't be certain that it works."

"Let Amanda come back. Then you can try it, okay?"

"No, Max. As you've seen, leaving my part of the city is too dangerous, besides, you've done this several times, right?"

"Yes, but—"

"Well, then...I'm sure I will be fine."

"We need the sun to help revive you, you're going to be, uh, *gone* for several hours."

"That's okay, right? What's the longest you've been...gone?"

"Eight hours."

"Perfect." Somnus smiled.

Mark was aghast. "Are you nuts, Max? Get Amanda back first."

"Yeah, if you go down for eight hours," Max paused, and glanced at an old-fashioned clock that hung precariously from the stone wall. It was nearly 9:00pm. Max mouthed something unintelligible, and twiddled his fingers, calculating. "That will only leave like two hours to get back."

"That's plenty of time," Somnus said, smiling.

Max sensed that Somnus would never yield. He hadn't known this man for more than a few hours, but he did suspect that he was the type who got what he wanted. He sighed audibly.

"Okay. But eight hours only, not a minute longer."

"Wait a minute," Mark interjected. "You're making a deal with the devil here, Max. It's bullshit."

Max stared intently back at him, directly into his eyes.

Mark sighed and waved his hand at Max as if to say *Oh the hell with you. You're hopeless.*

Somnus saw Max's eyes break their stare and move alternatively to look at the ground and then back at Mark. "Let's do this."

"What do I do?" Somnus asked.

"Take off your clothes down to your underwear."

Minutes later, Somnus shivered and gulped his last breath as cold water filled the cylinder and enveloped him.

Mark's face was completely colorless, as he watched Somnus struggle helplessly to hold his breath, and when Somnus's eyes went wide and his mouth opened to suck water into his lungs, Mark turned away. "Jesus Christ."

Max formed his hands in a triangular shape and placed them around his nose and mouth. He breathed out. "Shit."

Somnus was dead, and he had killed him.

***

Brock Patterson saw out of the corner of his eye, the head of one of his Knights explode, a conical red spray exited the base of his skull and spattered the pavement as if a giant mouthful of blood had been blown out a straw.

Snipers?

While Kyle had not seen any positioned snipers on top of the row homes, or near the complex, the angle of the bullet and the caliber with which his man had just been struck, told him that the shot had come from a long gun from a high-ground position. They had snipers, apparently, but only mustered them when needed.

Brock and his force had covered about half the distance to the target, so he knew that this development would thin his ranks, but hopefully not cripple them. As they continued running, more men had sniper bullets blow off their heads, contributing to the macabre red mural on the pavement. Given the rate with which Brock saw it happening, he guessed there was only one sniper.

In the back, a force of Rock-a-Bye men had emerged from the row homes and were taking positions behind storage containers, on top of sheds, and lying on the ground. They were actually advancing throughout the yard, bringing the fight to the Knights who had now finally managed to get everyone, not already dead, over the fence. The gun battle in the back was intense, with fire coming from every direction and from a variety of weapons.

Bullets *whizzed.*

Rifle shots *cracked.*

Shotgun blasts *boomed.*

A tossed hand grenade from one Knight took out a key position of enemies, allowing them to advance to a better, more defensible area.

Out front, no opposing force was coming at them. Brock hadn't expected it. Those inside would defend from within; it was, he knew, the tactically superior thing to do. As Brock's force finally reached the row homes, several of the windows exploded with gunfire, and a dozen Knights were lost in an instant. But, as Brock predicted, they had the advantage of numbers and soon breached each of the row homes. Carlos and Joseph were at Brock's side as they entered the middle home. Other Knights entered the other row homes, and everyone on the inside had the same mission: find Sedgwick. Each of the inside team members had committed his photograph to memory, and now they went, room by room, looking for him.

Out back, in the lot, the mission was to prevent the Rock-a-Byes from accessing the heavy weaponry Kyle had spotted and, but to a lesser extent, prevent Sedgwick from attempting an escape on the all-terrain vehicle Kyle had seen. The battle in the lot was taking on the shape of trench warfare. There were so many obstacles, it created a labyrinth of hiding places and defensive positions. Men and women who emerged were only visible for a split second before disappearing just as quickly.

After an initial surge by both forces, the fighting had reached a standstill with each side dug in to a variety of locations throughout the lot. The once constant barrage of gunfire now settled into an occasional burst or singular crack when someone on either side took a chance and left cover. The one positive for the Knights was that the container with the big guns was clearly in their sight and anybody who tried to approach its door would get shot at from multiple locations. The several dead bodies strewn in front of it were a good sign that they had it cut off. For now.

Inside was an entirely different and hectic series of encounters. Violent little vignettes played out like gruesome snippets from random movies.

Brock entered a kitchen, and a shotgun blast tore a hole in the wall next to him. Carlos who'd entered the kitchen from another entryway shot the man with the shotgun.

A Knight opened a bedroom door only to come face to face with a woman aiming a rifle at him. He died before he hit the floor.

Joseph climbed a staircase, and when he reached the second floor, a man ran at him with a knife. Joseph grabbed the man's hand as it plunged down. In the struggle, Joseph was stabbed in the arm. He shoved the man against the wall and then swept his leg out from under him. As he fell, Joseph managed to fire off a shot that blew a hole in his gut. The man didn't get up, and an increasingly large pool of blood kept growing in the hallway.

Carlos opened a bedroom door and saw a naked man standing behind a naked woman who was bent over with her hands on the end of a bed. Carlos then made a mistake. He judged the amorous couple not to be a threat, given that they were otherwise engaged, despite the unmistakable commotion around them. He simply moved on down the hall. But before he could open another door, the man with his penis still erect and glistening, put a gun to Carlos's head and pulled the trigger. Brock saw it, and as the naked man turned the gun toward him, Brock dropped him. He fell backwards, lying flat on his back with his erection, for a few moments longer, pointed directly at the ceiling.

Brock noticed that, as they moved, their encounters became less frequent. The other Knights in the other row homes noticed the same thing. At first, Brock swelled with pride, thinking *we're winning*, but when he opened a bedroom door and saw an open window at the back with some kind of hooks on it, he had a different thought. *They're retreating. They're running.*

He approached the window and peered outside. An emergency ladder dangled from this window, and as he scanned the backs of all the homes, he saw that many other windows did too. He quickly knew this meant that the fight out back was about to intensify. Just then, in front of a large shipping container, there was an explosion, and then voluminous amounts of thick smoke. Brock knew the fight on the inside was over. He yelled at the Knights around him, "Go down! Out back!"

For those in back, the smoke blocked their view of the container that held the large weapons. The Knights simply decided to fire into the smoke. Three bodies fell, but four others didn't. Soon the container doors were opened. Just minutes later, the back lot behind the row house encampment of the Rock-a-Bye Babies Blue Regiment exploded with a wall of sound that struck terror into the hearts of the Eight Hour Knights. Both heavy machine guns had been mounted to platforms in opposing corners of the lot, and as the belts fed ammunition at a rate of 600 rounds per minute, or ten bullets every second, the lot became a field of death. The caliber was heavy enough to penetrate many of the containers behind which the Knights had taken positions.

Brock knew the moment he heard the repetitive and thunderous firing of those heavy guns that, if they couldn't take them out, this battle was over. The one advantage he and those still inside had was that, technically, they were behind their enemy who had their backs turned. He grabbed Joseph who was about to run past him. "We gotta take out those guns," Brock yelled over the din.

"How?" Joseph yelled back.

"The roof," Brock said, remembering the sniper that had picked off several of his compatriots during their run up to the row homes.

Joseph and Brock ran up the stairs and frantically looked around for access. At the end of a hallway they spotted a staircase which had been pulled down from the ceiling above.

"There."

As they ascended, Brock thought there was a chance the sniper was still up there. He raised his rifle at the ready. They entered an attic, and at the far end was a dormer-style window, opened. As they stepped out onto the roof, the machinegun fire had another sound join its chorus, the sound of splintering wood. The Knights, dying next to each other, shredded to bits by the gun's fifty-caliber rounds, hurriedly climbed the fence. Their enemy trained the diabolical weapon on the climbers, and those same rounds ripped the wood apart like an industrial chipper.

Brock rested his rifle on the roof line and hunkered down. He took aim at the machinegun operator and fired. The side of the man's head splattered on the side of the house, and he crumpled.

Joseph, on the opposite side of the roof, did the same to the other gunner, but not before two other climbing

Knights died, and a huge hole appeared in the fencing. The sound of lone cracks of gunfire took over, once the machineguns were silenced. Soon, though, the singular shots were overpowered by a noise Brock wasn't sure he knew. He'd heard if before but it sounded otherworldly. Foreign.

Is that a gas-powered engine?

From another container, the surprising vehicle Kyle had seen lurched out. Brock knew instantly the driver was Sedgwick, the man he'd been looking for. Brock fired a shot at him in haste, which he would later come to regret. It struck near to him against the door of the storage container, making a loud *twang*, but also warning the man.

Missed! Dammit! Should have taken my time.

Sedgwick looked up. He and Brock made eye contact and Sedgwick smiled wryly as he twisted the handle of the vehicle and sped through a gate one of his men held open at the side of the lot.

The remaining combatants fired at the Knights as they ran out the hole. One ascended the machinegun platform but Brock ended him before he could man the weapon. Brock knew, with Sedgwick gone, continuing the battle was only a waste of lives. He stood on the rooftop and yelled for the Knights to retreat.

He and Joseph ran back through the row home and out into the street. It had been a good plan, but it had failed. He didn't relish sending this news to Somnus. He never imagined he'd get the chance to deliver the news personally.

Chapter 18

Somnus was still dead.

Mark and Max stood, stone-faced, for several minutes without moving.

The hours of waiting were filled with weak attempts at small talk, pacing, and mostly anxiety. Max did manage to tell Mark about their journey to Somnus's and how he'd kept Amanda hostage, but now there was silence as Mark investigated the defibrillator by moonlight while Max sat quietly, staring blankly ahead.

"Cool," Mark said. "It's battery operated. Looks like it can be recharged, too."

Max cradled his head and sighed painfully.

"When's the last time you've been inoculated?" Mark asked.

"It's not that. Just hungry, is all."

"I looked around for something while you were gone and there's nothing here. Oh, and you sort of ran out of whiskey."

"Ran out, huh?" Max smiled.

"I'll stay here while you go get us something."

"Don't you think I should stay?"

"This is your neighborhood. You'll be able to get back faster than I can."

"Okay. I'll be quick, promise." Max bounded upstairs,

out his door, and down the street to the nearest market. One advantage of a society not able to sleep is that nothing ever closes.

As Max entered the store, he was spotted by two men and a boy who'd been looking for him. The boy who'd seen Somnus enter the transport station, along with a dozen of his older compatriots, had followed them onto the train. Max's confusing route to his home had, without his knowing, shaken the tail and dispersed the group into smaller bands who now searched the streets by twos and threes. Max paid for his food and walked home.

The boy and the two men watched Max go through his front door. Minutes later, they approached the door and knocked.

"Who can that be?" Max put down the sack on the metal table in front of Somnus. It was 4:30am so Max knew that Somnus would need to be revived in just a bit more than thirty minutes. He also knew that would leave a scant two hours before 7:00am, the deadline to get back to Amanda. This thought was occupying his mind when Mark spoke.

"I'll check." Mark pointed at dead Somnus with his thumb. "This guy is giving me the creeps, anyway."

Max continued to unpack, laying out the wrapped sandwiches, grind-in coffees, and a bag of sugary candy. He was placing one of the large coffee cups down when a thud sounded from upstairs. He looked away and mistakenly placed the cup on the edge of the table. It teetered for a moment and then tumbled to the floor sending a gritty black puddle toward Max's foot. Another thud and a strange voice made him forget it altogether. He thought about calling out to Mark, but something told him not to.

Instead, he glanced around quickly looking for anything he could wield. Against the wall to his left leaned a piece of heavy pipe, a leftover from his device's construction. He picked it up and moved toward the side of the doorway just as way too many footsteps started coming down the staircase. Max breathed heavily and rapidly despite his best efforts not to. He held the pipe over his right shoulder and backed up against the wall out of sight. He was scared but determined to hit whatever came through the door. His muscles tensed, and he resisted blinking, keeping his eyes wide and focused.

The footsteps arrived at the bottom of the stairs, and he knew whatever was coming through the door had only to turn left and take a couple steps until they'd be there. Max tightened his grip and prepared to swing. He only hoped it wasn't Mark leading the way. He planned on swinging low to increase his chances of making contact, figuring that chests were easier to hit than heads. Also, he thought, if it *was* Mark, a blow to the mid-section probably wouldn't kill him. Seconds later, Max saw the tip of a shoe become suddenly illuminated by the pale bluish moonlight that filled the chamber. As Max swung low with all his might, he thought the shoe was relatively small.

The pipe, from its thin hollow core, let out a reverberating *gong*, as it landed on the side of the boy's skull. The force of impact lifted him off his feet, and he crumpled to the floor without any cry, or any visible effort to break his fall. His arms did not outstretch and his legs did not scramble in an attempt to put his feet back under him. The other side of his skull broke his fall with a horrid muffled *crack*—like stepping on a hard-boiled egg.

Mark had taken advantage of the attack and spun around to face the man behind him. They were locked in battle over the gun the man had let drop from Mark's back when Max had bludgeoned his comrade.

Max was shocked and hesitated. The other man had stepped in and was leveling his pistol at Max's head. Max blinked and thought of Amanda. He turned away from the boy whose legs quivered slightly, and lunged for the man. Max grabbed the man's hand, pushing it downward just as the weapon fired. The bullet whizzed by Max's ear and penetrated the cylinder holding Somnus. Water sprayed out of the hole in the clear acrylic. He managed to squeeze off two additional shots, both of which also struck the cylinder, the first shattering the weighting mechanism, and the second striking one of the door's hinges.

The man brought his other hand up to grip the pistol, and Max did the same. Mark and the man he struggled with had entered the room and, for a moment, the men appeared to be dancing with each other in some kind of macabre ballet. Mark's partner tried to shove him into the table behind him, but when he moved his leg backward to stabilized the push, Mark brought his knee up into the man's groin. The man loosened his grip on the gun, and Mark wrenched it free and crashed it into the slumping man's face in two quick motions.

Max wrestled for control of his adversary's weapon in

a shower of cold spray. The water in the cylinder had receded several inches, but Max didn't notice as he maintained focus on his formidable opponent. The water-coated slippery floor, combined with the man's superior strength, was making it increasingly difficult for Max to maintain his ground. He believed that if it were not for the new-found fortitude the cylinder had provided him, he would have already succumbed. Sensing that he would soon be overcome, he tried desperately to think of a way out. The gun moved from side to side and up and down, and along with it went four hands, all gripping tightly. They took steps forward and backward and leaned mightily from left to right.

The gun was pointing at Max's shoulder, and he decided one option was to force the gun to fire. He figured that once the trigger was pressed he would have an easier time pinning the man's finger down so that he couldn't release it for another shot. He worried that his resolve might weaken after the bullet entered him, and he was equally concerned about where the wound would occur. When Max's strength was nearly exhausted, the gun was right in front of his face, its barrel still aimed at his shoulder. He was about to allow the man to fire when he spotted the safety and had another idea.

A beam of moonlight from the chamber's ceiling shot across the weapon and Max could see that the safety switch was directly under his right index finger. He struggled to move his finger up, and when he was close, he let his left hand fly off the gun and land on the man's throat. He gripped and squeezed. The man used his left hand to easily pry Max's fingers free, but, as Max had hoped, he stopped looking at the gun. In that moment, Max wiggled his finger upward and threw the safety. Max tried to let go entirely and jump back, but the man he fought with didn't allow it; he kept a tight grip on Max's fingers and started to bend one of them backwards. He smiled and Max winced, biting his lip, when he heard the bone snap. The man, wearing a broad, devilish smile, let go and stepped backward, one pace.

Still smiling, he pointed the gun at Max and pulled the trigger. When nothing happened, he quickly figured it out, and with a flick of his own finger, turned the safety off. He squeezed the trigger again just as Mark struck the man's head with the butt of his newly acquired pistol. Max's would-be murderer slumped to the floor.

Max took a huge breath and examined his finger.

Mark nodded, bent over slightly and rested his hands on his knees, also breathing heavily.

Max noticed his finger beginning to swell, and as he was about to touch it, he heard a muffled gurgling from the corner of the room.

"Oh, Christ," he said, remembering the boy, the pipe, and the hollow sound it had made. He bent quickly, picked up the gun that had tried to end him, and moved toward the crumpled mass.

Mark stood tall again and stopped him. "Look." He pointed.

The water in Somnus's cylinder was half gone and still spraying out. The perfect hole made by the bullet was beginning to crack around the edges, and small lines, like tiny tree roots, were inching their way out, as if searching for solid ground in which to dig.

Max glanced again at the boy who shivered almost unnoticeably. "Damn." He turned away and stuck the pistol in his waistband. As he approached the cylinder, the man who'd broken his finger moaned. Without looking or thinking, Max kicked the man swiftly, high in the chest. The man went silent.

"Tie them up," Max said.

Mark scurried about until, in a pile of metal refuse, he found a bit of wire. Mark was binding the men when he asked, "what are we going to do?"

Max was inspecting the cylinder. "Anything we can." He stared into the dead eyes of Somnus.

Mark finished and rushed toward Max.

"I can't do anything with my finger like this...can you fix it?" Max felt panic rising within him; the adrenaline rush was wearing off, and his finger throbbed with each beat of his rapid heart.

"I can make it work," Mark said.

Max held out his finger, and Mark grabbed it. He twisted the knuckle slightly, and Max groaned deeply. When he set the bone, Max's groan escalated and he let out, against his will, an extended scream of agony.

Max's yell traveled upwards through the grating in the chamber ceiling and into the night sky. The three men who heard it, albeit faintly, didn't recognize the voice but headed toward it anyway. It was a ways off, and being unfamiliar with this part of the city, they weren't sure they'd be able to locate it without another auditory clue.

The Delta Wave

***

The bullets had rendered the cylinder's rudimentary, but automated, mechanisms useless. For well over an hour, Max and Mark had tried to pry Somnus loose. It was 5:47, forty seven minutes *after* Somnus was supposed to be revived. Max was panicking. In the back of his mind he knew what needed to be done but hadn't wanted to do it. He was trying to preserve the machine but now, with Amanda's time running out, picked up the same pipe he had used to strike the boy, and stormed toward the cylinder. "Fuck it," he yelled and smashed the machine's door.

Three men above them who had wandered the streets aimlessly, in the wake of hearing a scream, heard Max again.

Somnus fell onto the cold steel table but didn't slide forward. Max hadn't lubricated it, so Somnus stuck in its trough. Max waited, hoping that the fall would revive Somnus, but the body remained absolutely still. The table had not been warmed, and Max wondered if that might have something to do with it. Mark lifted Somnus's feet into the air, and a rivulet of water streamed from his mouth. They flipped Somnus over and pushed him downward, Max following Mark's lead. As he turned, a patch of skin stayed behind; like a tongue pressed against a metal doorframe in winter, Somnus's chest had stuck to the table. The patch, about the size of Max's palm, didn't bleed or turn red, it remained as pale as the rest of the man laid out in front of them.

Somnus's lips were puffed out and dark colored. Max knew intellectually that they held a bluish pallor, but they appeared black to him then. Mark held Somnus's nose, pressed his lips against the dead man's mouth, and blew. Somnus's chest rose and fell as Max threw blankets on top of Somnus's waist and legs.

"Push on his chest, like this," Mark ordered, "one, two, three, four, five. Count to fifteen."

Despite the pain in his finger, Max coupled his hands together and did as he was instructed, counting as Mark had done.

Mark rubbed Somnus vigorously, and whenever Max reached the count of fifteen, he'd blow two quick bursts of air into Somnus.

"What about that thing?" Max looked over at the defibrillator that Mark had been fiddling with.

"The battery's long dead. It won't even turn on."

"Damn it."

Between compressions, Mark dug through his leather bag, finally pulling out a large silver needle with some kind of a handle at one end.

"What's that? Eleven, twelve, thirteen."

"A bone marrow needle," Mark replied quickly.

"Fourteen, fifteen."

Mark blew air into Somnus then moved around Max to Somnus's legs. He swept aside the blankets, took one, and rolled it into a small bundle. He bent Somnus's left knee and stuck the blanket under it, propping it up. He moved around so that he faced Somnus's feet, took hold of his knee and angled it to the right slightly. Mark inserted the needle on the inside of Somnus's leg perpendicularly, just below the knee joint.

Max continued pushing and counting. "Thirteen, fourteen, what do I do? Fifteen."

"You've seen me, just do it," Mark said, clearly concentrating on what he was doing.

"But, I don't know exactly—"

"Just do it," Mark said in a way that made Max shuffle quickly to Somnus's head. As Max pressed his lips down onto the dead ones beneath him, Mark twisted the needle in a drilling motion until it gave way slightly, penetrating the cortex of the bone. Mark extracted the thin center of the device and with it came a single droplet of dark red blood. From his pocket he took a regular-looking syringe and inserted it into the core of the larger needle.

Max counted. "Ten, eleven, twelve..." He stopped to see what Mark was doing.

"Don't stop," Mark snapped.

"Okay. Thirteen, fourteen..."

"It's important you keep going. You're this guy's heart, the only thing moving blood around his cold body. I've just injected epinephrine into the bone marrow, so if it's going to work, it will work fast."

Max sent two bursts of air into Somnus's chest and watched it rise up. Despite the brisk night air, Max had worked up a sweat, and his forehead dripped. He moved to stand next to Somnus and resumed his compressions.

Mark took over the breathing, and one minute later, after four times of pushing and blowing, Mark stepped back and lowered his head. "It's over."

Max pumped Somnus's chest two more times and then stopped.

The night was quiet, and the chamber resonated with the overlapping sounds of inhaling and exhaling. It bounced around the room and whispered something to Max. His own voice spoke to him as clearly as Amanda cursing. He stared at Somnus, but that wasn't the face he saw. The words assaulted him again, just like the wind in the tube that had tapped him on the shoulder and beckoned him to go where he wasn't supposed to. He repeated them aloud. "You give up too easily."

"What did you say?"

Max raised his head. "I give up too easily." There was a determination in his loud voice that made him warm from foot to forehead, but also calmed him and stopped his perspiration. "Give him another shot." Then he swung his leg onto the table, pulled himself up, and straddled Somnus. His finger no longer hurt.

"Max, it's useless. We've done all that we—"

"Mark, please. Give him another shot. Everyone deserves a second chance."

"But Max–"

"Do it!"

The sound, like his previous outburst, signaled the three men who were now very close to the chamber's opening. They heard the cry and quickly found the grating.

"Hey," one of the men yelled down. "Who's down there?"

Max looked up and saw a shadowy figure looming over him. "Give Somnus the shot," Max said with an increasing calmness that Mark found troubling. He was in no rush to say the words, and Mark was suddenly afraid that Max had become suicidal in a brand new way; a way that might get *him* killed.

The three men above scurried away, and Max knew it would only be minutes before they found their way in.

Mark fumbled in his bag, found the syringe, and injected it into Somnus's cold leg.

"You give up too easily," Max said to himself. He looked at Mark. "I've got this, you get the door, don't let them in. Shoot anything that even remotely looks like one of these assholes. I mean it."

Mark walked toward the door and took cover in the shadows as Max vigorously pumped the chest of Somnus.

Mark whispered from his station. "Count to thirty this time."

Max's sweat came back quickly and was dripping off his brow by the time he'd reached his first count. The unmistakable noise of the front door being thrown open made Mark swallow. Max leaned forward and breathed for Somnus.

As his lips detached, he paused for a second. "C'mon, fight." Max compressed Somnus's chest with precision. He wasn't scared.

As footsteps pounded down the stairs, like a toppled box of lead balls, Max kept his attention on Somnus. "Sixteen, seventeen, eighteen..."

A man holding a shotgun entered the room, followed closely by another with a drawn pistol.

"Twenty, twenty-one..."

Mark fired from the blackness, and the back of the shotgun man's head exploded, and a small chunk of his cranium laden with dark hair and floppy skin landed and stuck for a moment on the pistol man's face. It made him duck instinctively, and the action saved him from Mark's second bullet, which whizzed past. He fired his pistol, twice, wildly. The chamber reeked of smoke, blood, and urine from the boy still dying slowly on the floor.

"Twenty three, twenty four..." Max remained focused and saw, out of the corner of his eye that the patch on Somnus's chest, the raw patch made by his initial contact with the metal table, bled. It was only a few drops here and there, but they made Max's counting get a lot louder. "Twenty five, Twenty six..."

Mark fired again and hit the pistol man in the chest, sending him spinning.

Somnus inhaled and opened his eyes. He tried to wriggle to the left but wasn't able. Somnus couldn't hear, or see very well, but he was able to make out a dark-haired man straddling him. His chest ached, and his back hurt. The man paid no attention to him; rather, he reached into his back waistband and, brandishing a gun, brought it around. Somnus blinked and took a second, long breath.

Max fired at the third man who'd entered the room but missed entirely. It wasn't only that the man was running forward and shooting, it was also that the gun recoiled badly in Max's hand, sending his arm upwards. Max realized that he would need to steady the weapon, not just aim it and fire.

Bullets went by Somnus's head, as he remembered. *It was this fellow, what's his name? M..M..Ma Max that held him down and fired a gun as if for the first time.* Max brought the weapon down, locked his shoulder, tensed his arm slightly and aimed the gun across the room. Somnus turned and saw a man with a birch tree insignia on his jacket, the traditional garb of the Rock-a-Bye-Babies. The man was headed straight for Max and shooting, as he ran. Max, with a stationary advantage, fired his gun repeatedly and, at last, the man fell.

Somnus saw movement from his left, downward, and he rolled his head to inspect it. Someone on the floor, another Rock-a-Bye with his hands bound, had just righted himself and was running toward them, his shoulder bent in anticipation of a collision. Somnus tried to speak, but could not.

Mark fired at the man he'd wounded, and the man fired back simultaneously. The bullet entered Mark's right shoulder, and he dropped his gun.

Max took aim at the man firing at his friend. He squeezed the trigger and sent a bullet into the man's neck. Blood sprayed out of the wound in a fan shape, and the man clasped both of his hands around it in a useless attempt to stay the bleeding.

Max heard a noise behind him and spun quickly.

One of the bound men was headed right for him. He was a short distance away when Max fired a bullet into his brain. The man's head snap backwards, but it didn't stop his considerable forward motion, and he collided with Max, knocking him off the table. Somnus watched the upside-down opera from his prone position on the bizarrely shaped steel table. Max got up and walked toward another man whose hands were bound. Max raised the gun to the man's head and pulled the trigger.

Max looked at Somnus, stood, and stuck the pistol in his waistband.

Somnus stared back at him. He hadn't thought Max was the type who could commit such violence but now, as Max wore the blood of those he'd killed on his face, Somnus reconsidered.

Max scanned the chamber and marveled at what had happened. He'd been dead more than once in this room, but as he surveyed the carnage around him, he thought he really ought to be dead now. *I've always worried my contraption might lead to violence. It has. I've always wondered how I'd react in a life and death situation in which I wasn't in control, one with no lever to throw. Now, I know.* He wandered about the room, making his way over to Mark. "You okay?"

"Do I look okay? I'm shot, damn it. Are you happy now?"

In the scenario he'd played over and over again in his head, it had always been Amanda that was in danger around him. Not Mark. He reflected on that scenario again...the one that haunted him. In that version, he'd simply frozen as the enemy approached. He'd remained motionless, causing Amanda to be killed. That wasn't, he now thought, what had come to pass. *I did it. I didn't freeze. I acted.*

His thoughts turned immediately to Amanda. *I love her. The next time I see her, I'm telling her that.*

The chamber, in the immediate aftermath of the battle, had smelled of gunpowder. The breeze coming from the grating above had washed that odor away, and the cold air now filled with the metallic-iron odor of fresh blood. The scent, as it invaded Max's nose, made a single thought come into his mind. *This violence, this tragedy, this murdering...it will change me.*

Somnus, fixated on Max and, shivering uncontrollably as he stared into Max's glassy eyes, read his thought. His own thought answered. *Yes, it will.*

Chapter 19

Mark groaned as Max helped him to his feet. The right shoulder of his shirt was bloody, and Mark instinctively pressed his left hand against it firmly. "Damn that hurts."

"It's a flesh wound. You'll be okay."

"Yeah. I'll live, but for how long? People want us dead, man."

Somnus's shivering and chattering were audible to both men, so they moved toward him quickly. Max arrived first. "Get up." He helped him off the table. "Take off the wet underwear. Put your dry clothes back on." Max handed them to him in a bundle.

"Move, Somnus," Max said more firmly. "You may be alive now, but just barely. You need to move around, get your blood pumping."

"I can't.

"Yes you can, c'mon."

"I'm frozen s-stiff." His words were slurred, and speaking took his breath away. He gasped several times.

"Believe it or not, that's a lot better than you were doing a couple minutes ago." Mark fashioned a triangular bandage around his own wound, simultaneously bounding and slinging it.

Somnus dropped his t-shirt and underwear to the

ground and dressed awkwardly, as Max held him up. The dry clothes made him feel instantly better, but he was still absent of color.

Mark slid toward Max. "He's extremely hypothermic. We should stay here and warm him slowly. He could go into shock if we let him move around too vigorously."

"We have to get out of here. More Rock-a-Byes will come. And soon. Besides, look at that clock. It's 6:05. Amanda has less than an hour to live."

Mark nodded, and the two men, without speaking, agreed to risk the life they'd just saved.

"Okay," Mark breathed out, "I suppose it's much riskier to stay here. Let's go."

Soon after, Max helped Somnus toward the stairs.

They were just about to leave the chamber when the boy that Max had hit with the pipe shifted and moaned weakly. Max left Mark to hold up Somnus and rushed to the boy, knelt, and turned him slightly. At the site of his face, Max sat back with a start, his eyes suddenly filled with astonishment.

It wasn't that the boy's head was ghastly misshapen from the blood that welled up in his skull, nor was it that the boy's eyes bulged out of his head and had turned dark red from the pressure of blood against his optic nerve. It wasn't even the visible crevasse in the boy's head where he'd struck the hard concrete floor. It was that Max recognized the boy as the one who'd saved Amanda's life in the Raven.

"Oh, Christ," Max said, "I know this kid."

"I do...too," Somnus managed to sputter. "Name's

Christopher. Killed one of my men not too long ago."

"I know."

The boy looked at him, and Max felt as if he was staring at an empty shell. The boy mumbled something and choked on the blood in this throat. He coughed, and some of it sprayed on Max's face. He immediately wiped it away but was surprised to see he already had blood on himself. He looked at it and then wiped his hand on his pants, smearing it off.

"I'm sorry." Max closed the boy's eyelids. A noise from the street refocused his attention on escape. "Let's move."

Somnus was confused, and his arms and legs hurt ferociously whenever he moved. His limbs were stiff, like steel beams had been installed in them. He was dizzy and without a good sense of equilibrium. He relied heavily on Max and Mark to keep him upright, though that too was difficult, as keeping his arm around Max's waist seemed to require more strength than he was able to muster. He slipped several times going through the living room, but Max and his friend simply dragged him along.

The three stumbled onto the street, and after several minutes of going as fast as they could through a confusing maze of alleyways and side streets, Somnus collapsed, bringing Max and Mark down along with him. The trio rolled onto the street and then scrambled into a doorway. They panted and sucked air as their exhaustion ruled them for nearly a full minute. The light of dawn peered over the horizon like a curious child, and Somnus's face, like the sky itself, showed signs of color.

Mark pressed his shoulder wound firmly. "How are you doing over there, Somnus?"

"Better." It was an exaggeration. The metal rods in his legs were still there, but now they seemed like strands of metallic filament. They still resisted his movements, but he could make them bend.

"We've got to keep moving," Max said. After such a cold night, the haze of dawn was a welcomed sight, but with it came the realization that Amanda only had minutes left.

Max moved to help Somnus, but he waved him off, struggling to get up by himself. He clawed at the wall and twisted his torso, attempting to keep his waist over his legs. They kicked-out and jerked about, as if he'd traded his old legs for a new set that had just arrived. It took longer than if Max had simply helped him, but he understood. Mark did too. They watched the battle of the "Somnus that was" versus the "Somnus that wanted to be" with a quiet respect despite the graceless spectacle it became. *Standing up isn't always pretty*, Max thought. Somnus, cheeks red from exertion, smiled as he completed the long ascension up by himself. Five feet and ten inches never felt so grand.

As Somnus's color returned, Mark's was slowly ebbing away. He coughed, and when Max turned to look at him, Mark shot him a look that said *I'm in trouble*. Max nodded and led onward.

Somnus's body was recovering quickly, and his mind wasn't too far behind. The three men rounded a corner, and when Somnus saw a transport station across the street, he grabbed the other two and shoved them behind the corner

RA Haskell

of a building. Max was impressed at how strong Somnus had become.

"What transport station is that? Hilltop?" Somnus asked.

"No, Hillsides." Max pointed. "Hilltop is that way."

Somnus looked down at his hand, momentarily, and his lips moved. His fingers twitched, each in turn, and he appeared to be counting.

Max looked at Mark who shrugged back at him. "What's up?"

"There's an Eight-Hour-Knight cell near here."

"How do you know that?"

"We use transport stations as markers. I invented a code which can lead us to them. Follow me." He led them down a street to his left.

He spoke while they walked and swiveled his head from side to side. "First, you take the station name, *Hillsides* in this case, and place each letter, in turn, on the directional arrows of a compass, starting at north. The last letter, the ninth, also ends there, so I know the second part of the code."

Somnus could see it in his head.

"Next, the second part of the code. You place each letter of the alphabet on the compass, starting with *a* in the **north** position. Then, find the first letter of the station stop, *H* in this case. That tells us to head west.

Somnus, again, could see it completely in his mind's eye.

Knowing that sanctuary was nearby, he looked at them. "I suspect that if we enter that station, they'll be

~184~

waiting for us."

"But we need to get you back so that Amanda won't get killed."

Somnus stood tall for the first time since being revived. He took a deep breath and let it out, smiling. "I'm feeling better...great, actually."

Suddenly, the import of the chamber, the shoot-out, the escape, everything about the recent past was clear to him. A cold vagueness that had impaired him was pushed away by the warm blood rushing through him. Millions of cells, nearly fluorescent and teeming with the oxygen they carried, went flowing through the ventricles of his heart with such force that Somnus reached up just to feel the impressive beating in his chest. He was no longer concerned with simply surviving. "Max..." He placed a hand on Max's shoulder. "We're going to change the world."

"But, Amanda."

"You have to trust me. We have to act fast or everything that's just happened will be in vain. Don't worry about Amanda...I'll fix it. This way."

Somnus bounded off in the opposite direction of the sunrise. He moved even more quickly now, the filament smelted from his legs. He hugged the sides of buildings as he went and slowed to walk nonchalantly past windows that showed signs of life. He reached an intersection and went directly to the street sign, which hung precariously from a bended pole. On the back, barely noticeable, were scratched markings. They were Roman numerals: *VII*. Somnus continued west for seven blocks.

"What are we looking for?" Max asked.

"Or whom?" Mark put in.

"Don't worry," Somnus said, "they'll find us."

The prophecy was immediately realized when, a moment later, Somnus, Max, and Mark found themselves surrounded by five men wearing white surgical masks and pointing guns at their faces. Somnus stepped forward. "West."

One of the men lowered his gun. "Where is Z?" His words were slightly muffled by the mask.

"East, by two."

All the men lowered their guns and pulled their masks down to hang against their necks. The man extended his hand. "Brothers. Welcome."

Mark and Max, despite Somnus's tutelage of the code, were too befuddled in that moment to make sense of what had just happened.

Somnus swallowed. "The Rock-a-Byes are right behind us. They just took a swing at Somnus."

"Bastards," the man said. "How do you know?"

Somnus didn't hesitate. "Because I am Somnus."

"Mother of God." The man staggered backwards and dropped Somnus's hand, then bowed reverently. He paused, and Somnus simply waited for the shock to abate. The man blinked and recovered. "This way, quickly."

The group entered a stone building with broken windows by using a street level staircase that led underground. They descended only a few steps to face a metal door with peeling red paint. The man who led the crew knocked on the door, and a second later, it opened.

Another masked man greeted Somnus, and they spoke softly before the greeter darted away. By the time Max, Somnus, and Mark walked through the door, word of their arrival was spreading rapidly. They rushed along a long metal gangway, which creaked and clanged, then passed through a guarded archway. The lead man acknowledged the masked guards with a quick wave.

Mark heard the two men whispering muffled inquires through their masks. "Which one is he?" "Is he the injured one?"

**

Kyle Green, still in agonizing pain, had forced himself out of bed, very much against Sharon's advice. If Somnus was really in the building, Kyle was dead-set on laying eyes upon him. He stood, along with the others and watched them walk past. *No,* Kyle thought, *he's not the injured one. Nor is he the tall one with the wavy black hair.* Kyle made eye contact with the only remaining man and knew, then and there, he'd just stared into the eyes of Somnus. There was a strength in those eyes. A determination. The eyes that had stared back belonged to a man that, if he told you he would summit a mountain, he would summit the damn mountain.

The hushed voices continued and grew in number, as they walked through an industrial kitchen, its original purpose long since forsaken. Pots hung from the ceiling on metal racks, but their luster was masked with an even coating of gray dust. Long steel tables, similarly clothed with the garments of neglect, were pushed against both sides of the wall. Shelving ran the length of the room and held a vast assortment of equipment, bowls and utensils. As the men trotted through, spoons on hooks bounced off one another with a startling metallic melody. The utensils appeared to be crying out to their kitchen brethren, beckoning stoves to light, knives to cut flesh, and forks to prod. The sound was soon drowned out by voices speaking the name *Somnus*; it filled the air as the curious spoke it to each other and drew closer.

The group passed through an open doorway, took a left down a narrow corridor, passed through an open rod-iron gate and into a stone chamber, the walls covered from floor to ceiling with shelves. The shelving was divided into hundreds of small cubes, obviously meant for wine bottles but now held candles that illuminated the cellar to reveal a small table and two chairs.

A trim man, bald, with a salt and pepper goatee, sat at the table. He wore no mask, though it was slung around his neck at the ready. Max stared at the man. Twenty others, unmasked, gathered behind him. They bustled and bumped each other as they vied for a better view. Kyle Green, owing to the condition of his broken body, wasn't able to jostle with anyone. He hung back and moved his head from side to side, looking around the heads of others that did the same.

The man with the gray goatee stood. "Let he who calls himself *Somnus* come forward and prove his identity."

Somnus stepped confidently out of the crowd and approached the table. The man with the goatee held out his hand, and Somnus, still walking, outstretched his arm. He approached the man holding out his hand with the palm down and his fingers outstretched and separated. The man reached out and placed his index finger and thumb on opposite sides of a slender silver ring on Somnus's finger. The goateed man gingerly twisted the ring from side to side and slid it up and down between the knuckles. Satisfied that the ring fit appropriately, he gently pulled it from Somnus's finger. He reseated himself and pulled a ring from his own finger, also silver, but with more breadth. At first glance, both rings appeared unexceptional, but upon closer inspection, one could see that their edges were slightly wavy and beveled.

The man with the goatee held one ring with the fingertips of his left hand and the other, in the same manner, with his right hand. He brought the rings together and twisted them until they locked in place.

The crowd behind Max all took a breath in unison.

The man placed the ring on its side on the table. He gave it a slight push, and it rolled forward for three revolutions, the last one laborious and slow. The ring paused, and then, miraculously, it rolled backwards for three revolutions, the last one laborious and slow. It came to rest exactly where it had begun. The man with the greying goatee grabbed the rings, separated them and handed one, unceremoniously, to Somnus.

"Welcome, Somnus," he said. "I'm Brock Patterson, designation two-four. What do you need?"

The crowd behind Max stirred with excitement, and just then, Mark fell to the side, his healthy shoulder hitting the wall, stopping him from fully toppling like a lumbered tree.

Nobody seemed to notice, but Somnus did. He pointed. "This man is injured and needs medical attention. How many cells are in this area?"

"Seven."

"And how many do you trust implicitly?"

Brock answered, "Three."

"Mobilize them immediately. Send units to the address of that man." He pointed at Max. "There is property there, a kind of technology that belongs to us, and the Rock-a-Byes will have discovered it by now, though I doubt they know its importance. Secure it and hold your ground. Post sentinel units at every transport station from Hillsides to MidTown. The Rock-a-Byes mustn't be allowed to replenish their number. This area of the city must be in total lockdown. Spread the word."

Somnus took a quick breath, and glanced at a digital wall clock. It was 6:45am. From the table he grabbed a pad of paper and pencil. He scribbled something on a page, tore it off and folded it. He scribbled something on the next page, tore it off and folded it. He did this four times.

"Send your three fastest men to the hospital with this message and make sure they all take different routes. Instruct them to ask for Leon, and when they see him, give him this. They must hurry."

Somnus gave the last piece of paper an additional fold, which made it small enough to fit in his palm. He leaned forward and put his hands down on the desk as someone approached Mark and led him away.

Max told his address to the person who asked him.

Somnus exhaled. "That's it, I guess."

The crowd dispersed.

"Wait."

The crowd halted.

"Something to eat would be nice."

"We have a small cafeteria." Brock shook Somnus's hand. "You should know that our attempt to terminate Sedgwick failed. He got away."

Somnus sighed.

"You should expect them to respond. Forcefully. I expect it'll be all-out war."

Somnus shrugged. "So be it. What you're securing for us at that address could very well make a war winnable." Somnus turned away. "Let them come."

Brock nodded and strode out of the room to do Somnus's bidding. The crowd dispersed quickly, except for Kyle Green who, smiling, shuffled back to Sharon's care.

Somnus walked to Max and handed him the piece of paper he had in his palm.

Max unfolded it, read it, and grinned.

The pain is sharp like fire.

Bring the girl. Keep her safe. S.

Chapter 20

In a cramped ground-level cafeteria, Somnus and Max ate a bowl of hot soup and shared water from a canteen. Max's finger was taped and splinted, and he babied it as he held the spoon. The room's two tables made the room look small but not crowded, as they were the only occupants. The window on the east wall was riddled with thin cracks, and the rising sunlight, now shooting through, broke into thousands of orange beams as it passed through the spider web of tiny fissures. The points of light bounced off a large mirror on the opposite wall and landed randomly on the faces of the hungry men. Max squinted.

Brock Patterson strode into the room. "Your friend is a pretty tough guy. He actually helped my people remove the bullet from his own shoulder."

"He wanted to make sure you did it right," Max said. "He's funny that way."

"The wound wasn't serious, but painful, I'm sure. He's eating now, and he'll be himself again in no time."

"Thanks for patching him up." Max slurped soup.

"Good work, Brock," Somnus said. "What about the property I spoke of?"

"It's secured. There were a handful of Rock-a-Byes scrambling around. We engaged, dropped two of them, and the rest realized they were in over their heads and ran off.

We captured one. He's being interrogated now to find out what he knows. So far he's claiming ignorance, but we'll break him, for sure."

"Okay. Excellent." Somnus stood and placed his hand on Brock's shoulder. "And the girl?"

"No word yet."

"Find her," Somnus said.

Brock acknowledged the order with a slight cock of his head, and then he turned and left the room.

Max stopped eating and looked at Somnus.

Somnus seated himself again. "She'll be fine."

Max had to trust Somnus...he didn't have a choice.

Both men went back to eating. Somnus finished, pushed his bowl away, and took a swig of water from the canteen. "Ahh...that soup was the best meal of my life."

"It gets better," Max replied.

"I could taste every spice, every nuance. The chef's loving care."

"It came out of a can."

"I'm sure it did, and I can't wait to taste a home-cooked meal."

Max reached across the table and grabbed Somnus's forearm. "You have no idea how close you came to never coming back."

"I think I have some clue." Somnus rubbed his sternum. "How did you get such a machine?"

"I made it."

"How? Why?"

Max had just finished telling Somnus about his experience in the aqueduct when Amanda rounded the corner. "Max! Max!"

"Amanda!" Max jumped to his feet.

They embraced and hung on to each other. Amanda was warm, real, and very much alive. Max put both of his hands on her shoulders and extended his arms. He inspected her with careful eyes that moved slowly and purposefully up and down her body. He took her face into both of his hands and tilted it, first to the left, and then to the right.

"I'm fine."

Max pulled her close, positioning his mouth over her ear. He kissed it. "I love you."

"Are *you* okay?"

Max didn't let go of her. "My finger is broken, but I'm all right. Mark got shot."

"Shot?" Amanda pulled back. "What happened?"

While Amanda and Max talked about what had gone down, Somnus walked over to the cracked window. The sun shined brilliantly, and the beams of light were intense in brightness and rich in hue. Somnus walked into the shafts and placed his hands over the part of his chest that ached. He breathed in slowly, wincing carefully, out of their view. The rays of light surrounding him appeared as if bullets were being shot at him from the other side of the sun and, after passing through its molten core, pulled bits of the corona in their wake, then whizzed past and struck the floor, walls, and Somnus himself.

He inhaled. "A new day," he whispered. "Indeed."

END OF PART I

PART II: *Excerpts from the Personal Diary of Mark Decker*

Chapter 21

Day 12.

There are so many books. For the better part of the past dozen days, I've sequestered myself in the hospital library, and I can tell already that it will take years to read them all, and a lifetime to understand even a quarter of them. I've begun to categorize and organize the collection and will keep that list under a separate cover. I don't know yet whether or not to fully trust Somnus, but he did tell me that there'd be books here, and he most certainly didn't lie about that.

There is a constant hum of activity, as men work to carve the earth under this building into a long, thin room. Somnus plans for it to be one hundred yards in length with the space to follow an enormous piece of the glacial-main infrastructure, which is to run perfectly straight along its ceiling. Only a few feet of the massive cylinder is yet visible, but enough has been done that I can now see what Somnus intends. With hammers, picks, and sweat, the men force the rock and soil aside, forging ahead almost entirely because Somnus tells them to.

The people here at The Hospital, at least two hundred strong, are loyal to Somnus, which is partly comforting and partly disturbing. I've had casual conversations with many of them, mainly as I stitch wounds or clean minor abrasions, and their loyalty seems to stem from the same basic quality in Somnus. They all use different words to describe him, but the common thread, the melody, is quite simply that the man does what he says. Somnus makes promises and keeps them.

He has made me only one promise, that if I decide to help him, decide to "join" him would be a better description, that I will never see my home again, but I will be part of something that will change the world. The rhetoric, even for a cynic like me, is tough to dismiss. And it doesn't hurt that my house is a shithole.

Day 13.

A bio-chemistry text in this vast hospital library has confirmed my belief that simple blood analysis will be sufficient to ascertain epinephrine levels. I've assembled an equipment list and will begin searching for the necessary supplies and chemical agents in the morning. Somnus has been apprised and has given me unrestricted movement throughout this facility. He is keen on understanding if his new-found tactical advantage is temporary. For different reasons altogether, I am equally interested.

Day 27.

Somnus begrudgingly agreed to my power allotment

request, and I will now have a functioning laboratory. I told him that I'd officially join his organization, so long as I was never required to participate in violence. I was protecting myself and my friend when we were attacked, but the images of that young man coughing a cloud of dark blood onto Max's face haunts me still. Somnus agreed without pause or exception to this condition. I believe him, though I'm quite sure I don't have the evidence to support it. It is, doubtlessly, my excitement at the prospect of what I might come to know. I'm learning by trial and failure, but even experiments that end in utter disaster leave me giddy. No entries for the next several days. I'll be heads-down on building out the lab.

Day 58.

The lab is complete, and none too soon. It's hard to believe I've been here a month already. Somnus insisted the lab be adjacent to the long room, which is progressing quickly. Somnus is pushing hard for me to understand and mitigate the mortality risks associated with the drowning devices. I have been consistent in my refrain; that they will never be safe. Somnus responds plainly that "life isn't safe," and I've stopped arguing with him. I've started concentrating on a set of procedures that will, as he wishes, increase survivability.

Ethically, I struggle with this position. On the one hand, I feel as if I should refuse to participate in any way with regard to this initiative. On the other hand, I know that Somnus will go forward and, perhaps with my involvement, I can save lives. It is this last thought that carries me and gives me a modicum of comfort.

Day 62.

Max and I have begun working together closely to improve the design of his cylinders. It's good to see him again, for more than five minutes at a time. He's been quite busy helping with the construction of Somnus's new room.

Somnus has stepped up patrols all over the city to gain reconnaissance he can put to use later. The result, from my perspective, is a cessation of laboratory time and hours of suturing and bullet extraction. Two died on my table yesterday. There is a rumor among the men that the Rock-a-Byes are planning to attack the hospital directly. After Brock's mission to assassinate Sedgwick failed, the Knights have been waiting for retaliation. Some are surprised it hasn't happened already. The fact that it hasn't happened yet provides no comfort to anyone. Everyone knows it's coming. Somnus is single-minded in his desire for the long room to become operational. I have found all the supplies I need to begin blood testing.

Day 63.

Amanda came to see me today. She's asked Somnus to allow her to go out on patrols, and he agreed only if I would clear her medically. This is normal, as Somnus now has me doing routine checks on everyone. She told me Max doesn't know and requested I not tell him, either. That seemed abnormal, and as much as I hate to keep Max in the dark, I will respect her wishes.

The Delta Wave

Day 70.

Max and I have made a major breakthrough that will increase the *safety*, though I find it nearly irresponsible to use that word, of his devices. We plan to add a heating element that will slowly heat the water and warm the body inside. The chances of successful resuscitation, by my calculations, will easily triple. The power required for the fifty cylinders to each have such a device will surely drive Somnus mad. I'm making Max tell him.

Day 71.

Somnus is expanding power production capabilities on the seventh floor to accommodate our design *and*, according to Max, he agreed to do it cheerfully. Several new rooms are being converted so that human muscle can charge huge banks of batteries. Every Knight, myself included, will now have to double our duties in this regard. Nobody is happy about it, but Somnus remains gregariously positive. His conviction is even stronger than I thought. When I speak to him, I sense something that I can't quite diagnose. I've tossed it around in my mind and finally decided that he either really believes these things will change the world, or he's bordering on a breakdown of some kind. I'm no expert on the inner workings of human emotion, blood, skin, bone, and muscle fascinates me, but with regard to Somnus, I'd say either of my theories is equally likely.

Day 86.

This week has been utter hell. Somnus has every Eight Hour Knight across the city scavenging for, or simply taking, the materials needed to build out Max's contraptions. And of course, that means crossing territorial boundaries of every other faction. There's been a steady stream of wounded and, until three days ago, only my two hands. A man with a broken foot who didn't want to end up with extended kitchen duties volunteered to help me. His name is David, and even though he hobbles around clunking his plaster cast against the linoleum with every step, I wouldn't have made it without him. For such a hulking man, he has a steady hand and a calming manner. The others like him and, quite selfishly, I hope he heals slowly.

Despite my disgust at the brutality with which a bullet rips into the body, there's no elegance to it at all, Somnus seems to have accomplished quite a lot. Three cylinders are done; all include Max's mechanical improvements and our safety features; and the materials for all the others have been collected. I'm particularly excited about the new landing tables, each equipped with a working defibrillator.

Max took months to build just one of the awful things, but Somnus got everything for fifty times that many in only a few weeks. Amanda enjoyed reminding Max of that fact.

I guess Max knows about Amanda's participation in the operation because he didn't seem surprised to see her, as she helped a man who'd been shot in the thigh get to my lab. She had a streak of blood on her face and a heavy looking rifle slung over her shoulder. Max saw her and I saw him mouth "Are you okay?" to her. She nodded, and he smiled.

I've begun blood testing, and several volunteers are already using the operational machines.

Day 99

The long room is half done, and my testing is way behind. Somnus, no matter how long it takes me, will surely begin using all the machines as soon as he can. I'm confounded by the test results, which is why I'm off schedule. Without doubt, I've ascertained that each of us has abnormally high levels of the stress hormone norepinephrine, and that, immediately following a session in the cylinders, the level declines. I'm convinced that the elevated quantity significantly increases the chances of surviving the *treatments*, and that repeated uses will eventually drop the hormone to a level that will provide little to no resuscitative benefits. I still have much to do to determine the safest interval between cylinder sessions, but something else has distracted me entirely. I learned about this quite by accident when several of my test candidates were complaining about the painful way in which a state official had recently inoculated them. Somnus employs a stringent schedule that allows the men, in groups, to leave the hospital compound to receive the required injections. Apparently, on a recent trip, an inexperienced young man was performing the service with a nervous brutality. The men, in fact, had some minor bruising at the injection site.

Out of simple curiosity, I made note of these men's samples, and what I found upon examining them is confusing. While there is absolutely no difference in epinephrine levels in proximity to the mandatory inoculations, something else is present immediately following them. In addition to what I would have expected, attenuated microorganisms and toxoids, there is, well, something else. I cannot positively label it, as no test I've conducted can identify it. I've conducted further tests, and all I can determine is that it seems to go away naturally.

When I reported this finding to Somnus, he turned over to me a staggering array of meticulous records he's kept for the past several years. Convinced that the doctors on the other side of the white wall have conspired against the rest of us, he started tracking every conceivable malady for all men under his charge. The details are mind boggling, every sniffle, every coughing fit, and every headache for hundreds of Knights are neatly organized and cross-referenced with the time of day and eleven environmental variables. I'm digging through it, but I'm not even sure what I'm looking for.

Day 103

Amanda came in complaining of nausea. She's pregnant. And stubborn. She refuses to cease her patrol duties. I suppose I could force her to stop by revoking her medical clearance, but I won't, as I'm afraid it would make her mad. And I don't mean angry. I mean certifiably mental. She ran off, smiling, telling me she couldn't wait to see the look on Max's face.

The Delta Wave

Day 121

Somnus's records have yielded little, other than to confirm that waiting too long between inoculations causes the headaches we all know too well. My little mystery will have to wait as all of the cylinders that are built are now being used. I don't expect it to take long for the rest to come online quickly. Somnus has opened the doors to the entire city's contingent of Knights, and they arrive daily. There was, understandably, hesitation on the part of many of the Knights, but word of the device's restful effect has quickly eradicated any trepidations.

Day 153

Until I collect more data I have advised that total downtime in Max's cylinder should not exceed eleven hours over a twenty-three day period. For now, this appears optimal.

Day 167

The number of new recruits requiring medical checks, all the cylinders now being used every day, and the injuries caused by constant violence have forced me to take on help. David works full time with me now, as does Amanda who has voluntarily withdrawn from patrol duty. I'm so exhausted I've actually considered a session in Max's cylinder. I need at least twenty more people, and then they need to be trained with basic resuscitation and first-aid skills. I joined Somnus to run a laboratory and provide basic clinic services to his crew, but instead I'm transforming this hospital-turned-headquarters back into a hospital. I'm so busy with medical recordkeeping that I'm even considering putting this personal journal on the shelf.

Day 233

I just read my last entry, and it was certainly prophetic. I did, indeed, put aside the narrative of my post-Somnus life, but, after what happened to Amanda today, I feel I need to put it down somewhere. Somnus's plans, it seems, have been both wildly successful *and* a miserable failure. Almost every faction in the city has either been forcibly overtaken by Somnus and his Knights or, and more commonly, they've joined him. But not every faction. The Rock-a-Byes have also grown in strength and number, and I suppose it's entirely because Somnus's ranks have grown. Rising up against a common enemy may be what Somnus had intended, but unfortunately, he himself has become one. Maybe duality is the natural order of things. Or, perhaps Somnus's total lack of respect for the Rock-a-Byes territorial claims during his search for long-room materials could have something to do with it. Certainly the failed attempt on Sedgwick's life is a major factor, too. Somnus's impudence around territory was very cleverly turned into a recruiting tactic by Sedgwick. Both sides are growing their number, and a large conflict is looming. Sedgwick is a man whose survived an assassination attempt. A man with a vendetta.

The Knights now number in the thousands, perhaps close to 10,000, and, we imagine, so do the Rock-a-Byes. I have a team of thirty, including Amanda, who's about halfway into her pregnancy. In addition to triage, we monitor and resuscitate soldiers during and immediately after their sessions in the cylinders. But they don't call it that. Those that willingly go under the glacial waters have come to refer to it as *Maxing*. I have thirty people who do what I say, and my friend is a transitive verb; not sure which is scarier.

Since full-scale operations began, we've lost three to the cylinders, one suffered a heart attack before the water fully engulfed him. Based on that, we now give a mild muscle relaxant to calm the nerves. I predict that while we may make some modest improvements in survivability, we will continue to suffer losses as use continues. Somnus remains dedicated to them, and based on my own observation and some limited testing, they do deliver tangible and often impressive benefits, increased cognitive ability, greater physical strength, improved dexterity, everything you'd expect to happen when a human sleeps.

And, in reality, I'm forced to admit that the most significant casualties of late have come not from Max's crazy invention but from the violence in the streets. There have been hundreds of deaths and the most brutal kinds of injuries. My team is ill prepared for most of them, but we do our best.

I can only describe what's been happening with one word, a word Brock Patterson used nearly a year ago: war.

And it's getting worse, not better. Somnus continues to attack and build, convinced he can defeat the Rock-a-Byes and then turn his attention to the "enemy" behind the wall. Max believed in him *and* in his intentions, but after what happened today, I think he'll lose faith.

We've discovered that the most efficient power usage occurs when all the tanks are run nearly simultaneously in rapid succession, and that was the situation today. All fifty cylinders were occupied and, as we neared the resuscitative phase, another wave of Knights was lining up for check-in. My team was taking positions at the drop tables. The newly redesigned cylinders are certainly reminiscent of Max's original but rely less on complicated gearing systems. The cylinders are hydraulically controlled and require an operator to initiate the filling sequence, begin the warming stage, rotate the unit for exit, drain it, and finally, pop the hatch. This process, combined with several minutes for resuscitation, means that the patients are submerged and evacuated using a staggered schedule. My team begins with the odd numbered tanks and then shifts to the even numbered ones. If there is a patient who stays down beyond the allotted time between odd and even, a rotating emergency team steps in.

While I'm used to the commotion, I do understand that the scene can be very troubling to witness. I guess that's why I didn't notice the man who left the queue. When fifty people are nearing the end of their *Maxing* session, the long-room is extremely intense. That someone would decide not to subject themselves to it seems, well, reasonable.

When the tank heaters engage, the overhead lamps dim to a mere tenth of their power, and when the first twenty five tanks violently expel their water, the sound lasts for an uncomfortable amount of time, the room's temperature drops by ten degrees, and the air fills with the smell of damp stone. The successive flopping sound of wet bodies falling onto tables is unnerving to say the least, and it's just the beginning; resuscitating the dead isn't glamorous. The tension in the air becomes thick as we battle to yank our patients from the clutches of death itself. We press violently on their chests, stick tubes down their tracheas with amazing precision, and drive needles full of drugs with a purposeful elegance. We chatter encouragingly, to them and to ourselves, as we use our entwined fingers and clenched fists to force hearts to beat again. We use our hands first, to save power, but nearly half end up requiring the defibrillators. With each shock, the lights go from black to brilliant creating a bizarre strobe effect in the long-room. Our success isn't met with words of thanks but with water-logged coughs, expectorant lungs struggling for air, and wide bulging eyes with splotches of red from broken blood vessels.

Despite how many times I've been a part of it, it's always distracting, and I'm sure it's why I didn't notice the man exiting the line and pulling a pistol from his waist. We know now, as he bore the birch tree marking, that he was a Rock-a-Bye infiltrator. His aim is less clear, though we imagine that he might have been sent to actually undergo a full-on *Maxing* and simply panicked at the spectacle of it. In any case, another Knight saw the pistol and jumped at the man, forcing him to about-face and run headlong into the long-room. My team was busy pushing on dead men's chests when the Rock-a-Bye realized he was cornered. He started shooting and, before several Knights had him subdued, Amanda got hit and it sent her to the floor.

The injury was minor, she was lucky. When I told Max he didn't seem angry, which is how I expected him to react, but instead he seemed afraid. It was as if in that instant he realized how connected they were, how much he needed her, and the thought of her being taken away from him was a reality he simply wasn't prepared for. He sank into a chair and cradled his head silently in hands. She is recovering in the clinic, and Max hasn't left her side.

END OF PART II

PART III: *The White Wall*

Chapter 22

Leon and Brock walked besides Somnus into the clinic and then took up positions outside the door. Somnus, Brock had insisted, was never to be without escort, and most commonly that was Leon and, for the past year, Brock himself. At Amanda's bedside, Max's face went plumb as Somnus approached.

"She could have been killed," Max whispered.

Quite unintentionally, his hands raised up to rest on his hips in the same way his father's did when young Max was scolded. He became aware of the exactness of the gesture and forcibly put his arms down straight.

"Mark told me she was fine...just a minor wound, nothing to worry about, right, Amanda?" Somnus said.

"*I'm* worried," Max said before Amanda could speak.

"My shoulder hurts, but I'm fine." Amanda reached out for Max's hand.

Somnus smiled at Amanda and patted her other hand. "Took one for the team, hey kid?"

Amanda smiled but Max glared at Somnus. "It's time to do something else."

"What are you talking about?"

RA Haskell

"Somnus, things are getting worse out there, and you know it. You've done everything you set out to *except* the one thing you really meant to. There are no more factions, save one. But did you really want to start a war?"

"War? What war?" Somnus was still looking at Amanda.

"Look around you, Somnus." Max's voice elevated. "Just look around."

Somnus saw a clinic with full beds of injured men and women. He saw, in the farthest corner, that a curtain attempted poorly to hide the bodies of several deceased. He saw, outside the door, a line of people waiting to die that they might fight more powerfully for him. Past them he saw a line of tanks filled with those awaiting resurrection. He saw Mark and two of his staff performing surgery on a man whose wound had soaked a gauze bandage to capacity, causing a thin trickle of blood to well up on the floor. He saw Max staring at him.

"What do you see?"

"Okay, Max...I get it, but what am I supposed to do? Surrender?"

"Do you really believe that our goal is beyond the White Wall?"

"I know it is."

Max frowned. "How do you know?"

"You have to trust me."

"Well then, let's concentrate our efforts there somehow. The Knights are as big as you could have ever imagined. Somnus, now is the time."

"Max, if I rally the Knights now, we'll do nothing but

lose ground. We are still vulnerable in the north, and I've just now received word that our position in the warehouse district is weakening."

A rattling metallic sound startled the men from conversation, and they and Amanda turned toward Mark, who knelt to pick up a fallen instrument. They watched him retrieve the tool and then stick it back inside the flayed open chest of the man on his table.

"Is that sterile?" Amanda asked.

"It doesn't matter." Mark looked at them solemnly.

Max leaned in toward Somnus. "What if we're thinking about this all wrong? Maybe an attack against the wall isn't the answer. Can we get a small group inside? You know, a couple of your best men to do some reconnaissance."

"There's no way in. We've tried hard to find one."

There was silence until Amanda's raspy voice broke in suddenly. "I know a way." She struggled to sit up. "My first job...after the change, was working in the great crop fields on the outskirts of West City."

"Yeah, I know them," Max said, "I've seen them from the top of the aqueduct."

"I've heard of them," Somnus added.

"The fields there were massive, and we worked them by hand every day. It was an incredible undertaking, but it made efficient use of excess water and provided sustenance and raw materials for the majority of the citizenry."

"And that helps us...how?" Somnus asked.

"There is a massive irrigation system out there. Thousands of gallons of water in open holding tanks scattered strategically throughout the fields. The tanks regularly would drain, and water would be carried, via a network of pipes and sprinklers to the crops." She paused and shifted again in bed, this time wincing. "But not always. Sometimes the tanks would drain, but the crops received nothing."

"We know," Somnus interrupted, "there are fields on the other side of the wall that receive the water but, strangely, not as often. It, like all the water in the city, flows through the Department of Transportation Purification facility. The crop water receives less scrutiny, but it flows through just the same. No one can go through that way because there are bio-filters in place. They function as redundant checks to prevent algae contaminations, but if the filter detects anything alive, the entire system shuts down until it can be manually inspected."

"Anything *alive*, huh?" A smug smile appeared on her face.

"Ah...alive?" Somnus stuttered and stopped. He turned around and gazed at the fifty dead men who seemed to be staring at him from inside their frost-covered tanks. "Holy shit."

It was the first time Max or Amanda had heard him curse. And it was the first time they realized that fact.

Somnus abruptly raced out of the room. Brock Patterson and Leon, like iron filings to a magnet, soon flanked Somnus as he stepped quickly down the hallway.

Max kissed Amanda in haste and gave chase. He strode up beside Somnus, who spoke rapidly to himself.

Max remained silent for the entire journey to Somnus's office at the top of the hospital. He knew that once Somnus started muttering, there was little else to do but wait. Somnus had elaborate conversations with himself because, he'd say, "the best ideas came from talking things out with people you trust, and," he'd add, "I'm one of those people."

Somnus continued talking and rifled through a large flat file in the corner of his office. He tossed some schematic drawings onto the floor until he discovered a stack of blueprints. He extracted them, made space for them on a nearby table, and then flipped the pages. He appeared like a small child looking at an oversized picture book. Finally he arrived on a page that interested him and stopped. He went silent as his hand followed one blue line that intersected with another and then another. He breathed in, backed up, and looked at Max. "You used to work there didn't you...at the Purification Plant?"

"Yes."

"Come here."

Max moved toward Somnus and stared down at the paper.

"Do you recognize this?" Somnus pointed.

"The Purification Plant and that line is Post-Inspected Tube 8, West Side."

"Look where it leads."

Max followed it a relatively long distance with his finger until it landed outside the city into something labeled, Receptacle A9. "What's Receptacle A9?"

"It's one of Amanda's irrigation tanks, and our way in. That tank represents the shortest physical distance between the plant and the other side."

"Okay, sure, it might work. We could get someone through that way, but we'd have to start in the Purification Plant."

"I know. But that's not the problem."

"It isn't?"

"We need someone else to get in, as well, just temporarily, to resuscitate whomever we send in. And to do it unnoticed."

"Good point."

Somnus snapped his fingers. "I think I know how."

"How?"

"Amanda."

"Huh? What do you mean?"

"She's pregnant."

"Even more reason to leave her out of this."

"I believe that if we feign a problem with her pregnancy, they will willingly allow her in. They *are* doctors, after all."

"Wait a minute." Max stepped away. "You have no proof that they *are* doctors...that may be nothing more than a myth. It's just a theory, perpetuated by yourself, I might add."

"I perpetuate it because I believe it."

"Furthermore, what evidence do you have that they'll simply swing a door open and let Amanda waltz on in?"

"Because I've seen them do it before."

"You what?"

Somnus sat down and motioned for Max to do the same. "You've asked me several times how I know that our aim is beyond the white wall. The reason that I know there are people behind the wall is because I've seen them."

Max, dumfounded, prepared himself to listen as Somnus described what he had seen.

"My mother, my father, and myself...I was maybe eight or ten...were seated in a restaurant. The locale was frequented, at that time, by a senior member of West City's leading faction. Without warning, a band of rivals entered the establishment and assassinated the man in a flurry of bullets. Both my mother and father were hit, my mom because she threw herself on top of me. Amid the chaos, somehow, my dad managed to grab us and get out."

"Where are you going with this?"

"You might remember, thirty years ago, medicine in West City was non-existent. Even tradesmen practitioners like Mark weren't available. Dad, with a shot in the belly, helped my mom, with a severe leg injury, through the streets. Eventually he couldn't hold her up any longer, and I had to do it. My dad, bleeding out and losing his pallor by the minute, directed me toward the white wall. When we reached it, my father could barely breathe, and mom collapsed. I fell next to her, crying. My father struggled to his knees and begged for help until he could no longer speak. I just kept crying."

Max, leaned forward. "Are you saying—"

"Suddenly, without a sound, an opening in the white wall appeared, and four men strode into the field toward us. They carried stretchers and carefully placed both my parents on them. I tried to follow them in, but they motioned that I wasn't allowed. I sat in the grass, whimpering throughout the night and into the dawn. Finally and silently again, the portal slid open, and this time two men came out, carrying a single stretcher. They rolled my dead father into the field beside me. One of the men spoke to me. *Sorry. We couldn't save him. Your mother's going to make it.*

Somnus told his story without emotion. His voice was monotone, his eyes steady, and his body motionless.

Max, amazed, asked, "What happened to your mother?"

"I never saw her again," Somnus replied in the same voice, then moved to shuffle some papers.

"Did she die, do you think?"

"Honestly, Max, I don't know."

"So, she could be alive in there...not allowed to leave."

"Maybe...that was thirty years ago."

Somnus's obsession was suddenly clear and logical. "Christ," Max said.

Somnus sighed.

Max saw his eyes drift aloft as if he was remembering the past, and Max remained silent, allowing him the reverie.

Brock and Leon entered the office from their posts outside. "Mark's here."

He stepped into the room. "What's going on?"

"Is Amanda alright?" Max asked, walking toward Mark.

"She's fine. What's all this?" He pointed to the blueprints.

Max looked at him wide-eyed. "You're not going to believe it."

Somnus smiled at everyone in the room. "Tell them, Max."

An explosion shook the entire building, and distracted, the five men huddled over Somnus's blueprints. Brock was the first man to the window, and his exasperation brought the rest in turn. "Holy shit," he said using a voice that seemed to drop the temperature of the room.

Max went to the window and looked down.

The streets were flooded with men and fire. Somnus, standing beside him, took in the siege then spun around. Max couldn't move at the sight of it. Directly across from the hospital were two buildings of about equal size in both breadth and height. They were in close proximity, creating a narrow throughway leading to the main entrance of the Knight's headquarters. The placement effectively shut off a direct frontal attack, which is partly why Somnus had chosen the locale. And it was working. The onslaught flowed through the passage into the hospital's main courtyard like raging water through a river bend.

There were thousands of them, and they hurled flaming bottles that broke and spread a liquid sheet of fire where they landed. Shots from rifles and shotguns peppered the air and struck the building. Max heard the shattering of glass, the ricocheting of metal, and the rapid succession of bullets hitting stone. He smelled smoke.

From one of the buildings directly across from the hospital, Max saw a flash and then a cylindrical trail of white smoke approaching him rapidly. "Incoming." He ducked.

The rocket struck the side of the building and again sent a tremor through it. Max remembered that hundreds of Knights were always stationed in those buildings, and the realization that they were all either dead or dying made him inhale deeply. The breath drew a pungent burning smell into his nostrils.

Somnus was speaking forcefully behind him, but Max only half-heard him. He glanced over his shoulder and saw him unlock a cabinet and retrieve two radios. He handed one to Brock. "Get down there and secure the south side...make sure they stay in front. Close the containment doors. Go!"

Another rocket struck solidly.

"I'm going to the communications room," Somnus said.

Brock headed out. He remembered leading the assault on the row-home compound of the Rock-a-Byes. It had been about a year since his failed attempt to take out the faction's leader. That encounter, along with the intel gathered by Kyle Green, had prepared the Knights for this attack. It had, most likely, also caused it. While most of the past year had been dedicated to building out the long room, Brock had also worked to reinforce the hospital itself. When metal could be found, he'd installed it over windows. The sound of the two fifty-caliber machineguns was a sound Brock would never forget. Those guns were heavy, so he knew his assailants would require time to move them and set them up, but they were coming, of that he was sure.

When the flood of men seeped around the sides of the blocking buildings, Max breathed heavily. The rivers of men would soon join to form a turbulent and uncontrollably violent wave that could crash into them and drown them all. Max suddenly remembered Amanda, bedridden and defenseless in Mark's clinic. Somnus might have said his name, but Max was running out the door.

Somnus rushed two doors down and burst in. The room was full of equipment, and one entire wall was covered from floor to ceiling with stacks of rectangular batteries.

A nervous man with headphones approached quickly. "What's going on?"

"I need you to send a message to all the cells. Rock-a-Byes attacking. Need immediate reinforcement."

"Is that all?"

"Keep sending it and don't stop sending it until the radio stops working, somebody shoots you, or the floor falls from under your feet."

"Okay." The man rushed back to his station and started hitting buttons.

The hallway was poorly lit, but Max ran as fast as he could toward the staircase. He had to get down to the long room. There was a thin layer of gray smoke hovering close to the slippery floor, and it blocked Max's view of his own feet. He turned a corner, and the stairwell door appeared in front of him. He ran toward it at full speed until an explosion erupted in front of him, engulfing him in dust. The blast, caused by a serendipitous convergence of rocket fire, pushed him violently off his feet and onto his back. He rolled slowly over, noticing the volume of the battle had been turned down precipitously. The explosion had severely damaged his ability to hear. His thoughts of getting to Amanda were growing more desperate, and it made him pop up off the floor, change direction, and speed toward the elevator shaft.

As he approached, Max saw the door was still open, so he used his momentum to leap the gap across the shaft and grab onto the metal ladder. As his bottom half swung, unattached, his feet scrambled to establish footing. Finally, fully on the ladder, Max scampered down it two rungs at a time.

As he passed by the middle floors of the hospital, he became aware of the overbearing ringing in his ears; he noticed that he couldn't hear his own feet strike the ladder. He smelled smoke again but heard no noises as to its cause. He looked down as he approached the main floor. There was a thick cloud of smoke rising up the shaft, and inside of it he saw the orange flickering of flames and the white bursts of pistol and rifle fire. He still couldn't hear much of anything.

Max jumped down the last few feet and dropped to his knees in order to catch a breath of air not filled with smoke. From his crouched vantage point he could see the chaos occurring in the hospital's main hallway. Knights peeked out from the door jambs lining the hallway just long enough to send bursts of gunfire into the never ending deluge of men that poured into the hallway from the mass outside. The men tripped over each other and scrambled inside, gaining a bit more ground by the minute. Max darted out of the shaft and ducked sharply left into the stairwell.

A dozen Knights rushed past him, and Max put his back against the wall to let them pass. They were yelling, and though Max couldn't make out the words, he did hear something. Max rushed down the stairs toward the long room and Mark's clinic.

Seconds later, Somnus, Brock, and Leon, having successfully navigated the damaged stairwell, burst through the doors into the hospital's main hallway. Somnus, with a drawn pistol, headed toward the wave of men crashing into his home. Brock headed for the elevator shaft, and then turned right toward the hospital's rear entrance. He spoke on a radio but ended mid-sentence when the belt-fed machineguns started. The sound, unmistakable and unwelcomed, sent a shiver down his spine. The large rounds annihilated entire windows, penetrated the thinnest metal sheeting, and created clouds of stone dust, which rolled into the hallway.

Max nearly collided with David who'd emerged from the long room with a look of concern on his face. Max saw over his shoulder that all the tanks were full. David was speaking and Max could make out his voice, though the words sounded muffled and distant. Max yelled, "Get them out of there. We're under attack."

"Is it the war?"

"Hurry!" Max raced toward the clinic. He rounded the corner and saw Amanda's bed was empty.

Chapter 23

Fighting panic, Max looked around the clinic. No Amanda anywhere. *Where would a wounded pregnant woman go in the middle of a battle? A back room, a closet, somewhere safe to hide. Shit.* None of that sounded like Amanda, in the least. *She's going to get herself killed.* Then he remembered David.

He rushed back to the long room and found David draining the tanks and the resuscitation teams were in their positions.

"Have you seen Amanda?" Max yelled.

David said something that Max couldn't understand, but he also pointed upwards.

"Jesus." Max breathed. He was about to spin around when, instead, he hurried into the long room, removed a defibrillator from its regular location, stuffed it in a backpack, zipped it closed, and slung it onto his back as he rushed out. *This might come in handy,* he thought. David was confused beyond words; his mouth moved, but nothing came out.

The smoke grew thicker, and Max could hear more distinctly now the firing of weapons and the occasional impact of ordinance. He burst into the hallway. "Amanda." Skirting the wall, he shouted her name and moved forward. Bullets whizzed past him, some struck the floor in front of him and the ceiling above him. A man leaning out of a door to his left, caught a slug in the belly. Max barely heard him scream as he crumpled.

Amanda, from a room across the hall, was yelling at Max, but he didn't hear her, just kept creeping forward, yelling her name. She leapt from her station, dove across the hall, and pushed Max into a room with a wounded Knight guarding the door.

"Amanda," Max shouted.

"Why are you yelling?"

"What?"

"Why-are-you-yell-ing?" Amanda shouted.

"Can't hear." Max pointed to his ear.

Amanda nodded.

The wounded Knight fell away from the doorway. He wasn't moving.

She took up his position as Max watched in total disbelief. With her arm in a sling, she used her good hand to fire a salvo of pistol fire toward the onslaught.

Max took the rifle from the wounded Knight and crept up beside her. Motion to their right made them both spin and train their weapons toward the elevator shaft. Brock and Mark emerged from around the corner, saw the pair, and darted into their room.

"The attack's focused on the front," Brock said. "They're throwing everything at it. Back's not secure."

"Where's Somnus?" Max yelled.

An explosion shook the building and sent chunks of ceiling tiles to the floor. The four covered their heads, and then Max, Amanda, and Brock leveled their weapons toward the entrance and fired. Another rocket blast impacted the opposite side of the building and sent a storm of dust into their faces, forcing them to cough violently. Some of the Knights wore their doctor's masks, though Max knew many of them wished they had remained merely ceremonial.

Mark moved toward the wounded man lying on the floor. He flipped him onto his back, put both of his hands together and compressed the man's chest.

Amanda pointed. "Look."

Somnus had zigzagged from room to room and moved up the line to the very front. He was looking back and signaling to Brock. Somnus pointed at the radio in his hand. The skirmish created a disturbing symphony with a gunfire melody punctuated by the deep bass of explosions and the guttural moans of the wounded. Brock jammed the radio to his ear and gave Somnus a thumbs up. He nodded several times and then signaled for the men across the hall to join him quickly, which they did.

Brock stood tall and shouted at them. "Step out and empty your weapons toward the entrance as you move forward. Follow me."

Brock jumped into the hallway, and the entire crew followed. They lined up and fired shot after shot after shot. They moved forward just until they reached the next room. Brock signaled the men to step out and take over. They jumped into the hallway and moved forward, firing. The push continued for another two doorways and then stopped. In the second of silence created by the offensive move of the Knights, Max and Amanda saw Somnus lead a small group into the hallway and toward the inset handles of a containment door on the left.

The huge steel door was the last in a series of four that Somnus had constructed to seal off the entrance to his headquarters. The other three were farther up the hall, and out of reach. His Knights, he thought proudly, had held their ground and given them this last chance.

Brock was frantically reloading. He looked at the others. "Cover him," he yelped.

Amanda, one handed, emptied her pistol and placed fresh rounds, clumsily, in the revolving chamber. The others followed suit.

The containment door, weighing at least a ton, rested on a bearing track, making it possible, though not easy, to move. Somnus and three others had pulled it out about a foot by the time the tide rose up again. Brock squatted in the door jamb and fired his weapon with ruthless precision. The door moved another foot and enough steel became exposed so that oncoming bullets from the enemy could strike it squarely. The sound was piercing, but strangely calming; it was the uncomfortable sound of hope gasping for breath.

The door was halfway shut when Somnus was struck. He stopped pushing and clutched his belly. He slumped to the ground, and the door stopped moving. Brock and the others kept up the barrage. Leon emerged from the room where Somnus had staged the retaliation. He looked down at Somnus with confliction in his eyes. Max, Amanda, and Brock knew that he wanted to attend to Somnus, but they also knew that Somnus had given orders to shut the door.

Leon passed Somnus and grabbed the metal door handle. It moved again until it finally met the opposing wall. The collision released a vertically oriented metal cylinder eight inches thick, which slid through the door and locked it firmly in place. The door was peppered constantly with bullets. A rocket struck several seconds later, creating a metallic reverb throughout the hallway. But the door held.

Brock jumped up from the floor and sprinted toward the door. Like Leon, he ignored Somnus who grunted painfully at his feet.

"First clan..." Brock radioed, "go to the third floor and move all personnel from this floor and the second to the east wing. Second clan...move from the top down and gather everyone to the west wing of floor four. Create a crossfire situation in the courtyard. Move!"

In a noisy scurry of feet and mumblings, the hallway emptied. Brock leaned down to Somnus and, rather than comfort him or even speak to him, he took the radio from his belt. He looked at Somnus briefly in the eyes. Somnus nodded.

"Leon," Brock handed him the radio, "take this and secure the back."

Leon nodded sharply and looked down at Somnus.

"Go!" Somnus barked at him, coughing.

Another rocket blasted the containment door.

"We need to move," Brock said, then turned to Somnus. "The door will buy us time, but they'll eventually get through. Can you walk?"

"I think so. Help me up."

Max was able to hear all the words the two exchanged

through a thick muffled fog.

Brock helped Somnus to his feet, and they shuffled down the hallway and into the second room on the left. Max noticed, just then, that despite the daylight outside, it was dark everywhere. The windows were blocked up, either by steel plating or shades that had been pulled shut. The metal, imperfectly aligned, allowed slivers of light to come through, but it was insufficient to illuminate the room.

Mark, with blood stains on his shirt and hands, turned into the room from the hallway.

There was a moment of silence interrupted only by the labored breathing of Somnus who sat on the floor, holding his stomach. Mark saw him and leaned down immediately.

Somnus stopped him. "No," he said, "it's bad. Trust me."

"What should we do?" Amanda asked.

Somnus looked at Max, Brock, and Mark. "It's time to breach the wall."

They were silent and looked at each other.

"Let's do it now," Somnus said. "I'll go with her." He pointed to his bloody mid-section. "This might even help us."

"Do what?" Amanda asked. "And go with me, where?"

A volley of rocket fire hit the containment door in rapid succession. They all covered their ears...except for Max. It ended, and Brock peeked outside. The door stood fast as smoke leaked in from the bottom, like breath in the cold.

Max leaned down. "But Somnus, what about what's going on right now?"

Somnus righted himself, wincing. "All that is in front of me is the past. You have the future in front of you."

Max sighed. "You won't make it."

"Yes I will, Max. Yes I will."

Max stood and turned around. Brock, Mark, and Amanda stared at him.

"Help me up," Somnus said.

Max helped him.

Somnus stood crookedly, pushing in on his belly with his right hand. There was wet redness between his fingers, and Somnus acknowledged it with his eyes. "We need to hurry," he said, looking at Max.

Max looked at Mark who nodded in knowing agreement. "We're doing this."

"Doing what?" Amanda asked.

"I'm going to the other side of the white wall."

Brock's radio crackled just then, and Leon's voice came through. "The back's clear."

Brock paused for a second and then raised his radio up. "Hold position. We're coming to you."

As the party moved out the door, more bullet and rocket fire rattled against the containment door, shaking the walls with vicious loudness. Cement dust spewed from cinderblock joints and sprayed onto the tile floor. Mark trailed behind to hurriedly open drawers and cabinets. He grabbed what he could find: syringes, random vials, a grease pencil, tape, and wads of gauze. Brock, progressing quickly despite Somnus's condition, soon yelled for Mark to catch up. Mark ran after them. As they proceeded, Brock ordered several men to come with them.

Leon had undone the intricate shackling at the only remaining back entrance to the building. Somnus had permanently sealed all other doors when he'd adopted the hospital for the Knight's headquarters, but he'd left this one entrance in working order, though nearly buried under old fashioned key locks.

The party approached the door, and Leon whispered to Brock, "It's strange, there's nothing out there."

Brock leaned Somnus against the wall, and Amanda helped him stand. The blood stain on his belly was growing larger and darker.

Brock approached the door, crouched slightly, and cracked it open. Yelling voices, cracking gun fire, the *phump* of rockets leaving their launchers, the rapid firing of heavy caliber machinegun rounds, all of them could be heard clearly, but it sounded to them as if they were close to it instead *inside* it. Brock removed a pair of binoculars from his vest and scanned the walkway to the street and the surrounding buildings that looked down on it. He removed the binoculars from his face and slipped them back inside his pocket. "If I were planning this, I'd have snipers up there."

Leon nodded. One of the men Brock had recruited during their scramble held a rifle. Brock took Leon's over-and-under shotgun from around his shoulder and traded it for the man's rifle. He handed the weapon to Leon. "It is imperative that Somnus, Max, and Amanda arrive at the transport station. Our future depends on it, and our duty is to ensure it happens. When you men joined the Knights, you swore to give your life if it came to it. Well, the time has come. For all of us. Leon, you stay here, and if there are snipers up there, take 'em out."

Leon nodded and put his hand out. Brock shook it firmly.

"Let's go."

Brock led the way out the door as the handful of recruited men formed a loose circle around Max, Amanda, Mark, and Somnus.

Leon leaned against the door with the rifle butt against his shoulder and his eye cast down its barrel, upwards toward the windows of the closest building.

Brock fully expected a perfectly aimed bullet to penetrate his skull and kill him instantly. He'd gone first, knowing that if he were targeted, Leon and the others could at least return fire in the shooter's general direction. The distraction might buy enough time to get the trio to the transport tube. He hoped that Mark would make it too. His skills could prolong Somnus's life, perhaps for a few critical minutes that would make a difference. Brock knew, however, that Mark was like him in this...expendable.

The party shuffled through the alleyway, as the sounds of battle became increasingly distant. Somnus's feet made all the right motions for running, but it was only that. Two men, one on each side of their dying leader, carried him along. The group rounded a corner and successfully took themselves out of range from the buildings that had loomed over them during their desperate dash.

The transport station was in sight, and Brock paused

briefly before rushing toward it. He scanned the intersecting streets to the west and looked up and down at the buildings he'd have to lead the group past. Surprisingly, the street looked quiet. He paused another two seconds to allow the group to catch up. When they were just a few feet away, he could see Somnus's face grimacing in pain. He'd stopped trying to run and now simply relied on the men carrying him. His face was colorless and his brow spotted with sweat that beaded up, but didn't roll; the droplets clung as if they were frozen.

Brock turned quickly and headed straight for the station. A minute later, he approached the stairs leading down. He was about to turn around when a crack of gunfire broke the silence and made him decide to keep moving forward. He jumped down the stairs just as a bullet struck the brick wall to his left, creating a small cloud of red dust.

He managed to keep his footing and bounded down the staircase until he was out of sight. He spun around, moved against the wall, crouched down, and climbed back up quickly, but carefully. The party was nearly at the stairs as he spotted the source of the shot. A band of Rock-a-Byes, at least twenty in number, streamed in from an alleyway from the east. They were shooting as they ran, and more clouds of red brick dust appeared over Brock's head. Brock returned fire just as his people came running down the stairs. None appeared wounded. If they'd arrived just a few seconds later, the Rock-a-Byes could have easily intercepted them. In an instant, Brock figured that, rather than posting a sniper, they must have positioned a spotter. That meant that the Rock-a-Byes were better prepared and more thoughtful than he'd ever given them credit for. It also meant that they were likely outnumbered and utterly cut off.

The Knights, without need for commands, went immediately into action. The two men, tired from carrying Somnus, handed him off to Mark. The recruited men, Amanda, and Max joined Brock and took up positions on the stairs. They shot their weapons as the band of twenty Rock-a-Byes grew closer. Bullets struck all around them, and clouds of grey concrete dust mixed with clouds of brick dust made it difficult to see. At least three of the attackers had been dropped, and this made them slow their advance and seek cover. They scattered to hide behind street lights, crouch in doorways, or lay flat behind curbs. The shooting continued, and Brock worried that perhaps the enemy was trying to capture them instead of kill them. His thoughts changed quickly as a Rock-a-Bye stepped out from behind a light post and threw a grenade toward the stairs.

"Cover," Brock yelled.

The grenade fell short, but its proximate explosion was sufficient to disorient Brock's men and kill one of them. The Rock-a-Byes took full advantage of the distraction and moved, en-masse, toward the opening. Brock ordered everyone to fall back. He guessed that they would all be dead within minutes. Just then, the swishing liquid sound of an arriving transport tube could be heard. Escape might be possible, and Brock ordered the retreat.

"To the tube," he yelled just as the Rock-a-Byes stormed down the stairs. Brock and his men fired with abandon as their enemy approached. Mark, Amanda, and

Max dragged Somnus to the sliding doors and waited for them to open. Bullets struck all around them, but they focused their eyes downward and didn't move. Somnus allowed a bit of spittle to escape his mouth and roll harmlessly down the side-cleft of his chin.

Brock was barking.

The transport doors opened, and at the sight of hundreds of gun barrels, Max, Amanda, and Mark closed their eyes, waiting for a flash of pain before eternal sleep. Somnus kept his eyes open and smiled. The mass of men with surgical masks came rushing up the stairs like a backwards waterfall, and the sight of them made Somnus gaze upward and blink with purpose.

Brock and his men walked backwards firing their weapons, as the enemy cascaded down the stairs like sharks led by the scent of watery blood. One of the men cast his gaze backwards long enough to stop paying attention. He crumpled as wisps of red mist exited his back from the bullet that destroyed his future. Brock heard a commotion behind him and then, suddenly a blast. He expected pain, or at lease euphoria, but was granted neither. Instead, his enemy fell.

"Brock," Max yelled.

Finally, everyone scrambled into the car after the last throng of Knight reinforcements exited the transport. The doors shut, and Max breathed.

Chapter 24

The stillness of the transport lasted only moments before Amanda faced Max. "What-the-fuck?"

"Somnus, when he was a kid, he saw them."

"Who?"

"The doctors. On the other side of the wall. They *saved* his mother."

"Really?"

"That's what he said."

Amanda bit her fingernail, then: "That's the craziest fucking thing I've ever heard."

"Really?" Max retorted quickly. "You want to talk about crazy? Running through the hall with your arm in a sling and shooting...now that's crazy. You should have stayed in bed."

Amanda sneered at him.

Max spoke under his breath as he cast his gaze sideways. "I almost lost you again."

Amanda stepped into Max and cupped his chin, turning his eyes to hers. "You okay?"

"I can't take much more of this."

"We're a team, right?" She touched her baby-bump. "You and me. We're going to make this a better world, for this little one."

"Yeah, but sometimes—"

"Then it's settled."

"It's just that... This could make a difference."

Amanda's lip quivered, her eyes watered, and her free hand stroked the shelf of her tummy. "I love you, and I don't want you to go."

"We owe Somnus this much. Besides, he believes the doctors there might save him."

"It's bad, you guys." Mark attended to Somnus. He packed the wound and bound it so tightly that his first attempt to tie it off resulted in a broken strand of gauze. He wrapped the roll again around his patient's back and then placed his knee on Somnus's chest for leverage as he tugged, somewhat more gently this time.

Somnus gritted his teeth, but didn't cry out.

"He's bleeding to death."

***

Mark had worked steadily to extend Somnus's life and, with it, his suffering. Mark knew that Somnus had to be in agony, but he didn't wince, cower, or grimace. Even when Mark's thumb accidently slipped into the bullet hole and fully penetrated Somnus's torso, the man's only reaction was an extended blink. When Mark extracted his thumb, and with it a dark chunk of liver, he knew that Somnus's bravery was bolstered by the onset of shock. Mark plunged a full syringe of morphine into Somnus's arm. The leader of the Eight Hour Knights made no noticeable reaction other than a meek smile. Somnus, Mark thought, would be dead very soon.

The transport tube sloshed into Prairie Station, and

silence overcame them all. As the doors opened and Somnus was helped to his feet, Max and Amanda kissed. Even though their embrace lasted several seconds, it wasn't passionate; it was, Brock thought, poignant. Their kiss was a lifetime of happiness and struggle. It was decades of the little things. It was comfortable vulnerability. It was goodbye.

Brock removed his coat and placed it around Amanda. Mark took the backpack strapped on Max's back, checked the defibrillator, and then helped Amanda put it on. From a long, thin pocket with a Velcro strap on his right thigh, Mark took a large syringe of epinephrine and secured it in Amanda's jacket. Max and Somnus stumbled toward her, and she positioned herself so that her good arm could provide Somnus some support. Before they exited, Max and Somnus made eye contact. It was a brief moment, but long enough for them to know they'd remember it forever.

Amanda and Somnus climbed the stairs laboriously, but with surprising quickness. Max stood at the bottom and stared up. Amanda saw tears in Max's eyes as the door closed like a curtain on some strange finale in the final act.

"See you soon," Max said as the doors closed.

The transport moved, and Brock was already briefing the men.

Mark walked up to Max and spoke softly to him. "Are you sure about this?"

"I'm not sure of anything," Max replied.

For the next several stops, the two friends simply stood next to each other. When the transport tube arrived at their station, Brock and his men stepped ahead of Max, readied their weapons, and tilted their weight to the balls of their feet, a move that gained them a two second advantage in forward motion. As the doors opened, Brock's team ascended, surmised quickly, and signaled for Mark and Max to exit. They moved through the station and into the street, all the while Brock and the other Knights provided flanking protection for Max. The Department of Transportation Purification Plant was directly across from the station exit, and Brock and his men kept moving toward it.

Mark and Max went along with them.

The men took up positions beside the entrance as Brock approached. At once, they rushed into the open hallway entrance. The entire crew ran up the ramp, pushing several people out of the way or down until they reached the main floor. The control room was in sight and its proximity hurried Brock. He paused briefly in order to signal the planned split of his team.

"Good luck," he said without looking, and then bolted forward with his remaining men.

As Mark, Max, and their escort, with fear in his eyes, broke to the left and climbed a thin metal ladder, the workers raised their weary heads. The team continued uninterrupted until the butt of Brock's gun broke the jaw of a man blocking the control room's spiral staircase. The blow caused a baritone aria that danced around the expanse with a metallic pang. Brock's men broke into the room while Max and Mark were still climbing.

The lights and sounds were foreign to Brock and somewhat disorienting. Somnus's communication array had impressed him once, but what he now beheld was as awe-inspiring as it was confusing. Luckily, he remembered what Max had told him, and bypassing the raised central part of the room, moved directly to his right, around a railing and to the third seat, occupied by a skinny, balding man. Meanwhile, Brock's men had secured the door behind them, confiscated two pistols from a locked drawer, assumed high ground positions, and leveled their weapons, sweeping them back and forth across the room.

Brock shouldered his rifle, reached into his pocket with his left hand, and drew a pistol from a holster with his right. He pushed the pistol's barrel into the bald man's head as he drew a piece of paper from his pocket.

"Confirm that you are the Pressure Chief," he said.

"Y-y-y-yes." The man barely managed to respond.

"Follow my instructions and you will not be harmed. Close flow to Post-Inspected Tube 8, West Side and then open Hatch 17."

"W-h-hat?"

"You heard me." Brock pressed the pistol harder against the skin and bone of the man's head. "And do it now."

"Alright." He pushed some buttons, turned some valves.

The roar of rushing water filled the air.

Mark and Max reached the summit of the ladder and scrambled onto a platform of meshed metal decking.

"Hurry," Max said.

Their escort was close behind. He walked backwards along the platform with his gun sweeping from side to side.

The men in the long cold tanks below noticed that something was wrong. They stopped moving and stared upwards.

Max slowed down as he reached a massive clear façade. The inches-thick transparency held thousands of gallons of water behind it, all of it receding quickly as Hatch 17 gulped it down.

Max stood still, staring at the outer hatch.

Mark spun him around. "Take your shirt off."

"Huh?"

"Your shirt. Now."

Max complied, and Mark went to work. From his pockets, he took some tape, the grease pencil, and his last dose of epinephrine. The epi-syringe was huge, and Mark used the entire roll of tape to secure it to Max's arm. He took the grease pencil and drew a series of concentric circles over Max's heart. The bull's-eye shape was connected to a long red arrow that started at Max's arm. The arrow had two ends with words that Mark had scrawled onto Max's chest.

This was inscribed near the syringe.

Here was neatly written just under Max's nipple.

"This isn't necessary, Mark. She'll be there." The hatch door opened behind him. A wet, cold breath rolled out and moistened his back.

"Just in case she—" was all Mark could say before the bullet struck him in the back.

Mark's knees gave way, and he pitched forward into Max.

The Rock-a-Byes stormed through the entrance,

shooting at everyone in sight. The escort to Max's right was flat on his belly and fired repeatedly into the surging mass. Brock's men stepped out onto an overlook deck and also fired down on the insurgents. They were again outnumbered, but this time had a significant positional advantage. A grenade from the outlook perch tumbled and wobbled through the air until it landed a few feet from the crest of the Rock-a-Bye tide. The explosion killed one man, injured another, and sent the entire band scattering back into the hallway. The invasion was stalled, for now.

Brock remained inside the control room, his pistol barrel leaving a deeper depression in the taunt skin of the Pressure Chief.

"What now?" the Chief asked.

"We wait."

Mark slumped to the ground, his right hand held as tightly as he could manage against a hole in his left pectoral muscle. The bullet had gone clear through and left a ragged opening that seeped quickly into his shirt. He made intense eye contact with Max. "Go. There's no time."

Max backed into the chamber. Mark gave a thumbs-up signal to the escort who was still providing suppression fire to keep the Rock-a-Byes at bay. The man fired a volley then rose to his knees. He passed the signal on to his compatriot on the overlook deck. In turn, Brock was informed.

"Close Hatch 17, flood Chamber 11A, and then re-establish flow to Post-Inspected Tube 8, West Side. Make sure you flood the chamber first...or else." Brock accentuated his last statement by nudging the gun barrel into the Chief's head. The cold reminder worked, and Brock's instructions were followed.

Mark leaned against the railing, his breathing erratic, as the chamber filled with freezing cold water. Max floated to the top and gasped a last breath before becoming submerged. His sense of panic was overshadowed, as he focused his attention on his friend on the other side. The water and thick containment material blurred his vision, and he couldn't tell if Mark had his eyes open. Max couldn't hold his breath any longer and, at last, succumbed to his body's urgent need to fill its lungs with whatever it could.

Mark, again, watched his friend die. He then resigned himself to the possibility of the same fate.

Chapter 25

Amanda used all her strength to keep Somnus righted as she dragged him through a field toward the white wall. The wall was monumental in size and loomed so grandiosely above them that they were shrouded in its shadow for an entire mile. Amanda had switched sides several times but was unable to keep Somnus upright.

He mumbled uncontrollably.

His bandaging was soaked through.

His eyes bounced from side to side.

His arms hung uselessly and heavily.

They moved much slower than the plan required and Amanda's heart beat faster and faster, and not just from exertion. She seriously considered leaving Somnus behind, but, she thought, it might actually be his injuries that would ignite a sense of compassion in those beyond the wall.

The pair was a little more than halfway to the wall, when an in-ground irrigation tank to their right echoed with the rush of water. As it filled, a cool mist rolled out over the field, like from a potion in a cold cauldron. If Amanda could have looked inside, she might have seen the lifeless body of Max, shirtless and frozen, bobbing just under the surface. The scanning system engaged with a high pitched *whine* and it acted as the proper impetus for Amanda's resolve.

She spun the backpack to her front, threw her sling aside, positioned Somnus behind her, wrapping his hands around her neck, leaned forward, and dragged the man until the white wall stood before them...immense and seemingly impenetrable. Amanda was exhausted, and the two crumpled to the ground. Amanda rolled onto her back and gasped for breath. Somnus moaned, but did not move. Amanda rolled Somnus, propping him against a large grey stone. She tilted his head so that his face was pointed at the massive edifice, and approached the wall confidently. Amanda pointed.

"This is Somnus, leader of the Eight-Hour Knights," she said, loudly, her chin raised. "He is gravely injured and requires assistance. You once helped his mother, and now *he* needs your help." Amanda walked for several strides in each direction along the wall, repeating some variation of the same story.

The wall did not answer. No porticos opened. No lights turned on. Not a sound could be heard.

Amanda's heart pounded and her palms sweated. She thought of Max, cold and dead and alone inside an irrigation system. She had felt that the plan relied too heavily on things out of their control. *What if she couldn't get to him? How much longer did she have?* Amanda screamed at the wall. She screamed about Somnus, and then she screamed about herself, about her pregnancy, about her arm. She cursed at the wall and demanded that it be opened. Finally, she wept and begged, dropping to her knees.

The wall did not respond.

Somnus muttered something and moved his hand. He waved his hand, meekly, beckoning Amanda to come closer. Tears welled in Amanda's eyes as she leaned down to hear Somnus speak.

"You have..." Somnus swallowed hard, struggling to continue. "You have to tell them about Max."

"What?" Amanda stood and stared downward at Somnus, her hands on her hips. "What did you say?"

"You heard me," Somnus breathed.

"That was your plan all along, wasn't it...wasn't it?"

"I knew it was a possibility."

"You bastard," Amanda yelled, fell down and grappled at Somnus's clothes. She grabbed his collar and pulled it without regard for her arm, moving Somnus away from the rock upon which he rested, and then let him fall back toward it. He winced when his back slammed against it.

Amanda walked away from Somnus, held her face, and wiped away tears that filled her eyes uncontrollably. Talking to herself and thrusting her fists into the sky, she walked randomly about. Amidst her tearful realizations that Max might die, she cast hateful glances at Somnus. The glances were brief and full of desperate, flailing venom.

Somnus saw them and reacted. "Tell them. It's the only..." he coughed, "way."

Amanda couldn't think of any other options. The air dried her remaining tears, and it left a white trail of salt, marching down her cheeks. She wiped and scratched at it clumsily, and approached the wall. Amanda stood still, cleared her throat, and looked directly ahead.

"I need your help," she said plainly, mentally telling herself to control the pitch of her voice.

Be passionate, but not radical. Animated, but convincing. Save Max.

"A man named Max Dyson is trying to get to the other side of this wall. Your side. Many people have died or been injured in this attempt. Myself, Somnus, the leader of the Knights, and even Max himself. Max is using the crop irrigation system to get through. To bypass the security systems, he has temporarily stopped his heart from beating. How he did it isn't important, but he needs your help to survive."

Amanda nearly cracked. She almost broke down completely. *Hold it together. Save Max.*

"Max needs you to find him and resuscitate him. If you are really there...if you can hear me...I beg you to do this. Save him. Save him."

Amanda walked twenty yards to the right and repeated her speech. She walked another twenty and spoke again. And another. And another.

When Amanda returned to Somnus, his eyes were closed. She shook him and he awoke, smiling. "Don't worry," he burbled, "he'll be okay."

Amanda wanted to strangle him, but she didn't have the energy. "I hope so. Did your mom really go through the wall?"

"Both my parents did. That's the way I remember it."

"But did it actually happen that way?"

Somnus struggled to raise a hand to his head. "I see it

that way..." he pointed clumsily to his head. "here." He let his hand fall. "And I feel it that way..." he used his fingers to claw his hand over his heart. "Here."

Amanda sighed, and put her hand on top of Somnus's. She felt his clammy flesh and thought how cold he had become. She wriggled her body between Somnus and the rock so that his back was leaning against her chest. Wrapping her arms around him, she whispered in his ear. *Shhhhh.* She held him, until he stopped shivering.

"Tell Max...something for me," Somnus said in a voice that was eerily crystalline. "My name...isn't Somnus....it's Thane."

He spoke no more and, after a while, Amanda's tears stopped falling.

***

Dazzling white silhouettes moved inside a white storm even more brilliant. The maelstrom pulsated, enveloping the silhouettes and then revealing them again. The silhouettes moved too slowly and then too fast, and then too slowly again. They spoke to each other in a familiar rhythm, but with incomprehensible vocabulary. At first, the scene seemed two-dimensional, like sheets of paper in front of a lamp. Suddenly, one of the silhouettes turned and moved toward him, reaching out. And then, one of them spoke a word that Max understood.

"Doctor," it said.

And then more words he knew, though not a phrase he'd ever used.

"He's waking up."

Another voice joined, and another white silhouette moved.

"That's not possible...with the amount of Triazolam."

"Of course it's possible." A third voice cut off the second. Max could not attach it to another silhouette, moving or not. "Look at the gamma acid levels."

There was a pause, a silence...

"I'll push this in, and we'll see if that does the trick."

Moments later, the whiteness, and the silhouettes floating around inside it, disappeared.

***

Max's eyes opened synchronously with a large exhale lasting nearly ten full seconds. He was propped up in a white hospital bed with his head surrounded by clean, antiseptic smelling pillows. He was disoriented and confused. His limbs throbbed and his chest ached, especially, and in a strange way. He thought, perhaps, he'd been wounded. He wanted to reach up and touch his torso, but his hand wouldn't cooperate. He exerted extreme effort to simply roll his head to the right. Beyond a few feet was nothing but white haze. In a chair close to his bed sat a man with his arms crossed, staring.

Max blinked. He thought that man in the chair had his eyes closed. The man's chest rose and fell with a regular and deep rhythm. If the man had been a child, Max would have guessed he was sleeping, but he'd never seen an adult do it, so he wasn't sure what to call it. Max blinked again and this time the man was staring back at him.

The man rose from the chair, raised his left wrist to

look at it, and then turned his attention to something behind Max's head. Seconds later, Max felt nauseous, and the light faded away again.

***

Amanda's apartment smelled of lilies. The giant flowers should have suffered in their basement home but, with Amanda's meticulous care, they rose upwards with a magnificent defiance. Their pungency was thick and noticeable. It wasn't possible to navigate the forest of them without emerging covered in yellow-orange powder. Max, already smeared with the stuff, sneezed and kept moving toward Amanda's bedroom. There was a disturbing quietness that hung in the cold air like an untold secret.

Max wondered why Amanda wasn't on the street to greet him; she was always on the street. The lilies were too. At least during daylight anyway, he thought. And why was the door open? Max heard a strange noise from the other side of Amanda's bedroom door. A guttural rasping. His head, against his will, filled immediately with images of the butchery; Amanda was being murdered.

Her nearly lifeless body rattled in its final attempts for oxygen even though her breaths simply made a labored and bloody escape from the gashes in her throat.

It made sense, Max thought; they had been found out after all, and now the enemy was coming. Another faction had discovered the cylinder technology and was hunting him. Better to find the creator first and then deal with his creations.

Max was careful not to make any noise. He knew that

if he did, the killer would find him.

He envisioned a man just barely stronger than he. That thought sent a droplet of cold sweat down the small of his back. If the man was only slightly more powerful than he, and if he killed with a knife, then it was very possible that the blade, at least the first time, would penetrate him slowly, as he struggled to reverse it. He thought about allowing it to come quickly, but he knew he didn't have the nerve. Max pushed the door slowly, praying it would open silently. The creaking was almost loud enough to bend the lilies.

Max closed his eyes, surprised at how willing he was to let it all go. He waited for the pinch on his chest, but it didn't come. Light from a small window illuminated Amanda's leg. She lay on her side in the bed, one leg sticking out and the other underneath covers. Her body moved in rhythm, smooth and peaceful. Amanda slept. She breathed and raised upwards.

Max scratched his neck because it felt like a cold set of lips was kissing him. He moved closer to the bed. She had a stupid smile on her face. She was blissfully unaware. Her breathing was deep. Max was shocked to see that her eyes were moving underneath her lids. They shot from side to side. They vibrated upwards. They circulated. He leaned in and gently peeled a lid upward. Max stopped breathing when he saw the empty cavern of her socket. It was clean and dark and vast. And then the other one, identical, snapped open.

Amanda's hand touched Max's shoulder and sent him reeling. "Max, it's okay," she said. "Come with me."

Max spun around and saw Amanda, smooth and creamy-skinned, her eyes still and calming. He glanced over his shoulder at the empty bed. Amanda took his hand and led him out the door. The lilies had become a jungle and filled every inch of his path. They were growing still, pushing upwards, penetrating the ceiling, advancing through the wall, and climbing up their legs. Amanda kept walking until she reached the front door. Max noticed his feet were wet. Water forced its way under the door, and a rivulet ran from one end of Amanda's apartment to the other. The water gurgled through the bottom and sprayed out through the sides. The door bulged.

"Open it," she said

"I'm afraid."

"I know. But it's the only way out."

Max opened the door, and a wall of water faced him. Amanda squeezed his hand and Max waited for the push. Instead, the water remained in place, wiggling and shimmering.

"Go ahead." She kissed him lightly on his hand before letting it go.

Max walked into the water and turned around.

He saw Amanda smiling and staring at him.

He saw a man with a knife rise up behind her.

***

When Max's eyes opened, the same man he'd seen before was waiting for him. He leered at Max. Max blinked repeatedly and the man rose slowly from a thin white chair. Everything was blurry but the man's voice was clear.

"Hello."

"Hello." Max managed to gasp. There was a constant beeping noise. There was tremendously sharp pain whenever he moved his eyes, but Max searched for the source of the sound anyway.

The man reached over Max's head, turned the knob of a machine, and the beeping became quieter but did not go away. "You're going to be okay."

"Okay."

"We weren't sure at first, but now we are. You'll be all right."

Quiet beeping.

Beep.

Beep.

Beep.

Without fully knowing why, Max asked, "Was I sleeping?"

The man stood straight. "If you want to call it that."

Max was not sure what to make of the cryptic answer. He then asked the simplest, yet most complicated, question of his life. The answer, no matter what it was, scared him. "Are you a doctor?"

"Yes, most of us are...of one kind or another, anyway."

Max was suddenly strong and struggled to swing his legs out of bed and onto the floor. He stood up, steadfast in will, though shaking in body.

"You should really lay down."

Max resisted and stood anyway. His eyes filled with tears and he thought of Somnus. *Doctors,* he thought, *all*

Doctors. Max wept for Somnus. The heaving hurt. He wept on. He wept for the truth Somnus knew but would never see. *Somnus is dead.* "How was I sleeping? Was I dreaming? What is this...place? Where..."

"Yes, yes...questions." The man placed a hand on Max's shoulder, gently guiding him back to lay in bed. "I understand you have questions. And I have answers. I do. But first, you must eat something. You've been down for days, and you must regain your strength."

Max wondered about Amanda. "Is Amanda okay?"

"Who's that?"

"Never mind." Max sighed.

A woman with a white plate entered the room. Her black hair was heavy, thick and shimmering. Not a single strand was caught in the breeze of her motion, not a single strand showed the slightest sign of waviness. Max knew that there were no straight lines in nature, but this woman's hair might have been the exception. She approached him, extending the plate. "I hope you like it," she said with a smile. "It's my daughter's favorite."

Max realized that he was very hungry; the smell of the food sent his stomach tumbling. He rudely devoured what he was given, but the woman with the straight hair seemed exceedingly pleased, happy that she was the one to satisfy Max's savage appetite.

The face of a teenage child peered into the room, whispering to herself with only a perceived discretion. Max made eye contact with her and she retracted her stare, finally, but only after looking Max in the eyes.

The man spoke. "Sorry about my daughter. She's

curious, is all."

"That's okay. What's her name?"

"Mabel." The man stepped back. "Once you've cleaned up, the washroom is over there," he pointed, "we'll help you into the study..." he pointed again, "and then I'll answer all your questions. Well, as best as I can anyway."

Max, with the dark-haired woman's help, stepped forward into the bathroom. She turned on a light, and the brightness made Max squint noticeably. She flicked it back. "Sorry."

"It's okay."

The woman left, closed the door, and Max was alone in the dark room. His eyes adjusted, and the mirror before him reflected an unnatural pallor. The robe he wore parted naturally at his neck, and Max noticed a bit of strange thread poking out. He spread the robe apart to reveal a thick suture down the vertical length of his sternum. He touched it gingerly, and it ached so intensely he had to hold back from vomiting the meal he'd just consumed. Turning on the sink, he splashed water in his face. He wanted colder water but even though he let the faucet run, it remained tepid. Max stared at his own sick ugliness, grasped the sink for stability, and smiled widely.

He was about to sit down with one of the doctors on the other side of the white wall. He was about to learn everything.

***

The black-haired woman heard Max shuffle out of the bathroom and met him as he approached the door. She offered him her arm, and as he placed his hands around her, she was amazed at the strength of his grasp. The woman led him forward.

Max looked around.

The space was warm in temperature, color and texture. Max could see electric lighting recessed into the ceiling of the hallway they traversed, but they were not working. Instead, large lamps at either end guided them. The shades were draped with red cloth, presumably to prevent the brightness from wounding Max. The floors were wooden, but not cold. His bare feet shuffled along them, and he could feel their smoothness. They passed by a room with a closed door, and the hallway eventually opened to a large den. The room was angular with large windows at the far end covered by rich fabric. Two throw rugs, each thick and curly, were positioned in the center of the room. Around the rugs sat a series of leather furniture: a couch, two chairs, and a bench. The chairs were positioned in front of a fireplace, but no fire burned. Behind the couch were bookshelves stuffed with volume after volume. A small side table held a glass of water, and Max went to it immediately. In the other chair sat the man he'd seen before.

The man rose up. "Please...sit."

Max sat and grabbed the water simultaneously. He gulped it down.

The man sighed. "Here's what I know about you. Two days ago I was summoned to a place in this facility to which I'd never been. There you were, freezing cold, soaking wet, and well, dead as far as I could tell. We used

The Delta Wave

every method at our disposal to revive you, including plunging the syringe strapped to your arm directly into your heart ventricle. We finally had to crack your chest open and massage your heart by hand." He held his left hand up to face level. "This hand, actually."

"Thank you doesn't seem enough."

"It's astonishing, if not miraculous that you are sitting there. I'm Dr. Nichols, and that is the entire extent of what I know about you."

"I'm Max Dyson, and that's more than I know about you."

"Fair enough." Dr. Nichols smiled. "I assume that you are from the other side of the wall, but that's just an assumption, not something I know."

"Yes, that's true."

"Max, I know how you got here, I just don't know why."

Max asked for another glass of water, and when it arrived he drank it. He then told Dr. Nichols everything. He told of Somnus and Amanda. He spoke of the first cylinder in his basement and of its origin and construction. He spoke of the long room. He told of the Eight-Hour Knights, and of the Rock-a-Byes, and of the battle that, he believed, claimed Somnus. He spoke of his decision to cross the wall, and how he'd done it. "Have any of you been to the other side?"

Dr. Nichols cast his eyes down. "We've never dared."

"What are you afraid of?"

He chuckled, looked up. "You sound like my daughter. I don't know exactly. It's been nearly two generations since the wall went up, and we still hear rumors of revolution. We're still the target of animosity, are we not?"

"Some maybe, but mostly, well, curiosity."

"There are many of us here who've wanted to breach the wall and even bring it down. Maybe this conversation is the beginning, what do you think, Max?"

"Maybe."

Max and Dr. Nichols talked into the wee hours of the night.

"Let's see..." Dr. Nichols said just before sunrise, "we've talked about literally everything under the sun. You know that we, on this side of the wall, prefer savory meals while you, on the other side, graze throughout the day on sugary snacks and strong coffee. I also learned that..."

Max, rather than listen to the man's words, studied his physical appearance. Dr. Nichols was a short, middle-aged man with a full head of wispy hair and a round face. His eyes, strikingly blue, were set back but perfectly proportioned to the rest of his visage.

"Does that about cover everything?"

"Yes, I believe..." Max had started to answer when Dr. Nichols yawned.

That's not that strange – everybody yawns, Max thought, but was then surprised when the man appeared to actually *sleep* for a brief moment. His head fell listlessly downward as if his neck forgot what it was doing, his eyes closed, and he breathed deeply and rhythmically several times. After a few seconds his head fell deeper, his chin hit his chest, and then, as if his neck suddenly remembered its job, his head popped up. "Sorry. What did you say?"

"I said, yes..."

Dr. Nichols's listless head and forgetful neck became more and more frequent. This continued. He kept apologizing each time he awakened.

Max kept going, talking about Amanda and the baby on the way.

Finally, Dr. Nichols's neck gave up entirely.

Max sat there watching him breathe noisily. Finally, he stood up cautiously despite the nauseating discomfort it caused. He shuffled toward Dr. Nichols and stared at him from a standing position. Struggling against pain, he bent slightly closer. The man remained still, breathing. Max waved his hand in front of Dr. Nichols's face, but again, he remained unaware. He stood there for a moment, dumbfounded.

It can't be that...

Max moved around behind him and walked slowly away, checking over his shoulder frequently. He saw the same hallway he'd taken to arrive here and another, more to his right. He took that one. It was dark except for the light reaching out from two doorways, both slightly ajar. He approached the first and pushed it gingerly with his index finger. It squeaked, and Max froze. He shot a look toward Dr. Nichols who was still in the chair, now making louder noises from his mouth, which hung down, fully agape. The door swung open and Max saw the doctor's daughter, Mabel, curled in a bed with one leg outside the covers and another hanging off the side nearly touching the floor.

She slept.

Max didn't think much of it; children could sleep. He still wasn't sure what to make of Dr. Nichols. He cast a glance over his shoulder, and the doctor remained seated, slumped and open-mouthed breathing. Mabel looked peaceful, and Max smiled at her akimbo position. He moved down the hall, continuing his investigation, and stood in front of another doorway. Max extended his index finger and laid its tip on the door. He could feel the wood grain meshing with the ridges of his fingerprint. He pushed.

The doctor's wife slept on one side of a large bed without covers and faced away from him, her knees drawn up. Max stared at her rhythmic breathing and gasped, covering his mouth as tears welled up in his eyes. They were tears of longing and jealousy as much as they were tears of happiness. A sleeping adult. A dreamer. Dr. Nichols in the other room wasn't some aberration; he was asleep too. Max stared at the doctor's wife. She wore a long silken camisole with thin straps and a scalloped bottom with lace fringing. There was a shimmer of pale lavender made possible from the light Max had let in. Her right buttock was exposed while the rest was covered with bunched up fabric from the cami, the cost of rolling over. Max raised an eyebrow and turned around. His heart brimmed with a cocktail of emotions. Joy at the sight of people breathing with easy contentment. He was also filled with curiosity and, increasingly, a sense of injustice. *How can this be?*

He moved quickly away, without regard for his pain or his hosts. He walked through the room with Dr. Nichols, who'd further succumbed to both his chair and his sleep. Max turned down the red-lit hallway and toward the door. He approached and slowed, wondering if it were locked, or alarmed. He grasped the knob with as much faith as force and turned it. It swung outward, silently and easily. He stepped into a clean, sterile white hallway that expanded as far to the left as it did to the right. There were doors at regular intervals. He thought he heard noise coming from his right, but he couldn't be sure. Not wanting to waste time, he decided to move in that direction anyway. He closed the door, remembering its number and stepped down the hall.

As Max approached the end of the hallway, he could see that it flowed out onto a balcony with a short railing. As he got closer, he could see that it swept both to the left and to the right, adjoining massive staircases. The ceiling of the hallway gradually gave way to an expansive space. It kept rising up. And up. Max moved to his left and hugged the corner of the entrance to the balcony before stepping onto it. He paused and rotated his gaze slowly. The brightness made him squint at first, but after blinking hard, he was able to see clearly.

The space was impressive, widely open, and brilliantly alabaster. The outer walls rose up with an increasing curvature meeting at an apex of octagonal glass, now lit with the messy dots of stars. The floor space was chopped into a confusing geometric series of squares and rectangles by short walls interconnected in a labyrinth pattern. In the larger squares there were scattered folding chairs, all basically facing the same direction, while the smaller squares held one or two chairs and an odd table or desk.

It's an office?

Despite the vastness, there was no noise or movement. Max moved onto the balcony and placed his hands on the railing. His arms were fully extended, and his back was straight; any position that required him to bend was intensely painful and nearly impossible. Max could now see more of the left part of the space. It was similar except for the farthest left corner, which included a large and out of place architectural element. In the midst of a right angle maze, a long cylindrical structure ran horizontally against the wall, ending at the room's mid-point. Then, as if his gaze caused it, a loud sound erupted from the cylinder. Max let go of the railing and stepped backward. The noise, an increasingly pitched rushing sound, intensified as a yellow light at the end of the cylinder illuminated and rotated. It pulsated around various locations in the room as if he'd closed one eye and held his thumb against the sun, toggled it away, then back over it, away, and back over it again. A door at the far right corner opened, and Max quickly climbed down a few steps to his left where he ducked behind the solid railing. He peered over and watched several men walk toward the cylinder. They talked and laughed. Max froze for a moment and then descended the entire staircase.

He focused his hearing on the voices of the men, and used them to guide himself through the space. As he drew closer, he slowed down to listen more intently so that he could position himself to maximize his vantage point without detection. He rounded one last corner, climbed a short metal staircase very slowly until reaching a small office with a half wall overlooking the cylinder and the men. The yellow light hit his position every two seconds. Max, despite the intense pain of the motion, crouched.

The men moved toward the cylinder and worked together pressing buttons and turning handles mostly out of his view. He caught an errant arm swing in one second, and an extended index finger in the next. An alarm sounded and Max's heart leapt. He saw a massive door swing open and away from the end of the cylinder, and he realized that the alarm was only a warning, a precaution, likely on account of the door's excessive mass, as it was huge. The men scurried around, throwing levers, cranking handles and pushing buttons on now-open panels on the side of the cylinder. Suddenly, there was a burst of air, followed by a rush of water and the unmistakable scent of transport lubricant.

Max breathed in the familiar scent. It seemed that centuries had passed since he'd last smelled it. The water rushed out and fell away immediately through the grated rectangular floor that met the cylinder's end. The men continued to work, cranking at handles on each end of the grated floor until a metal bearing track jerkily rose up. Max watched in amazement as a transport tube partially emerged from the cylinder, sliding out onto the track. Max had had no idea that the transport system went through the white wall. He was stunned, his eyes wide. The yellow light went off and three more doors on the right wall opened, as hundreds of people walked in, forming an orderly line leading to the transport tube.

The transport tube was opened but there was nobody inside. Instead, there were neat stacks of boxes. The three men Max had watched, moved to unload the boxes, while another man and a woman from the line stepped up. They wore white coats and latex gloves, and carried inoculation instruments. It made sense, suddenly, that even those on this side of the wall would need to be inoculated. He couldn't figure out why the transport tube was necessary, though it was possible, he thought, that the transport didn't actually break the barrier of the wall at all. He was about to accept his own explanation when he overheard someone, just as they were being inoculated. The latex gloved woman inserted a needle into the base of another woman's neck, and she sighed deeply with relief.

"Oh, I need this," she said. "I haven't slept well for days."

***

Dr. Nichols awoke with an incredibly stiff neck. He'd stayed in his study chair for, he didn't know how long, and not until a ray of sunshine sliced through the room and onto his face did he stir. He smacked his mouth, rubbed his eyes, and righted himself with a grunt. He yawned and rubbed his eyes again. Max sat across from him with fixed eyes that burned with intensity.

"You sleep," Max said, "you all sleep."

"Yes, Max, we do. Let me ask you, do you know why the wall was built?"

"Not a clue."

"It was all about resources, and one very important one most of all, the resource of *time*."

Max didn't understand, and his blank expression made that obvious.

"Max, let me show you what we do here then you'll understand." Dr. Nichols stood and walked toward Max. "Better let me have a look at that." He pointed to Max's chest.

He unbuttoned his shirt, and Dr. Nichols came in for a closer look. He had soft, warm hands, and they gently examined the sutures. "Not a bad job if I do say so myself." He walked away, smiling, and then paused and turned around. "Let me get cleaned up, we'll have something to eat, and then I'll take you on the grand tour, okay?"

"I'm in."

Dr. Nichols's wife handed Max a bundle of clothes. "I think these will fit you."

Max changed in the master bedroom and then stepped out. His chest still ached, but he felt better than yesterday. He stood and paced around the room, fingering several of the books on the tall shelves. He turned around and was startled by Mabel who had seemingly appeared out of nowhere.

"Max," she whispered.

"Yeah?"

"Later tonight, when everyone's asleep, I want you to come to a secret meeting."

"What kind of secret meeting?"

Mabel shushed him. "People like you who've been on the other side of the wall. Look, there is a movement here.

A movement to—"

"Ready, Max?" Dr. Nichols entered the room from the hallway.

"Uh, yeah." Max walked away from Mabel who casually put her finger up to her lips.

Max and Dr. Nichols left and walked down the hallway together. Max looked over his shoulder at Mabel who watched them intensely.

Dr. Nichols led Max through a series of hallways punctuated by wide open rooms with desks, chairs, cabinets, and whiteboards, all of which had caster wheels and were often clustered together in one section of the room or another. People were in the rooms, and they worked together, some sitting motionless, some rolled from one desk to another, some formed semi-circles around a board, others stood with their hands on hips.

"It's collaborative free spacing," Dr. Nichols said, "to do our work we need instant access to each other, so this is how we accomplish it. There are no offices here...with a couple exceptions...no desk belongs to anyone, no chair either. It's an entirely shared work environment that fosters the highest levels of interaction. There are no positions, no titles, and no hierarchy either. One space, like this one we're passing through now, simply flows into the next...just like good ideas."

They passed through two more free spaces before a short hallway finally ended at a t-intersection. The hallway went left to a short, steep staircase, right to another expanse of open space, and directly ahead stood a simple white door with a silver knob.

Dr. Nichols paused. "How are you feeling, Max? Not too much for you too soon?"

"I'm fine." Max inhaled. "Feeling much better."

"C'mon then." Dr. Nichols took two steps, grabbed the door knob and swung it open. "After you."

Max stepped inside and was awestruck at the sight.

The room was tiered into three semi-circular levels each with rows of computers, screens, and other equipment, much of which he didn't recognize. People moved freely around each level, stopping now and then to pick up a piece of paper, type something on a keyboard, or to converse with one another. At each end of the rows were stairs connecting the rows vertically. The main wall to his left rose at least four stories up and contained brilliantly lit statistical readouts, maps, moving graphs, scrolling text, and other data on a series of screens. Above the room, at the same level as the top of the giant wall, a series of glassed-in areas went around the room. These too were filled with the bustle of moving people. Often Max would see someone approach the glass, gesture toward the giant wall, and then a portion of it would move from an obscure location on the side and take prominence in the center of the wall; a chart barely readable would suddenly come into focus.

A man descended the stairs from the second level and approached them. He carried a clipboard stuffed with papers, stepped around Max, ignoring him, and handed the papers to Dr. Nichols. The doctor thanked him and the man went back to tier two. Dr. Nichols looked at Max, recognizing the look of astonishment on his face: eyes wide and his mouth open.

"Quite something, huh, Max?"

Max was dumbfounded. The operations center at the Purification Plant had always intrigued him, but what he saw now stunned him into inquisitive silence. There were so many questions it simply overloaded his ability to ask even one. *Where did they generate enough power to run this facility? What did they do here? What didn't they do here?* There were pieces of equipment he'd never seen. *What did they do? Were all of these people really doctors?* The questions kept coming, piling on top of each other like a damn about to burst. And finally, "There's no lock on the door?" he managed to say.

Dr. Nichols laughed and put his arm on Max's shoulder. "No, Max, there's no need for locks here. This is East Operations. Come, I'll show you around."

Max followed his guide with unsure footsteps and eyes stuck in a wide open position. Dr. Nichols was talking, but Max was so overwhelmed he only picked up a word or two here and there. They moved up to the third tier, and Max stopped dead when Dr. Nichols said something about the "global glacial water management system."

"What did you say?" Max blurted, "the water—"

"Yes. From these two stations we monitor pressure in three of the seven mains in the global glacial water management system."

"My father helped construct that system, and I worked in the Transportation Plant before, well, I don't know. Just, before."

"You should be very proud of your dad. The water

management system was an important stopgap that bought us valuable time. It's probably the most stunning achievement of human engineering in the past one hundred years. It should've taken fifty years, but we got it done in ten. We had to get it done in ten. When the icecaps really started to deteriorate, it became exponential. If you pour water over ice it accelerates the process, and that's exactly what happened. Dr. Forrester worked from this facility, and it was his schematic design that enabled the transportation system. It was ingenious really, to turn that much water into such an expansive and efficient public transit system. We knew the old systems would need to be shut down, and Dr. Forrester was a truly inventive scientist. He really did kill two birds with one stone."

"What about the smell?" Max asked.

"Oh that." Dr. Nichols sighed. "A chemist from the same facility came up with that one. Dr. Stevenson, I think he was. The viscosity was perfect, built in temperature control, and a self-cleaning micro-organism, as well. Everyone complained about the smell, but he never could fix it and maintain the same results." Dr. Nichols chuckled. "They call it the *Stevenson Stench.*"

Max thought about what he'd just heard. He thought about his father.

Dr. Nichols moved on and started to talk again, but Max interrupted him quickly. "What about the sleeping? Tell me why you can sleep. Do you dream too?"

The bustling room suddenly became still, as they all turned their heads toward Max, awaiting the doctor's reaction.

RA Haskell

Dr. Nichols tisked his tongue. "Okay, Max." He gestured behind him toward a bank of elevators. "Come with me."

Max followed, and they were silent, as they waited for the elevator, entered, rode up toward the glass areas, exited, walked down a narrow hallway, and entered the corner room. Dr. Nichols closed the door which bore his name, walked toward the glass wall, pointing casually at a chair, but not looking at it. He strode toward the glass and stopped just inches from it. He sighed heavily and whispered loudly enough for Max to hear. "We've saved billions of lives."

Max didn't respond. Dr. Nichols turned around and wasn't surprised to find Max standing, staring at him. He wasn't sure if Max was the one he'd been waiting for, but he was about to find out.

"By the time the world's governments agreed to work together and fully fund the Centralized Atmospheric Science Project, it was already too late. The polar ice caps were melting at a rate far faster than we thought possible, and it was feeding on itself. Water currents were changing in unexpected ways, which exacerbated the problem. Ambient temperatures were increasing the world over, while humidity levels plummeted. We estimated that at least a centigrade degree increase per annum was attributable to the spike in forest fires alone, the decreased humidity had that unforeseen affect. The program spent the first two years simply remodeling the scope of the crisis and developing projections about how much time remained. And I mean that literally. The best minds in the world were trying to determine how much time the human race had to save itself from annihilaticn. Independently constructed models from several ops-centers generally agreed that within ten short years, the crisis would reach a tipping point from which no feasible recovery would be possible. Global leadership argued about the validity of the projections, but ultimately C.A.S.P. convinced them all. The first step was runoff diversion. It only rercuted about 10% of the volume from the caps, but that isn't why it was done. By removing and repurposing that small amount, it succeeded in slowing the deterioration just enough to buy time for the real solution."

Dr. Nichols stopped talking for just a moment and motioned with his hand. "Won't you sit down, Max?"

"I prefer to stand. Sitting kinda hurts."

"Ah, okay. Turns out, *time* was the real issue. The first atmospheric stabilizer went into use eighteen months later, and that's when the real problem started. It worked actually, but it had the unanticipated effect of changing the mathematics of the crisis. C.A.S.P. realized that the work required for remodeling and re-engineering each of their devices as they went live would require either more time or more scientists. Unfortunately, every scientist and academic with any skill even remotely related the world over, was already part of the effort. Every idea to buy time was tried. Construction for a space station diversion lens was attempted. Algae farming in the Antarctic. Everything. Every effort was made to increase efficiency. C.A.S.P staff was co-located to the ops facilities, collaborative free spacing was mandated to speed communications, the entire power grid was taken offline, industries and businesses that contributed to the problem were subsumed and dismantled, and hundreds of other measures were implemented, but they only provided nominal improvements. It seemed hopeless until the sleep avoidance program was suggested. If C.A.S.P. membership could stop sleeping, but remain at least 80% productive, then the program could work. It created time when there wasn't enough."

Max remained still, staring, listening.

"Max, it worked," Dr. Nichols continued, joyously. "By the end of the decade, C.A.S.P. had deployed enough stabilizers that we saw real and measurable improvement. Temperatures stopped going up and the cap melt slowed. Still, though," Dr. Nichols became suddenly solemn, "millions died. Despite hope that we might be wrong, the models were right-on, and the rising tides overwhelmed island nations and the coasts of every continent."

Dr. Nichols turned away from Max, casually made a few strokes on a keyboard and faced the large screen-wall out the window. Images and video appeared. Max saw what he'd always heard about: tragedy, desperation, death, sacrifice, and the power of a tide that knew no master. Dr. Nichols, without looking backward, reached toward his keyboard and made another stroke. A blurry video clip magnified and took the wall's center position. The staff working in the tiers stopped and stared at it. Their faces wore a melancholy familiarity. Max watched the video. A helicopter—Max had seen pictures of them—lifted off shakily, and then a woman inside with large headphones over her ears looked directly at them. She was speaking in a high pitched, nervous voice.

"Christ," she hollered. "It's worse than we thought. Look at that."

The helicopter noise was constant and overbearing. The video skipped, and several voices filled the space, but Max couldn't understand a single word. The picture scanned a cityscape and then zoomed in. The sea was overtaking it. It was quietly violent. It didn't rage, but it rose quickly in the streets and engulfed everything. It was like a pair of loving arms engaged in a deadly hug.

The woman shrieked. "Over there...look," she shouted. The picture moved blurrily, her face, then her finger, then the street again.

From a great distance, the video showed a line of cars positioned on the curb of a gradual hill. Halfway, there was motion.

"Zoom! Zoom!" The young woman's voice was breaking.

The picture steadied and framed the front seat of a sleek red vehicle. Inside, an injured woman struggled to unbuckle herself from a restraint that lay over her left shoulder. The water was rising. In the passenger seat was a small boy, much too small to sit on his own. He fidgeted with the restraint that held him. The woman looked down. She must have noticed the water at her feet. Her frightened face with bulging eyes noticed the helicopter, and she looked directly at it. She said something but could not be heard. *Do something! Help!*

Max noticed all the tiered workers mouthing along. *Do something! Help!*

Water sprayed lightly through the closed doors. The child noticed and laughed. He put his small hand over a stream, then placed his hand on his mouth. He tasted the saltiness and scrunched his face. The tier workers smiled. Dr. Nichols dropped his head, and Max saw him smiling, with a single tear running down his cheek.

The mother unbuckled the boy, brought him to her lap, and opened the moon-roof above her.

The water rose.

The mother waited until the water reached her neck before lifting the boy up.

The child, only now becoming upset, squealed, squirmed and cried. His shrieking, though faint, was the first real noise that could be heard from the scene. The affect was stunning. Several of the tiered onlookers, and Dr. Nichols wept audibly.

The shot zoomed to the mother who wrenched her body to remain above the flood.

Help! Help! She screamed.

Over and over and over.

Until the water overtook her.

"We have to get down there!" The woman's voice screeched, off camera.

"We'll die," another answered. "We can't. This is all we can do."

The young woman, in the shot for a moment, removed her headphones and looked away.

The small boy, whose drowned mother still clasped him, sat atop the car as the water rose. He screamed and cried, and it was nearly louder than the helicopter blades.

The shot was fuzzy, but still, even when the water took him.

The woman with the headphones screamed, "Noooo..." and then the video stopped.

Dr. Nichols turned around and faced Max again. The tier workers were back in motion. "All the resources were, were..." Dr. Nichols choked, and more tears welled in his eyes.

Max stared at him, statuesque.

Dr. Nichols breathed in. "We've often wondered. No...we *still* wonder if some of our attention couldn't have been focused on better evacuation and relocation plans."

Max didn't move. "Tell me about the sleep avoidance program."

Dr. Nichols knew he couldn't turn back now. "The human brain produces a chemical called gamma-Aminobutyric acid, which we now know is the singular compound primarily responsible for enabling sleep. It signals the brain to rest and simultaneously makes it possible. Through complicated, groundbreaking actually, bio-chemical manipulation, a team of C.A.S.P doctors were able to effectively suppress the production of this chemical. Using other drugs, they were also able to trick the brain into believing it had rested. They fooled it so well for the most part that everyone under the regiment maintained 90% of their physical, emotional, and intellectual capacities. The treatments turned 10 years into 20 and enabled the first C.A.S.P teams to finish the initial phases of the water management and stabilization programs.

"But because so much of this was experimental and

untested, there were, well...ramifications. What nobody predicted was that the chemical concoctions would have a permanent effect. A permanent and a genetic effect. Those under treatment the longest, showed serious signs of mental breakdown, physical illness, and emotional distress. The real problem was that these men and women were the most valuable...they'd been there since the beginning. When Dr. Franken, a brilliant mathematician and largely responsible for the stabilizers re-sequencing algorithms, shot himself in front of his wife, he knew the situation was fast spinning out of control. Many attempts had been made to reverse the damage but they all failed. Only one solution remained. They needed gamma-Aminobutyric acid."

Dr. Nichols paused and then sat down. Max remained standing, listening.

"Many members of the populous volunteered, but not enough of them. Those who did volunteer showed us that the procedure could work. Supplemental treatments given with regularity could induce and maintain sleep. The situation was becoming more desperate until..."

Dr. Nichols stopped again. He became visibly nervous, his hands shaking slowly. He laid them flat on the table in front of him, pressing them down hard to satiate the shake. "They added something to the water to increase the amount of gamma-Aminobutyric acid produced. It had an adverse effect. It systematically increased the blood flow to the brain but failed to compensate for the pressure."

"The headaches." Max spoke quickly, the epiphany rolling off his tongue accompanied by the anger it produced.

"Yes, Max. The headaches. It was so poorly done, not well researched. Rushed. Just, poorly done. So poorly, poorly done."

"Is it still—"

"No, definitely not."

"But the headaches?"

"Yes, I know. The effect was permanent, apparently. Among other things, it decreased delta wave production for the post-pubescent population." Dr. Nichols rubbed his brow. "Delta waves are a bio-electric phenomenon occurring in the brain during deep sleep." He then sat back in his chair and looked up. "It seems even the smallest attempt to fiddle with Mother Nature has consequences that last for generations. It's like a pendulum that knows no center. Even the slightest touch sends it soaring this way or that."

There was silence. Max sat down and looked at Dr. Nichols. "But you still take it from us, don't you? This gamma whatever."

"Yes. But Max, we have to. We haven't solved the problems that started it. For us...or you. And, well..."

"What?"

"There is still so much to be done. Years of work, decades, have only bought us more time, it hasn't solved anything. This planet reached a point from which we still don't know how to recover. We have the best minds on this. The best minds. But here is my feeling, a feeling I wouldn't ever share with them." He stood and pointed out to the workers in the tiers. "We will probably do nothing more than buy time. We will extend our existence but not save it."

Silence.

Dr. Nichols sat again. "I want to bring the walls down, Max. All of them...in all the cities. I believe we can expend the necessary resources...or I feel that we should expend them to find the cure for what ails us all. There will be resistance. There will be arguments about losing our focus, but I think this work is our most important, and that's the argument I'll make. If we are to buy time for living, then we should get about doing that, and *divided* is no way to live."

Max righted himself in the chair, leaned forward. "Do you believe we can sleep again? Will we ever dream?"

"I know it."

"Once word of what's happened gets out, keeping the peace will be challenging at best."

"I know that too, and frankly I think that is the greatest fear around here. That's how you can help, Max, that's what you can do. Carry a message of solidarity...of unity...of cooperation. We will not be able to do this if we don't work together."

Max lowered his head and stared at the floor. Then he moved forward. He extended his hand toward Dr. Nichols. "I'll die trying."

"I believe you would." Dr. Nichols accepted Max's hand and smiled with a glimmer of hope in his eyes.

Chapter 26

D inner at the Nichols's was loud. Max could barely hear anything under the din, but Dr. Nichols, his wife, and daughter seemed to communicate just fine even though they all spoke at the same time. Bowls, plates, glasses, bottles and baskets moved around the table just as fast as the words, and from a distance Max thought he must have looked like the only person there serenely sitting amidst a dizzying array of color, whipping lines of motion, and swatches of skin. Mabel would frequently break from the routine whenever Dr. Nichols and his wife parlayed so that she could stare at Max, nod her head slightly, and open her eyes widely as if to say, *don't forget.*

Dr. Nichol's laughed suddenly. He set down his fork with a clink, leaned back, and smiled. "I never said that." He gulped from his wine glass.

"Yes you did." His wife pointed her fork at him. "You said it...absolutely."

"When?"

"Last week. Tuesday, I think."

"Eleanor, I never said that."

"Craig, Yes. You. Did."

"I never promised that because if I had, it would have been done."

The table was silent for the first time in minutes.

Dr. Nichols spoke again. "I am a man of my word, Eleanor." His seriousness stilled the room momentarily.

"I think we both know that isn't true," his wife said calmly, but with a steady conviction.

The doctor's face crinkled in anger.

Eleanor shifted her focus. "Max, tell me, do you have someone special over the wall? I don't mean to pry, but I differ with my husband in this regard. I know he believes that good reasoning, honest negotiating, and a common understanding of each other's goals will form a foundation strong enough to bring the wall down. I think that a common understanding of each other's *hopes* will be the bridge we need. So, do you? Have someone special? I mean, love is, after all, the greatest hope there is."

Max stopped chewing. "Yes."

Eleanor Nichols smiled and hunched toward the table. "Oh, good. Tell us everything."

"Her name is Amanda." Max's eyes watered. "And, ma'am, I honestly don't know if she's still alive."

***

Craig and Eleanor Nichols were fighting in their bedroom when Mabel and Max climbed into the ceiling.

"You've done this before, huh?" Max asked as they quietly inched their way through ducting in a crouched position. The position hurt Max's chest, and he wasn't sure he'd be able to stay that way for very long.

"Lots of times. The door is coded, so this is the easiest way."

"Shouldn't we wait until they're, uh, asleep?"

"No way! This is perfect. Trust me."

Mabel stopped and gently pried up a ceiling tile and peered under it. She then slid it fully aside, and light poured upwards. Mabel hung on to a steel beam as she extended her body toward the floor. She let go and dropped, bending her knees to cushion the impact. She looked up and motioned for Max.

He followed, though his descent was decidedly more clumsy, owing to the pain he struggled against. Mabel stood on her toes to reach the edging of the door jamb to her immediate right. She retrieved a thin metal pencil-shaped implement, held one end and pulled the other to extend the device, and then she pushed it upward to its full length. Using the metal stick, she gently nudged the ceiling tile back into place. She collapsed her tool, slipped it inside her pocket, and trotted off. "C'mon."

Max followed.

After a dizzying number of stairs, doors, double-backs, and hallways, Mabel finally slowed down. She motioned for Max to be quiet and stand still as she stepped in front of him several feet. Looking up and down the hallway at first, she then struck her foot against the floor firmly, but not recklessly.

Two seconds passed.

An equally firm knock was heard from the floor.

Mabel remained still.

Two seconds later, another knock came.

Several more seconds passed, and then a door in the floor slid open.

Mabel jumped down and directed Max to follow.

Everything was pitch black beyond the perimeter of a small light held by the unknown person who led them. Max hit his head twice before he and Mabel finally emerged into a dimly lit room filled with rattling pipes across the ceiling and a cracked cement floor. It was damp and smelled of earth and the chemical attempts to mask it; it smelled natural at the same time it smelled falsely sweet.

A young man with wispy blond hair, a serious look, and badly acned skin approached Mabel. "Is this him?"

"Yes, it is."

Everyone in the entire room stared at Max, gasping and muttering to each other.

The young man left Mabel and walked confidently to Max.

Max started to extend his hand, but realized the serious blond wasn't making the same effort.

"I am called Theo...and I welcome you."

"I'm Max. Thanks."

The bustle in the room amplified, as Max spoke, and finally the wave of rumblings crashed and sent a question rolling to the shore.

"Is the Raven a *real* place? Have you actually been there?"

Max tilted his head, thrown off by the question. "Yes. I've been there. Lots of times."

The blond young man named Theo grabbed Max and pulled him along. Behind a twisted mess of air vents and pipes, Theo pushed a piece of concrete blocking away from the wall. Moonlight shown in, and Max realized that he was staring through a hole in the great white wall, a chink forged by a group of curious kids. He saw that several of the other blocks were misaligned, meaning they'd probably been pulled away at some point, as well. Theo scrunched down and looked at Max directly. "Can you take us to the Raven?"

As soon as Theo's question was asked, it was followed by a burst of other questions, of equally banal and youthful import. Max surveyed the room behind him carefully and realized that this resistance force, this *revolution*, was nothing more than the culmination of dozens of privileged childhoods. Max grumbled, then sighed.

"What's wrong?" a voice asked him.

Max realized he was definitely the tallest person in the room.

The kids stared at him.

"Have any of you actually gone out there?" Max pointed to the hole.

"Yes, I have," Theo said. "All the way to the fence, too." He smiled and crossed his arms.

Max looked out and saw a fence perhaps a hundred yards away. He looked around for a place to sit down and cradle his head in his hands. He couldn't find a place, so he simply sunk down and moved the stone back, closing out the moon.

A boy ran into the room, holding a flashlight. He was breathless and sweaty. "There's something going on. The Ops room is full, and Dr. Nichols just arrived."

The children flowed around Max like water across a rock, and seconds later, he found himself in the wet room all alone. Mabel stuck her head around the corner. "What are you waiting for? This is huge. Let's go!"

Max sighed and followed.

They traversed the twisting innards of the complex with a speed that only comes with great practice. The kids snaked around dirt-floor passageways and pipe-laden alleys in a messy single file that broke apart whenever a corner was too tight, or too sharp. They came back together and slowed down on a straightaway littered with scraps of metal and concrete. Theo, leading them, turned and signaled for everyone to be quiet. He then flapped his arms about in a series of ridiculous looking hand gestures that Max didn't understand, but everyone else apparently did. The group quickly split into three parts; one scurried down a dark corridor to the right, another to the left, and the third group climbed up a service shaft using a metal-rung ladder covered in rust. Max walked toward the ladder and Theo came to meet him.

"This is right above the Ops room," he whispered. "Wait here and I'll send word."

"I don't think so," Max said, moving forward confidently.

Theo glared at Mable who shrugged, grabbed something from Theo's hand, and followed Max up the ladder.

At the top, Mabel directed Max to the right. The shaft diverted into three directions, each equally small. Max lay flat, wincing softly in pain as his chest hit the metal. He pulled himself along until the ducting reached another three way intersection. The ambient whirly noise of exhaust fans made it difficult to hear but likely provided auditory cover for their travels, as well. Directly ahead of him, he heard voices rising up through a large grate.

Mabel tugged on his leg.

He turned around.

She handed him a small square mirror that articulated on top of a metal rod, about a foot long. She motioned toward the grate.

Max crept toward it until his face was near its edge. He looked quickly with his own eyes and then snapped his head back just as fast. The grating was at the far end of a room, and all Max could see was a wall with shelving. The shelving was covered with electronic equipment that produced a constant waft of heat that rose through the grate.

Max could stare directly into the grate, and unless someone was pressed up against the shelves, then he would be undetected. Max leaned the side of his head on the grate and then positioned the mirror just below it, inside the room. He heard Dr. Nichols speaking, and swung the mirror around until he could see his back. The room, like the wall under the grate, was also full of equipment that blinked, bleeped, and flashed. There was a large semi-circle table, in front of which Dr. Nichols and several others stood. In front of that was a sprawling wall with multiple screens. A person sat at the table, wearing a small earphone mic and typed rapidly on a keyboard. The room wasn't nearly as big as the one he'd seen before, but was similar in layout and, Max guessed, in purpose. He held his breath and listened.

"Where are we?" Dr. Nichols asked.

"We just went in," the seated operator said. "See?"

Max toggled the mirror a few degrees until it caught the picture on one of the screens. It was dark, yet strangely familiar.

"Any resistance?"

"Not yet—"

The screen suddenly came alive with bursts of orange and yellow. It crackled and shook. Voices yelled but were incomprehensible. Repeated gunfire and muzzle flashes filled the screen.

The operator touched her ear and tilted her head, listening. "Understood. Lighting it up. Confirmed."

The screen was blinding white for just a second and then retreated into itself, revealing a scene that made Max open his mouth and blink hard. A familiar corridor of the Central Hospital stretched out toward a staircase that led, ultimately, to the long room.

Mabel, lying in back of Max, sensed his body tense up. "What is it?" she whispered.

Max didn't respond. He saw several Knights lying on the hallway floor. They appeared dead, but he didn't see where they'd been hit. Max twisted the mirror left and then right, trying to maximize the field of vision. *Stupid little thing, can't see shit.* Suddenly more Knights scurried out of a room. They had something over their noses and mouths, towels or cloth, Max couldn't tell.

"Firing," the operator said.

A thump sent a canister hurling toward the Knights. It landed and exploded with yellow gas, engulfing them. One managed to escape out the doorway at the hallway's end, but as the cloud quickly cleared, the others were prone on the floor.

"Affirmative. You are authorized to advance," the operator said.

The scamper of feet gave way to images of identically dressed men, crouching and advancing in formation down the hallway. There were as many as twenty five, and they appeared well equipped.

The squadron moved with caution down the stairs and paused at the landing on the long room floor.

"Confirmed. East. To the right, 100 meters," the operator said.

Max adjusted the mirror again, and this time found an angle that afforded a better view.

When the invaders rounded the corner to the Hospital's long hallway, Max saw what he expected. Resistance. He'd hoped to see Amanda, but she'd not been in any of the shots. He knew they were Knights, though, so the question of who prevailed over the battle he'd fled was certainly answered. *Get 'em, Knights.* In one split second of clarity, Max spotted Mark limping away down the hall, clearly favoring one side as he ambled. Suddenly, gunfire filled the screen.

"Man down," the operator said.

"Another."

"Firing two."

Thump. Thump. Thump.

Another volley of canisters followed. The hallway, the screen, and the reflection in Max's mirror were nothing but an amber noxious fog. The gunfire crackles became less and less until they stopped. The fog dissipated to reveal a pile of Knights, unconscious. *Or dead.*

Max winced at his uncomfortable position, and shifted. Mabel asked again what was happening, and Max again ignored her. The soldiers entered the long room without further resistance, stepping carefully over the Knights.

The operator turned slightly toward Dr. Nichols. "We're there."

Dr. Nichols folded his arms. "Good. Get it done."

The operator turned back around, hit a button, adjusted her microphone and spoke. "Confirmation. Set charges."

Max had never dreamt in his adult life, though his images of Amanda and the man with the knife certainly reminded him of what he remembered from his childhood, though that one would certainly have been classified as a nightmare. What happened to him now, in this moment, also felt dreamlike. Part of him was cognizant of his movements and the pain in his chest, but a bigger part of him was nothing more than a spectator to his actions. He watched himself drop the mirror, drive his elbow repeatedly into the grate, every blow producing excruciating pain. The grate finally gave way, and he saw his body falling loudly through. Max watched himself make a controlled tumble into the room, the impact blinding him in several seconds of agony. He saw everything as if he wasn't living it but watching it on a screen. Max walked toward Dr. Nichols, and when he made eye contact with him, that's when the screen-version faded away and he, once again, inhabited his own body. "What the hell are you doing?"

"Jesus. Max." Dr. Nichols stumbled back two steps, his eyes wide with surprise.

Max stepped forward as strongly as he could and repeated himself. "What the *hell* are you *fucking* doing?" He was now face-to-face with Dr. Nichols.

Mabel stuck her head through the hole in the ceiling.

Dr. Nichols backed up another step, but tripped over his own feet. His bottom lip quivered as the other people in the room stepped back even farther. The operator kept peering over her shoulder but remained seated, listening.

"I'm...I'm...I'm paving the way for peace," Dr. Nichols said finally.

"By invading our home and destroying the only thing that gives us hope?" The fact that Dr. Nichols answered his question and stared him in the eye had calmed him slightly. He was still apoplectic, but less out of control. The pain in his chest was acute.

"Hope? They aren't hope. They are instruments of war. How can we begin a peace process when they exist?"

"War?"

"Didn't they cause the greatest battle between the factions that's ever occurred? Isn't that why the Rock-a-Byes attacked the hospital?"

"How do you know that?"

"What does it matter, isn't it true?"

"Yes, but how do you know that?"

"Max, together we can find another way. Those,

RA Haskell

those, *devices* aren't the future, it's up to us to make them part of our past."

Max thought about Amanda. On the large screen he saw soldiers in the long room, placing explosives on each of the cylinders. On a smaller screen near the operator he saw two soldiers in a hallway in the very facility in which he stood, running. *They're coming for me.*

Max walked away from Dr. Nichols and toward the door. "You want the wall to come down but you don't want it to mean anything. You want our permission, you want our blessing. Hear me now because I speak for all of us. No. No, Dr. Nichols, No. You don't have our permission, and you won't have it. Ever."

Max turned and ran out the door. The soldiers were there, but startled. He squirmed away, kicking one of them off. Max ran, taking every turn he could. His chest pounded with every footfall, but the adrenaline coursing through him allowed him to persevere. He remembered that the facility was under constant surveillance, so he slowed his pace and thought. He heard footsteps in front of him, and seconds later, two soldiers rounded the corner. They were coming. There was a thump and he ran, holding his breath. After he rounded a corner, he saw another person coming at him. He was trapped. Breathing in again, he realized the person running at him was Eleanor, Dr. Nichols's wife. She was signaling him to hurry. He ran to her.

"I can get you out," she said. "This section of the hallway is a blind spot."

Max nodded, huffing.

"Hit me in the lip. Make me bleed," Eleanor said.

"What?"

"Just fucking do it. Do it right now. Both our futures depend on it."

Max punched Eleanor in the mouth, splitting her lip badly. It bled immediately and profusely.

She didn't fall, but stumbled. She spit and then told Max, "Go there."

Max followed her instructions and ducked into a doorway to hide.

Eleanor took several steps forward and flung herself on the floor.

The soldiers ran around the corner. They came up to her, gently. "Mrs. Nichols, are you okay?"

Eleanor was tearing. "I'm okay, I'm okay. He just hit me. He just hit me. He went that way." She pointed away from Max's location down a long hallway. The soldiers ran.

Silence, but for the breath of Max and Eleanor.

Eleanor spat again. She pulled the silken scarf from around her neck, wadded it, and pressed it forcefully against her lip and moved to Max. "We need to hurry."

Max followed Eleanor through a series of turns until she reached a door and opened it.

"This hallway will take you to where my daughter had her 'secret' meeting with you."

Max remembered the hole in the wall. "But, how do you—"

"I'm smarter than a thirteen-year-old."

"Right." Max started down the stairs when Eleanor grabbed his hand.

"Max, take this." Eleanor placed a small leather book into Max's hand. It had a long leather strap that wrapped around the book several times. Embossed into the worn leather cover was, "E.N."

Max went down the stairs into the room. He moved the concrete blocks, squeezed outside, stood up, tucked the leather book into his pants and ran as fast as he could manage. The sutures in his chest had come loose in several spots and his shirt, a clean white button-down given to him by Dr. Nichols was spotting with blood. *Prophetic*, he thought as he moved over the field in the moonlight.

The Knights had won. Amanda could still be alive.

EPILOGUE

Excerpts from the Personal Diary of Mark Decker:
Undated.

I just don't know how to tell Max; his instincts were completely right, and I can now prove it scientifically. But here's the thing, it isn't going to make him happy. Being right about being wronged isn't a revelation. It's a self-inflicted condemnation. The extractions that make our headaches go away aren't just extractions. A very subtle chemical compound is also added. It self-replicates over time in the base of the brain because it interacts with our gamma-Aminobutyric acid. It feeds on it, actually. It boosts the production of GABA and uses it to grow simultaneously. It's not an additive in the water, at all; it's something they put in us directly. If I hadn't been looking for it, I wouldn't have found it. Max was right. They are using us like production facilities and have implemented a clever incentive for us to comply. And more than that, I think its sudden removal could be damaging. There's no telling what would happen if we stopped our complicity. All evidence points to significant risk of a wide variety of psychoses. But just how do I tell Max?

***

Max dropped the diary onto a desk, just as Mark entered the room. The two men, best of friends, stared at each other.

"I-I didn't know how to—"

"It's okay." Max left the room slowly, placing a hand on Mark's shoulder as he passed. "Wish me luck."

"Where are you going?"

"To find Sedgwick."

"The leader of the Rock-a-Bye Babies?"

"The same."

"Whatever for?"

"To propose an alliance."

***

A month later, after taking control of the Transportation Purification facility for the second time, fifty Eight-Hour Knights and fifty Rock-a-Bye-Babies were shirtless while Mark and his team used waterproof glue to place electrodes on their chests. They strapped a small box to the men's arms, connected the electrodes, and set a digital timer. Max smiled as Mark attached one to him.

"You sure about this?" Mark asked.

"We'll see," Max said. "You sure about this?" Max motioned with his head to the contraption Mark was attaching to him.

"We'll see," Mark said, smiling. In reality, he didn't expect all these men to survive the trip. But he simply kept smiling.

Max could still taste Amanda's lips on his own, as the water rushed in. If there was one thing Max had learned from Dr. Nichols, he'd told Amanda when saying goodbye, was that sometimes you have to make your own future.

Minutes later, the hundred men were dead, nearly frozen, and on their way to the other side of the white wall. They were on their way to a new future of their own making, a future Max hoped one day to dream about.

He didn't know it then, but it was a future that would include a son.

Amanda's water had broken.

About the Author

RA Haskell built a career in marketing high-tech and amassed over a million miles traveling the world. He's published many business-oriented articles including the results of a market research project in an academic journal. His short stories and flash fiction have been published on the internet. Besides his aspirations for storytelling, he's a father, a husband, a runner, a U2 fanatic, and a lover of single malt scotch. He resides in Middle America, Wichita, Kansas.

RA Haskell

Enjoy more short stories and novels by many talented authors at

https://www.twbpress.com

Science Fiction, Supernatural, Horror, Thrillers, Romance, and more

www.ingramcontent.com/pod-product-compliance
Lightning Source LLC
Chambersburg PA
CBHW051243260626
47162CB00002B/577